A SIMPLE LIE

MARY BUSH

Print ISBN 978-1-913419-15-8

7289 6466   3/20

For P — love always, M

1

Francine Donohue slipped out of bed and grabbed her gun from the top of the nightstand. *What in the hell was that?* With her finger poised on the trigger, she glanced around the room but couldn't see much in the darkness.

It sounded like a door slamming. She was sure of it.

She waited for another minute, remaining still, alert. Prepared. Listening hard for anything more.

The only sound was her pulse thumping, echoing in her ears. Every nerve stood on edge as she peered around the dark room. Her gaze lingered on shadowy outlines of suitcases she'd packed just hours ago. She listened again. All was quiet and she breathed deeply, trying to calm down.

In the last couple of days, she'd been jumping at every noise. The slam must have come from the apartment next door. *Goddamn neighbors again, either drunk or high, always fighting, always smashing something. It never ends.*

Francine checked the time. The numbers on the clock flashed from 2:59 to 3:00am. In a few hours she would finally be out of this hellhole.

Even though everything seemed all right, she couldn't

relax. She crossed the room to the door and quietly pulled it open, hesitated for a second, then stepped out into the hallway.

She moved slowly, her hand tight on the gun, turning on lights and carefully checking each room. In the kitchen, she parted the curtains above the sink and looked out from her first-floor window. Several cars were parked on the street. A lone neighbor had the lights on. No one was outside. No one was in her apartment. Everything was fine.

She walked back into her bedroom and shut the door behind her, locking it this time. She looked at the suitcases again and thought of leaving now, but was just too exhausted to start a long drive.

For the last thirty-six hours she'd been anxious and awake, drifting off for only momentary reprieves. Delirium was setting in. She had to hold it together. Things were going as planned so far and she just had to keep her head straight. A few hours of sleep, that's all she needed. As she got into bed, she slipped the gun under her pillow this time.

Francine didn't even remember closing her eyes when the sound of another slam dragged her out of a deep sleep. This time she didn't jump. She couldn't. Her hand darted under the pillow for the gun, but her fingers fumbled, sliding off the handle as she tried to grasp it.

What the hell? She struggled to lift herself, but could only get partway up. Her body felt strange, heavy, as if she was trying to move through thick mud. Every movement was a chore, an exertion that was becoming more difficult by the second. Then suddenly her body froze, and she slumped, falling back on the bed.

Oh my God! What's happening to me? She attempted to move her arms, her legs, but a loud bang grabbed her attention and she gasped for air. When she heard the next sound, her heart began to pound wildly, racing as if it would jump out of her chest.

A voice was calling her name.

Seconds later, Francine felt someone standing over her, watching her. She tried to turn her head and speak but couldn't do either. There was no need to see the person who was now just inches from her face. She knew who it was. She knew what was going on.

"You didn't check your bedroom closet when you got up. I was in there the whole time. I'm surprised at you, Francine. Who checks their entire apartment and then neglects the closet? You really ought to be more careful. Don't you know the closet is one of the places monsters hide?"

Jesus Christ. The gun. I need the damn gun! Francine's thoughts spun uncontrollably as she fought panic. She forced herself to focus. If she didn't she would die.

"I slammed the door a couple of times to get you going. I could have just woken you up in an ordinary way, but really, where's the fun in that?"

As Francine stared at the ceiling, blinking rapidly, her fingers twitched and her body began to feel lighter, like she was regaining control. Frantically, she tried to move. She longed to feel the cold steel in her hands. It was so close, still hidden under the pillow.

Hands prodded at her hard and fast, assessing her muscle tone. "I'm sure you've figured out by now you've been drugged. I did it while you were sleeping. Thank God for chloroform and muscle relaxants. They really do make things easier. But you've been able to blink your eyelids all along and now your fingers are moving. It shouldn't be wearing off yet. I might have miscalculated the dosage."

Francine curled her fingers into a fist and then opened them again, repeating the motion, hoping to awaken her arms. She froze when she heard the sound of a zipper opening, followed by a loud clank of metal objects hitting together, then the rustling of plastic.

"You're probably wondering how I found you. You must be. Any smart person would. That's what I like about you Francine —you're smart. That's how you got this far, how you've managed to hide for so long. But unfortunately, you have a really stupid side too. And that's why you're not going to get away."

Her whole body was tingling. It was coming around. In just a few minutes she'd be able to grab the gun.

Francine didn't have a few minutes.

2

D r. Valentina Knight, DDS, walked out her back door and checked her watch again. The interview was in an hour. The drive would take twenty minutes. She had plenty of time.

Val looked up at the clear sky, squinting from the glare of the sun. A beautiful day like this should have been a sign of promise, of good things to come. But she just couldn't get in the spirit. Promise had betrayed her more than once. No, she didn't believe in promise anymore.

She reached into her bag and pulled out a pair of sunglasses. After a sleepless night her eyes were heavy and the bright sun only made them burn. Though Val tried to remain positive, stress gnawed at her stomach, creating waves of nausea. If she didn't get a job, she wouldn't be able to pay her growing pile of overdue bills. This week alone four desperate interviews had led to nothing. The one scheduled for this morning was her last chance. No more were lined up; nor would they be for the immediate future. With all of her potential prospects exhausted, everything rested on the outcome of today.

The advertised pay wasn't great with this position but Val

could manage with it, plus benefits were included. Jesus, this would be a lifesaver until she could find something better. Unfortunately, anything better wouldn't be in the dental field. She hadn't practiced in over a year. She couldn't anymore.

Damn. When did that happen? Val took a deep breath, attempting to calm herself, then picked up a broken piece of clapboard hanging from the side of her house. She turned it over, revealing a large section of rotted wood. A quick inspection of the adjoining pieces showed that they too were about to fall apart.

It was just one more problem, and at this point, definitely not a minor architectural detail. The place was in need of a major overhaul. Advertised as a handyman's special, the 1,100 square foot fixer-upper wasn't just reasonably priced, it was cheap for the address of West River Road on Grand Island, NY. The properties along this road on the west side of the island face the Niagara River, allowing a view of the water before it inevitably drops over an edge twelve miles downstream, creating Niagara Falls.

Val had thought that she had a good investment when she'd bought it last spring, after moving back home from Clearwater, Florida. She'd assumed she would eventually be able to pay someone to fix the house up. But this was yet to happen. She had never imagined she'd go so long without getting some type of work. If she didn't get this job, the bank would take the house soon. The number of foreclosure notices sitting on her kitchen counter said it all. In the shape it was in, the bank wasn't getting a gem. But they'd be getting her house. Her home. She dropped the clapboard and headed towards the garage, ignoring the two gutters also hanging loose.

Traffic was light for the late-morning commute and she drove down the highway quickly, heading east towards the city of Buffalo, New York, to the Erie County Medical Examiner's

Office; the county morgue. The position was described as a medico-legal death scene investigator, something she'd never even heard of before. From what Val learned through an internet search, the death scene investigator assists the medical examiner by investigating the nature of any suspicious, or violent death, and determines if any additional investigation is needed. Usually there are no formal educational requirements, unless stated otherwise—thank God there were none in this case—but some knowledge of medicine and law was highly recommended. This ad did say they were looking for someone with "a medical and/or legal background," though the specifications were a bit vague.

Val knew she could be stretching it a bit with her qualifications but hoped her dental training was close enough to claim a *medical* background. More importantly, the ad said nothing about needing experience. Lack of experience in any field outside of dentistry had been a curse so far. She'd spent the last year applying for various positions, but was always either underqualified or overqualified. Even the local grocery store chain wouldn't hire her as a manager, well not without a degree in business management. Nor would they take her as a grocery checker. "You're a doctor. We can't hire you for that job," they said, as if they were doing her a favor. All of her interviews had gone the same way.

Val had never thought her life would come down to this. But who does? No one sees the end until it's too late. *Promise* can be very deceptive. A pied piper for the unsuspecting. She gripped the steering wheel tight and put on her turn signal. The exit leading to the hospital that housed the medical examiner's office was coming up.

A little more than a year ago she'd had a thriving practice in Clearwater, Florida. With an income climbing well into the six-figure range she enjoyed her lifestyle as one of the "up and coming" professionals in her area. Four years at college, four more years in dental school, then ten years in practice had got her to the point where, for the first time in her life, she didn't have to worry about money, her future, her confidence.

It only took thirty seconds to end it all.

She often replayed those last seconds in her mind, searching for something that could have been done differently. But nothing could have turned this twist of fate in her favor. There was no way that she could have ignored Mr. Tate's injury. He was her patient, for God's sake. And there was no way anyone could have predicted what he'd do to her, especially with the cops right outside the examining room door.

Three surgeries and six months of physical therapy had helped restore most of the mobility to her left hand. For all outward appearances there was nothing wrong with her, except for the ugly scar that ran down her thumb and partially across her palm. She was not disabled. She could work, at least that's what the doctors said, which led to the decision of the disability insurance people to deny her any benefits.

It was when it came down to the fine, intricate, detailed work demanded in dentistry that she couldn't perform. Val had to face the fact that being a dentist wasn't an option anymore. With her life falling apart all she wanted to do was go home, to Buffalo, hoping to find salvation in the comforting feeling of familiarity, of life before dentistry, before success. Of *promise*.

She had found a career once. She could do it again. Couldn't she?

Rounding the corner in front of the Erie County Medical Center, Val pulled into the parking lot. She checked the clock on the dash. As anticipated, the drive didn't take that long. Now what to do? She was early. But early is a sign of a good employee. Val opened the car door and stepped outside.

It was unseasonably warm for the middle of April, the

temperature cracking seventy degrees already. As Val walked towards the building, beads of perspiration formed on her forehead, the heat adding to the effect of stress, which had already caused her to feel as if she had soaked through her blouse. Pulling the clingy material away from her body, Val worried about her choice of dress. Agonizing over every detail, second guessing herself—Jesus, she couldn't help it.

Today she wore a little more makeup than usual, mostly to hide the dark circles under her eyes from lack of sleep. Her silk blouse was slightly too fancy, and her snug black pencil skirt was perhaps a tad too short. She'd bought these items while climbing the social ladder in Florida. Patients came to her office to spend thousands of dollars on cosmetic dental work. What would they think their teeth would end up looking like if their dentist had a crappy appearance?

She had no money to buy a conservative suit for interviews now, but her shoes were a sensible height, and the briefcase she carried was professional. This should balance things out. Val tried to reassure herself that being petite, she could pull off wearing something short without appearing inappropriate. Plus, her long brown hair was demurely pulled back in a barrette and she wore black-framed glasses over her dark, almond-shaped eyes. When she was younger, men found her attractive, mostly because of her eyes, which gave her a slightly exotic look. Now, at thirty-six, she wasn't sure where she stood with the opposite sex anymore. Other than seeking a job, she hadn't been out of the house much in the past year.

As Val entered the building, she wiped her sweaty palms on her skirt and pulled down on the hem, then approached the secretary, who was sitting behind a large window of what appeared to be bulletproof glass. A speaker in the middle of it was attached to a microphone on the other side. To the left of the window were large metal doors, presumably to enter the rest of the building. They had big warning signs: "Alarm will sound" and "Restricted area" and "Wait for lock to open".

Jesus, is this the medical examiner's office or the goddamn U.S. Mint?

Val waited as patiently as she could, her foot tapping anxiously on the floor, but the woman behind the glass ignored her. The nameplate on the desk read Betty Fletcher. Betty had a telephone pressed to her ear and made no effort to discontinue her conversation to greet her.

Val wondered if Betty knew the microphone was on because she could hear everything Betty said. "DNA results are pending on that skull found in Chestnut Ridge Park. The one missing all the teeth."

Pause.

"A hiker found it on one of the trails. From what I heard, you couldn't miss it. Detective Gavin thinks it was put out in the open on purpose, that it was supposed to be seen. He talked to several people who were on that trail only the day before, and it wasn't there."

Pause.

"It must belong to Jeanne Coleman. You know, the murdered woman that had all her teeth ripped out."

Val's ears perked up at the mention of *teeth ripped out* and listened closely, waiting for Betty to say more. "After two months with no leads, nothing at all, the case was getting cold. And then this happens? Reporters were here most of the day yesterday. All hell broke loose after that."

Val knew the case Betty was talking about. You could hardly miss the coverage, which had been on every news station. Several months ago, Jeanne Coleman had been found dead in her apartment, the victim of a savage attack. She had been stabbed repeatedly, and then dismembered. The killer photographed the victim throughout the murder and left the pictures behind so that cops, and everyone else, would know exactly what happened to her. Given the brutality, let alone advertisement of the crime, initial speculation focused on the possibility of a gang-related killing. Someone was sending a message. But nothing about Jeanne's lifestyle fitted with this theory. The fact that she was murdered like that made little sense.

One of the oddest issues of the case was that she'd had her teeth removed and then placed on the bedroom pillow. The rest of the body parts were missing, and so far, none of the pieces had been recovered.

Well, not until now.

Now, murmurs of a serial killer spread across the headlines.

Betty finally glanced up and quickly put the phone down. "Can I help you?"

Val jumped to attention, her pulse quickening. "I'm here about the death investigator position. I have an interview today. I'm afraid I'm a little early, though," she said, holding her head high, back straight. Then, leaned one elbow on Betty's counter with as much careless confidence as she could work up.

"Interview? Today?" Betty checked her computer. After a few seconds she smiled, got up from the desk, and pushed a button on the wall. The large metal doors opened. "No kidding about being early—we weren't expecting you until next week. Please come in."

Val entered through the doors, confused, correcting Betty immediately. "Next week? No, my interview is today."

"I wish they'd tell me when these things change. I'm always the last to know." Betty made her way back to the computer and searched through the schedule again. "I don't see you listed for today." Her face focused on the screen. "Your original appointment for next week is still here."

Val narrowed her eyes, still trying to comprehend what was going on. *Did I get the day wrong?*

"Oh well, I'm not surprised to see the scheduling mix-up. I was off sick and we had a temp in here last week. I'm still trying to fix things. I'll call Dr. Blythe and see what I can do. Oliver spoke so highly of you that I know Dr. Blythe will be happy to meet with you today." Betty picked up the phone. "This should only take a few minutes."

Val felt her stomach nervously flip. She did call last week to inquire about the status of her application for the job, so that would explain the scheduling error by this incompetent temp. But who was the person who spoke so highly of her? She didn't know any Oliver. She was so deep in thought she jumped when Betty spoke.

"So, I heard you met Oliver when he was in Rochester. He was such a great man. I can't believe he's gone. It just goes to show you never know when your time's going to be up," Betty said, dropping the phone down a little from her ear. "Anyway, with Oliver's glowing recommendation, Dr. Blythe will be relieved to have you start. Things have just been so hectic around here."

Met Oliver in Rochester? Glowing recommendation? Relieved to have me start?

Suddenly it all became painfully clear. Betty thought she was someone else. This job belonged to someone else. Her own interview was probably a courtesy interview to satisfy human resources and state hiring guidelines—in other words, a waste of time for anyone not promised a job internally or "on the side."

In an instant, all hope disintegrated. Val became lost, overwhelmed by circumstances beyond her control. Her life was falling apart, the last bits shattering and falling in a chaotic heap as she stood in the front office of the county morgue. She was broke, and without the promise of a pay check soon, she was about to become homeless too.

Val didn't say a word. She couldn't. The room felt like it was swirling and she was about to fall over.

Betty just stared, her eyes wide. Then her expression seemed to turn sympathetic. "Oh my God, I'm so sorry. I didn't mean to startle you. I thought you knew Oliver had died."

Betty's voice sounded far away. Val managed to answer, confused. "Died?"

"It was an aneurism. He went so suddenly."

Val felt outside of herself with no control over her own faculties, and then without realizing what she was doing, said, "So Oliver had good things to say about me?" As the words left her mouth, she couldn't believe the outright lie she'd just told. But hopeless situations call for desperate behavior. Survival instinct forced her to focus.

Betty smiled and placed her hand on Val's shoulder. "Yes, he said Gwen Carmondy was one of the best."

The seconds ticked by as Val thought of what to do next. Desperation clung tightly, making the decision clear. What could be lost at this point other than dignity, and dignity wasn't going to put food on the table or a roof over her head. Val was pretty sure the next lie she was about to tell wasn't criminal. Besides, what was the worst they could do? Have security escort her out? If she was coming back to the morgue anytime soon it wouldn't be under circumstances in which she'd have the capacity to really care about. "I think there might be some confusion. I'm Dr. Valentina Knight, a dentist. Oliver must have told both Gwen Carmondy and me about this job. Gwen *is* one of the best, but he thought I'd be better suited for this position."

Val breathed hard as perspiration rolled down the back of her neck. Her face felt hot and she began to wonder if her lie was showing.

"I'm so sorry. I had no idea. Oliver only mentioned one person," Betty stammered, then suddenly turned her attention to the phone and Val took the opportunity to try to steady her breathing.

"Yes, Candace. Is Dr. Blythe available to speak to a Valentina Knight?" When Betty responded, she lowered her voice, clearly sounding uncomfortable speaking in front of Val. "She's here about the death investigator position. It seems Oliver recommended her." There was a longer pause.

"I know that. But apparently Oliver spoke to her about it too." Betty's voice became still as she listened. Clearly, there was more discussion going on the other end of the line. She finally said, "Okay, I'll send her back."

"Dr. Knight, please come with me. I'll introduce you to Dr. DeHaviland."

"Dr. DeHaviland? Didn't you mention a Dr. Blythe?"

"Dr. Blythe is the chief medical examiner and is in the middle of an autopsy right now. Dr. DeHaviland, the deputy medical examiner, is just finishing up and can talk to you."

Betty led Val down a long corridor and into an office, saying nothing as they walked. Val was thankful for the silence. She wasn't quite sure how she would have responded to any questions. The only thought on her mind was keeping this house of cards from crashing down on her.

"Please have a seat. I'll tell Dr. DeHaviland you're here. She should be right in."

Val sat in the chair, heart in her throat, wondering how on earth she would pull this off. She needed to stay calm or this would just go from bad to worse.

As she waited, she anxiously looked around the room, searching for anything she could use to start small talk with, anything she could use as a distraction if she got backed into any uncomfortable corners regarding this Oliver person. The only reason they let her in today was because of her supposed connection to him.

There were diplomas in thick wood frames on the wall. The largest one, above the desk, displayed a medical degree from the University of Michigan to a Julia DeHaviland. Across the room was another diploma, this one for a PhD in pathology from the same university.

The room was furnished in dark mahogany. Persian carpeting in shades of gold, blue and burgundy covered the floor, completing the effect of an inviting office. For all of the pleasing colors, there was only a thin veneer of warmth in the room. The rest gave off a sense of sterility. There were no pictures on the desk or on the bookcases. In fact, other than the degrees, nothing personal was in the room. It had a feeling of remoteness, a distance at odds with the welcoming décor.

Val began to chew at her nails. There was nothing in this room, no photos of children, a significant other, nothing to help move a conversation away from the topic of Oliver if need be. *Jesus Christ.* Val's heart pounded harder. *I don't even know what this man's last name was. Or what in the hell his job was here.*

Without realizing it, she bit down again, this time a little too much, and winced in pain. She pulled her hand back and checked to see if she was bleeding. When she did her eyes froze on her scar. Mr. Tate's tooth marks were still engraved on her skin. He was the reason she would never practice dentistry again.

He had been her patient for only a couple of weeks when he was arrested in connection with the deaths of three young girls. One victim had bite marks on her breast. The local police asked if she could get a set of dental molds of his teeth so that they could be compared to the wound. Val agreed.

Mr. Tate was brought handcuffed and shackled to her dental office. He looked like he had been beaten. His right eye was swollen nearly shut and his lip was fat. Dark purple bruises covered his face. The cops left the room for only a minute to take a call. When they did, he pleaded with her to help him, confirming what she thought. The officers had used him as a punching bag. He said he was in terrible pain and thought his jaw was dislocated. Could she please check it for him?

She put on gloves and inspected the inside of his mouth. Three teeth were broken. The jagged edges must have been cutting his tongue, which had nasty lacerations near the tip. She had to put her entire thumb in his mouth to reach his jaw joint. Her index finger rested on his cheek and she began palpating the area for injury. After this point, it all became a blur, but she remembered the change in his eyes. He wasn't pleading for help anymore. He was happy.

He bit down hard, the sharp teeth cutting through her latex glove and skin. She tried to pull her hand back and as she did, he clamped down harder, making a crunching sound.

She screamed in pain and the cops rushed in. The first one grabbed the suspect's head, trying to pry open his jaws. The second began punching him in the face. But Mr. Tate fought back fiercely, his teeth still locked in her flesh. This was all she remembered. She passed out right after that. It was only later at the emergency room that she learned her mangled thumb was nearly torn apart.

A woman's voice snapped Val to attention.

"Just get everything prepped and I'll look at it later." The woman stood in the doorway, talking to someone in the hall. There was an inaudible response.

"Take the X-rays. We have to wait for DNA anyway," she answered, clearly irritated. After a second of silence she entered the room.

"How do you do. I'm Julia DeHaviland." She was slightly taller than Val. Her brown hair extended just to her shoulders and thick bangs came down to the top of her glasses. Makeup might have helped to hide the worn, pale complexion of her skin, but she wore none.

"I'm pleased to meet you, Dr. DeHaviland." Val stood and stretched out her hand.

"Call me Julia otherwise I'm going to have to call you Dr. Knight. I prefer to not be that formal." She took Val's hand, shaking it firmly, and then sat down at her desk. "I was told you are here about the death investigator position."

"Yes, I am."

Julia sorted through the papers in front of her, sighing as she moved them around. "Do you have a copy of your résumé with you? It looks like Betty didn't give it to me. With the scheduling screw-up, I'm not surprised."

"Of course, I have one right here." Val reached into her bag, pulled out the requested document, and slid it across the desk. It seemed like conducting this interview was the last thing Julia wanted to be doing.

"Thanks." Julia leaned forward, put both elbows firmly on the desk, and briefly read the lines. When she frowned and then narrowed her eyes, Val sensed there was a problem. She swallowed hard when Julia thumbed through it a second time.

"Betty tells me that you were a friend of Oliver's, and that he sent you our way." Elbows still rigidly positioned on the desk, her eyes fixed on Val's.

"Yes," Val replied simply. She felt her cheeks tighten and jaw clench. She said nothing further.

"I also hear he tried to get two of you to apply for this job. To be honest, I only knew about one. We have an ad posted too. Did you see it?"

Val smiled and shook her head, maintaining as much composure as she could. "No, Oliver told me about it."

Julia appeared to be satisfied with the answer and continued with her next question, sitting back in the chair now. "So tell me, why does a dentist want to become a death investigator?"

"I'm looking for a change in careers, something new. Something where I can use the medical knowledge I've obtained." Val exhaled in relief. Julia was more relaxed and it seemed like there weren't going to be any more questions about this Oliver person. She leaned back herself, crossing her legs, adding casually, "To tell you the truth, I've always been fascinated with forensic science and would love to do something in this field." The response came out with an air of credibility. Val knew she'd be asked why she wanted a change in careers and had learned, from previous experience at other interviews, not to admit that her injury was the reason.

People tended to act differently once they knew what happened. Oh, they were always kind at first, congratulating her on her courage. But Val would find them catching their words, apologizing at every turn, treating her like she was a victim. They also seemed skeptical that she would be a good employee. That maybe her injury was a little more serious, and the use of her hand was a lot less than she let on. Convinced that it had cost her several jobs over the last few months, she just couldn't take any chances right now.

"I can understand that. From what I hear, dentistry can be routine," Julia said.

"It is." Val laughed, accentuating her light-hearted response, though dentistry was anything but routine.

Julia laughed too and added, "I was in private practice at one time, in medicine, though. It's all the same. I know what you mean. Sometimes you're just ready for a change."

"What kind of medicine did you practice?" Val asked with interest.

Julia didn't answer immediately. She shuffled papers again and then said quietly, "I was a surgeon." She didn't elaborate on what kind of surgery she did. Val sensed something was off and strategically changed the topic, talking again about how interesting forensics was and now how much she admired Julia's position as a medical examiner.

Julia leaned forward, engaged in the conversation. Val began to grow comfortable as she spoke. She seemed to be winning Julia over and felt her chances of getting this job increasing.

"You know, as I look through your résumé, I just have one last thing to say," Julia said as she closed the document. Julia smiled as she spoke and Val felt secure the job was hers.

"What's that?" Val responded enthusiastically.

"You have no experience as a death investigator." The statement was blunt and the smile vanished from Julia's face.

"The ad didn't say experience was required." As soon as she said the words, Val wanted to retract them. A knot formed in her stomach and her chest constricted as she tried to correct the error.

"I have ten years' experience as a dentist. I have a lot of medical training." Her voice came out sounding guilty. Perspiration formed as the temperature in the room seemed to increase. She continued to ramble, digging the hole deeper with each word.

Julia sat back in the chair, crossed her arms, and frowned. Val couldn't help but think that she was going to have her thrown out of this office. But as Val talked, Julia's irritated expression changed, and now she had a quizzical look on her face.

Once the babbling stopped, Julia spoke. "Are you actually practicing dentistry?"

That question took Val by surprise. *What does that have to do with anything?* It took a second before she answered, "In Florida, but not since I've come back to Buffalo."

"That's an awfully long time."

"Like I said, I'm looking for a change in careers."

"Yes, you did say that. What part of Florida were you in?"

"Clearwater," Val said slowly, still not seeing the point.

"That's a very nice area. I've been there many times. So, you must have licenses to practice in both New York and Florida?"

"I have one for Florida but haven't gotten around to applying for New York yet," Val lied. Her Florida license was expired. She couldn't afford to renew it.

"You keep your Florida license current, but are now living in New York with no means to practice?" Julia seemed confused and Val didn't know what to say. Julia's question was valid.

"My Florida license is due for renewal soon. I think next month," she continued to lie. Julia knew the truth about Oliver. This interview was over. Why else would there be all of this off-topic talk? Val didn't feel like being interrogated on her dental license now. It was just too humiliating. She envisioned living on the street, her life over. Reality was hitting hard. Tears were starting. This job was her last hope and now all hope was gone.

She rose from the seat in an attempt to get out before the tears ran freely, but it was too late. They were already streaming down her cheeks. As Val wiped them with the back of her hand, Julia reached into her desk drawer and pulled out a tissue.

"Thank you for your time. It was very nice to meet you." Val kept her head down and stretched her right hand to pick up her bag, reaching for the tissue with her left hand.

"What happened to your hand?" Julia asked.

Val didn't reply. She didn't know what to say. Her mouth opened, trying to form words, but nothing came out.

"I'm sorry I was digging around with the questions. But honestly, you could make more money one day in practice than in two weeks in this position. It's not the kind of job people lie to get. There's a reason why you want this, and it goes well beyond a desire to work with the dead."

In a moment of much-needed relief, Val let it all out. Once the first words tumbled, she couldn't stop, describing the attack and how she couldn't practice anymore. She finished by confessing that this job was her last hope and as she came clean, she caught herself, embarrassed at exposing so much to a stranger. She wanted to die on the spot. Val hated to be seen as a victim, but for the last few minutes, she was just that.

Julia wheeled her chair back from the desk, her face sympathetic. Val had seen this reaction a number of times before. This is the point where she would be told, "We'll call you if we're interested."

Julia took a deep breath. "Being a private practice dentist is very different from what this job demands."

Oh no. Val cringed. *I'm going to be lectured before being shown the way out.* There was nothing left to do but sit and take it.

"Most busy offices like this one can't have one of the medical examiners going out in the field every time someone dies, so we hire death investigators to go in our place to analyze and report on the circumstances of the death."

"I'm so sorry. I didn't know. I thought a degree wasn't necessary. The ad stated you were looking for someone with a medical background. It didn't say medical doctor." All Val wanted to do was hide her head and crawl out of the room.

"That's because a medical degree *isn't* necessary. The death investigator responds to the scene of a death not as the medical examiner but as a representative of this office. Evidence is acquired from the scene to help someone like me determine cause and manner of death, as well as any information to identify the decedent, if that's unknown."

"So, this is kind of like being a cop?"

"Not at all. Cops catch criminals and solve cases. The death investigator's responsibility is to document the when, where and how someone died—in a medical context—but in suspicious cases he or she does become the link between this office and law enforcement."

"Again, I'm sorry. Had I known all of this I wouldn't have wasted your time." Val picked up her bag. Maybe if she made it obvious that she was ready to leave, Julia would let her go.

"You're inexperienced, but not unqualified. It's certainly not out of the question to consider someone with your background. Honestly, many people are trained on the job and learn that way." Julia hesitated and took a deep breath. She looked at Val's hand and then shifted her eyes, locking them on Val's. "I know what it's like to need a new start. So, actually, I think you might work out for us after all."

"Excuse me?" Val heard Julia's words, but they didn't register.

"Part of being a death investigator, as I said, is to help determine the identity of the decedent. With your dental background, you are definitely someone who could do that. Dental ID is so helpful in many cases."

Is this really happening? Is she thinking of hiring me? Val couldn't believe it and spoke quickly. "I can handle anything you throw at me. I'm willing to do anything. If you give me a chance, I'll prove it to you." She couldn't mask the eagerness in her voice and hoped that she didn't sound pathetic as she pleaded for this opportunity.

"The hours are variable, nights and weekends. Plus, you'd be on call."

"I can work anytime, day or night."

"Good. I'm assuming you can start tomorrow?"

"Absolutely," Val said.

"One last thing, your *relationship* with Oliver Solaris will be our secret. But the fact you have no experience in this field is something I won't be able to hide, as you'll have to be trained and people will notice. They'll wonder why Oliver would have recommended someone like you for this job. The best advice I can give you is to be ready for this."

"Thank you so much, Julia. I will. You won't be disappointed."

"Great. There's a floater waiting for a dental ID as we speak. He was just pulled out of the river about two hours ago. So, I'll see you tomorrow at 7:30am and we'll get started."

Julia hesitated for a moment before going into Dr. Phillip Blythe's office. She had no choice but to meet with him. He needed to know about the new employee. He wasn't going to be happy and had every right to say no. The first thing he would probably do is yell. Phil always yelled first. Julia braced herself.

"Good news!" she sang as she walked through the door.

Dr. Blythe looked up from his desk. A pile of paperwork sat in front of him. "I could use some good news." His sunken eyes clearly showed the stress he was under.

"I've hired someone for the death investigator position." Again, Julia was positive. Her plan was to get in and out as quickly as possible.

"We were down to the wire on that. I wasn't sure how we were going to function with just Howie."

"This new person is also a dentist, so she'll be able to do dental identifications too. With how busy we've been, this should help."

Blythe raised his eyebrows. "A dentist? Why does she want to work here?"

"She can't practice anymore. She had an accident." Julia kept her answers brief, hoping to leave Blythe's office unscathed. Once this was out of his hands and into that of the administration, she would be free and clear.

"I don't remember Oliver mentioning this about her."

"Apparently, Oliver promised the job to two people. This isn't the one you're thinking of. Here's her résumé. I'll have Candace get going on the paperwork. Dr. Knight can start tomorrow." Julia handed him the document, turned and walked away. She made it as far as the doorway.

"Julia!" he called out, résumé in hand. "This seems to be missing something."

"What?" she asked innocently.

"Experience?" He shook his head in disbelief. "How could Oliver have recommended someone like this?"

"She's trainable," Julia said, trying to appear as if this was no big deal.

"Damn it, Julia! How could you have hired her? I am up to my eyeballs in crap here. Can't you see that?" He pointed to the papers littering his desk. "In addition to all of this, I'm now hounded by the hour on the Coleman murder. Since the press announced that toothless skull was found, it's been nonstop. They're not going to ease up until I give a positive ID."

"Aren't you ready to make one?"

"I have no doubt the skull belongs to Jeanne Coleman. I'm just waiting for the DNA results, which have been difficult to get. There's been a lot of issues with it."

"Like what?"

"It's far too degraded."

"It can't be. She's only been dead for a couple of months."

"That's exactly the problem. We're to believe this skull's only been exposed to the outside environment for two months but the amount of breakdown isn't consistent with that. There was no tissue left on the bone. That was purposely stripped off. Deep linear marks from a knife are evident. But the skull itself is dried out. If I had to guess, it had been outside for two years, not two months. This skull is either too old to belong to Jeanne Coleman or someone is trying to make it look like it's too old. Honestly, I think it was purposely dehydrated, by baking it."

Julia narrowed her eyes. "Are you releasing that information?"

"Absolutely not. We're keeping this private for now. Can you image the additional hell we'd have to endure if the public found out that the killer ripped out Jeanne Coleman's teeth, dismembered her, then *cooked* her skull?"

"Good decision," Julia said. Blythe went quiet and she took the opportunity to get back to the topic of the new employee. "So, can I get Candace going on the paperwork for Dr. Knight?"

"Julia, we need competent, well-trained professionals for this job, and you want to bring in someone so green she's useless. I can't have someone without any experience running around causing more trouble than they're worth. We can't afford to babysit someone right now."

"I can train her. Howie can—"

"Howie can't. You can't. Neither you nor Howie have time for this. How is this person supposed to be able to do this job? I have no one to hold her hand."

"On-the-job training is very common for a death investigator."

"Yes, when there is the time and resources to do it. Right now, I am understaffed and underbudgeted."

"But—"

"I understand what you're going through, I really do." He rubbed his temples. Taking a deep breath, he continued, "And I sympathize with you, but I can't have your bleeding heart run my office."

Julia swallowed hard. "That's not why I want to hire her."

"No? Then what is it? Do you honestly expect me to believe the similarity of her situation to yours didn't influence your decision?" Julia detected an accusatory, sarcastic tone in his voice.

"Not at all." She said the words slowly. Her eyes didn't leave his.

"The fact that both of you no longer practice had nothing to do with it? She, because of what did you say? An accident? And you because of your... *situation*."

As soon as he said "situation," Julia just glared at him. How dare he throw *her* situation in her face? It was so like Phil to do this kind of crap.

"Look, I feel a camaraderie with my fellow professionals, and maybe you want to give this person some of the advantages you've had, but this is not the time or place for that," Blythe said.

His words only made her angrier. "If you want to talk about a situation, Phil, we can talk about one." She crossed her arms. "I finished the O'Rourke case."

The muscles in Blythe's face tensed and he drummed his interlocked fingers repeatedly. "And?"

"The wounds were in conical-shaped pairs. Most are located to the head and neck area. Death was by exsanguination. The carotid was lacerated and he bled out. This kid didn't have a chance." She paused. "The scratches are in lines of four and the bruises resemble a paw. Plus, there are six incisor marks between the conical punctures of the canines that are easily detected in the bites. I have no doubt it was a dog attack. Looks like you were right."

"I know I am. This was that dog's second assault." His expression remained rigid. From the case file, Julia had learned that the same rottweiler was to be euthanized for attacking its seventy-year-old owner. The dog was so friendly at the pound that instead of putting it down, it was put up for adoption. The O'Rourkes were the unlucky recipients. Two-year-old Billy O'Rourke paid the price when he was left unattended with the dog.

She also found out that Dr. Blythe was the only person who

claimed it was a dog attack. Two other pathologists stated it was a child abuse case. The wounds, the other doctors said, were created with various kitchen tools. The gash to the neck was made with a box cutter. The parents had spent the last year in jail, their other three children placed in foster homes.

Dr. Blythe's career, which had once been a prestigious one, was now swirling around the toilet bowl. Several significant errors on other cases where he rendered wrong conclusions made the problem worse. Julia suspected he might be heading in the same direction with the Coleman case.

"Looks like you were right on that one, Phil," she said, adding, "I've told Valentina Knight she's hired. I know she can do the job."

He stared at Julia. "I'll give her one week. I'm only doing this because Oliver seemed to have had some confidence in her. There will be no special treatment. If she can't do this job, she's out."

"Fair enough." Julia couldn't argue with that.

3

The next morning, Val stood outside Betty's window, waiting to be let into Erie County Medical Examiner's Office. First-day jitters were nothing compared to the anxiety she was feeling right now.

Julia had promised to keep the fact that Val had never met Oliver a secret. She was forced to take this guarantee at face value. The problem was what to say to everyone else who thought she knew him. Right now, that was Betty and anyone she might have told. Val stared through the glass. Betty wasn't alone. There was a woman standing with her.

As soon as Val was inside the metal doors, Betty said, "This is Candace Drapier. She's our head administrator and pretty much handles everything going on here. She'll show you where to go and get you sorted out."

Candace was tall, an easy five feet ten, with short blond hair and wide-set blue eyes. She came forward, hand outstretched to greet Val. "I'm so happy to meet you." With the opposite hand on her hip and the other taking Val's in a firm handshake, she squeezed a little too tight, then peered down. It had a carnivorous feel and Val couldn't help but sense she was being appraised, questioned and evaluated all at once. *Candace suspects something,* she thought. *Or she wants to suspect something—which honestly, is worse.*

"I have some paperwork for you to do. It's all the standard first-day-of-work forms." Candace handed Val a folder filled with various documents. "I need you to complete these and give them back to me ASAP." She continued to rattle off the itinerary.

"We'll get your ID done at some point today. You'll need that for just about everything you do. The ID swipes to open all of the doors here, and you will have to display it at any death scenes you go to." She pulled on the strap around her neck and showed Val her own ID card.

Val nodded, trying to make a mental note of the rapid-fire instructions.

"Well then, come with me. I'll bring you by Dr. DeHaviland's office first. I know she wants to say hello, and then I'll take you to your office so you can get started," Candace said.

As they entered the hallway, Candace pointed to an open door to their right. The sign outside the entrance read "toxicology department". "This is where we perform all of our drug testing. Dr. Beauchamp is our head toxicologist. It's amazing what they can find in tissue samples nowadays, isn't it?"

"Yes. It is." Val had a decent knowledge of medications. She had to prescribe them for her patients when she practiced. She poked her head in the room and was surprised by the large size. "They must do a lot of drug analysis here."

"A lot is an understatement. This is a pretty busy morgue. We handle about a thousand autopsies per year. All of our departments are worked to the max. You'll be a welcome addition for Dr. Blythe and Dr. DeHaviland." Her tone seemed sincere and Val felt her tightly wound nerves ease a little.

They continued down the hallway.

"In addition to the toxicology lab, we also have a histology lab so we can check for pathology in the tissues quickly. Of course, most autopsies take place in the main morgue area. There is one private room for high-profile cases, but only Dr. Blythe and Dr. DeHaviland use that."

"DNA testing isn't performed here?"

"Oh, that's done at the Erie County Crime Lab. Everything DNA goes there."

As the two walked together, Val began to relax around Candace. Convinced now she was just being paranoid, assuming everyone would be suspicious of her.

"So, there were two of you fighting for this job? How odd."

The question came out of nowhere and Val felt her stomach drop. She had no idea what to make of this. Her voice faltered as she said, "Excuse me?"

"We had a devil of a time getting anyone in, and then all of a sudden there were two of you. What did you do to win? We didn't even interview the other girl. You must have some spectacular credentials." Her tone implied interest and admiration for Val. But Val couldn't help but sense something darker in it too.

Fortunately, Val didn't have to answer because at that moment they arrived at Julia's office. The door was partially open and Val could see her speaking on the phone. "I don't care if you file for divorce. I was expecting it anyway, just like this bullshit lawsuit." There was a pause and then Julia spoke again. "I had nothing to do with that disfigured bitch. Go ahead. Try to sue me."

Candace grabbed Val's arm and led her away quickly. "Dr. DeHaviland seems a little busy right now. Why don't I show you your own office? We'll catch up with her later."

They were barely away from the door when she whispered in Val's ear, "I'm so sorry you had to hear that. Poor Dr. DeHaviland. Her story is so sad. Everyone in this office knows about it, and I'm sure you'll hear it sooner or later. Let me just set the record straight for her. I don't want you to fall prey to any office rumors."

"What is it?" Val asked reflexively. She couldn't help it after hearing the words *divorce*, *disfigured bitch*, and *lawsuit*.

"As you just heard, she's being *sued*. And that's not the whole story. The person who's suing her is her husband's girlfriend."

Val's eyes opened wide.

"Don't look so shocked. Julia should be commended. Talk about revenge. This woman was one of Julia's patients—that's back when Julia used to practice. You might not have known this, but Julia was a plastic surgeon before she came to work here."

Val remembered that Julia had said she used to be in private practice and waited to hear more of this story.

"The girlfriend had a mole removed and ended up getting a nasty infection that started to destroy the skin and tissue on her face. The doctors thought it was some weird type of flesh-eating bacteria. Of course everyone assumed Julia did it on purpose, that she gave *the other woman* something that caused the infection. But no strange species of bacteria was found, so no criminal charges were brought against Julia. They couldn't prove anything. It didn't take long before the civil suit was filed. I'm not sure for how much, but I know it's a lot."

So that was Julia's story. Val had never thought someone else's problems could be as bad as her own. Hell, Julia's problem was even worse. She felt sorry for Julia. And then realized that perhaps Julia had felt sorry for *her as well*. But it was more than that.

Everyone had sympathized with Val, but no one saw her as anything other than a victim. Therefore, no one ever gave her a chance to be anything other than that, until Julia hired her. Val never wanted sympathy. She wanted an opportunity, and Julia had finally given her that opportunity.

She felt a sense of loyalty towards Julia. Even though Candace had said she was telling this story so that Val wouldn't be subjected to office gossip, she couldn't help but notice that's exactly what was going on.

Candace stopped and turned to Val. "You know, it's funny. I used to talk to Oliver all the time and he mentioned several of his colleagues that would be good for the job, someone named Gwen Carmondy being his first choice. But now that I think of it, he never mentioned you."

"I guess we're even because he never mentioned you to me either," Val said without hesitation. She held her breath, waiting for a response. Candace's smile was immediately retracted and Val couldn't read the expression that replaced it. After a second or two, the smile returned. Candace continued as if nothing had happened.

She led Val to an office the size of a large closet. It wasn't much more than two Formica counters lining each wall. Both were strewn with folders.

"I know it doesn't look like much. Why don't you put your things down in here and get into a pair of scrubs. You'll find them on the shelves in the hallway. Howie should be here shortly. He'll take over from here."

Eager to be rid of Candace, Val didn't bother to ask who Howie was and as soon as Candace was gone Val breathed a sigh of relief. She knew to trust her first instincts. Candace was trouble. Trouble, as it turned out, she could handle. *Hell, I've handled worse before,* she thought. Val quickly changed her clothes and waited. She was busy thumbing through the folders on the countertop when she heard a knock on the open door and glanced up.

"Dr. Knight, nice to meet you. I'm Howie Watts. Your fellow death scene investigator. Dr. DeHaviland asked me to show you the ropes. Some of this can be confusing at the beginning, so feel free to ask me anything you need to."

He was a big man, over six feet tall and easily 250 pounds, but had a clean-cut, boyish appearance that didn't fit with his size. "There are no death scenes to go to right now so we'll be working in the morgue instead. Are you ready to get to work?" he asked.

"Nice to meet you too, Howie. I couldn't be more ready," Val said eagerly, relieved that Julia was the one who had sent Howie. He seemed to have an understanding of what her experience level was, and that she needed to be trained.

"Well, then come with me. I'm going to show you the autopsy room. Dr. Blythe's about to do roll call. That's where he goes through the bodies that came in last night and decides which ones need a post-mortem exam. He's ready to start."

Val had never been inside a morgue before. After seeing depictions on TV shows, she had her own idea of what one should look like and expected there to be one body per room, kind of like an operating room. Instead, she was surprised to see eight stainless steel tables placed one after the other in this big open space.

In the center of the morgue, five dead people were on gurneys. Two of them were in white body bags, the zippers open, lifeless faces exposed. The other three were not in bags, but were wearing hospital gowns, obviously patients of the hospital who had died during the night. One still had EKG tabs on his chest. At the far end, a sixth body lay on its own, separated from the rest, the white bag completely closed. Beyond this person was a steel door with a sign that read Autopsy Isolation Room.

In the corner of the room, a female photographer was standing almost on the top rung of a stepladder, taking pictures of clothing laid out on the floor. The clothing consisted of a pair of jeans and a T-shirt. Both were blood-soaked.

A man walked in with clipboard in hand. He wore scrubs and had surgical booties over his sneakers. His dark hair was cropped short. With a square jaw, taut muscles and intense blue eyes, Val couldn't tell if he was intimidating or attractive. Or both. He appeared to be in his mid-forties. Without question he had a commanding appearance. The staff snapped to attention. Howie explained that this was Dr. Blythe. Val watched him as he went over to each of the three bodies from the hospital and for two of them, stated the names and causes of death. "No post-mortem needed. These can go."

"They don't need an autopsy?" Val asked Howie.

"It's not required in all circumstances. Just because someone ends up here doesn't mean they need to be opened up, especially if we already know their cause of death."

Val continued to watch Dr. Blythe as he inspected each corpse. The person with the EKG tabs as well as those in the body bags would need an autopsy and he cleared those to begin.

"The one at the end of the hall is yours," Howie said, pointing to the one on its own. "Our job is just to take X-rays of the decedent's teeth."

"What's she doing over there?" Val asked, pointing to the photographer on the stepladder.

"She's documenting the clothing worn by that victim." Howie motioned towards the gurney closest to them. A dead teenager lay on top. "From that height she gets all of the items in the proper orientation for the photograph."

"What happened to him?"

"He was killed in a gang fight. Poor boy was only sixteen." Howie shook his head in regret then grabbed the gurney and wheeled it over to a steel table, finally transferring the teenager's body onto it. "This kid's one of my cases. I picked him up off the pavement last evening as he lay dead outside the house where he lived with his grandmother. She was inconsolable when I took him away."

Two doctors were standing around the table, waiting to get to work. Howie introduced them as medical residents, Dr. Chen and Dr. Phelps. They said polite hellos. "Val, I have to get a couple of signatures before we start. Why don't you hang out here until I come back."

Val nodded without looking in Howie's direction. She couldn't keep her gaze off the face of the victim. She thought of his grandmother and the pain of loss, of family that now only existed as memories. *Jesus, he was just a kid. What a waste of such a young life.* In his chest was a small hole. Dr. Chen began to describe this as the entrance wound.

The victim was rolled to expose his back. There was no exit wound.

Dr. Chen picked up a scalpel. In one motion and without any hesitation, he cut from just below the shoulder on the right side to mid chest. The skin immediately gaped open. In another sweeping motion he repeated the cut on the left side, continuing down the middle to just above the belly button.

Val watched intently, speechless as Dr. Chen picked up a pair of long-handled garden loppers, wondering what on earth he was doing with those. He placed the blades under the bottom rib, starting on the right side and cut upwards towards the top. Val stared, shocked, as each rib snapped easily, like Dr. Chen was pruning small branches from a tree. He did the same thing on the left side. Then lifted the entire ribcage off the body.

"I know it looks crude but the loppers are quick and, most importantly, leave little mess," Dr. Chen said.

Val smiled nervously, aware that he saw her expression. "Of course," she said, as if she was well versed in rib removal. Oliver recommended her for this job. Why the hell the morgue used garden instruments should be commonplace knowledge for her. *Jesus, there is a lot to learn here.*

Dr. Phelps picked up a long, thin, straight instrument and she inserted it into a hole in the boy's heart. "The bullet entered the left atrium, crossed through to the right ventricle and then both lungs to the lower right quadrant. The trajectory is left to right and downward. He probably died within minutes of being shot." She worked for a few minutes to free the bullet, finally reaching in with her fingers to grab it, then placed it in a plastic container. "The cops will want this," she said, handing the container to Val.

She took the container slowly, carefully, as if Dr. Phelps was passing over evidence that solved the crime of the century. "The cops should be happy. The bullet will be able to tell which gun fired the shot," Val said. She'd watched a few episodes of *Law & Order*. She knew what this kind of evidence meant.

Dr. Phelps ignored her and continued with the autopsy, removing organs, taking tissue samples. Val looked around. There was no sign of Howie yet, but she did notice the table where the man with the EKG tabs was being dismantled. The doctor there was dissecting the heart. Intrigued, Val moved in closer. She was still holding the plastic container with the bullet and had no idea what to do with it.

"I'm Dr. Jim Stedman. Nice to meet you," he said. "I'd shake your hand but I'm a little messy right now." He set down the heart and held up his bloodstained gloved hands.

Val smiled. "That's okay, I'll catch up with you later, after you wash up."

"I clean up pretty good," he said.

"No amount of cleaning could make *you* look good," Howie said, laughing. Val hadn't even seen him come back into the room.

Val held out the plastic container for him. "This is from the boy who was shot."

"Thanks. I'll get this to the cops for ballistic testing." He took the container, and placed it on the morgue counter, next to paperwork that appeared to be his. "We have our okay to get started on the next case. Your case. I need you to put one of these on." He held up a white disposable jumpsuit. It had a zipper up the middle and looked like the kind of thing people wore for biohazards. This one was complete with a hood. "We're going to start you off easy with something that should be second nature for you. It's a dental ID."

"Why do I have to wear this?" She looked around the room. No one else had on anything like it. They were all in hospital scrubs.

"That's because we have to work in the decomp room."

"Decomp room?"

"I mean, the autopsy isolation room." Howie continued with instructions for dress. Shoe covers for her sneakers were next. Once those were in place he gave her a surgical cap for her hair and a thick mask to cover her nose and mouth. She was grateful for the mask. There was a stench in the air, like raw sewage mixed with rotten eggs, and it helped to block it out.

"Let's get your gloves on now. Make sure to pull them up over the arms of the suit."

Val did as Howie instructed.

"You only need to see how this is done once. You'll be able to do it yourself next time." Howie dressed himself in the same manner, then took the gurney and wheeled it into the autopsy suite.

The room was bigger than Val thought it would be, and quite cold, much more so than the main morgue area. "Why is it freezing in here?"

"They keep it colder in here for a couple of reasons. The big reason is it gets hot as you work. With all you're wearing, you'll realize as soon as we start how quickly you'll sweat."

While he moved the gurney into place, she inspected the room, wondering what the other reason was. High on the wall was a small window. On the sill were many dead flies. She immediately began to feel itchy.

Howie picked up the file and started to read the report. "John Doe # 457987. Found washed ashore on the banks of the Niagara River by a couple of kids fishing. That will give them nightmares for the rest of their lives."

Val eyed the body bag, eager to see what was inside. This was her own case and she couldn't wait to get started. "Can I open the bag?"

"Yeah, but when you unzip it, make sure to stand back."

Though it seemed like an odd thing to do, Val again did as she was told. As soon as she slid the zipper down, she was immediately overcome by a repulsive smell. The odor was so fetid that her knees became wobbly and she broke out in a clammy sweat. Her stomach turned but she managed to control the nausea, only because the condition of the body distracted her. But there was something else. Something was on it.

The body was a foul greenish-gray color and severely bloated. Patches of skin were missing. What remained was slimy. The body was dotted sparsely with white spots, but the eye sockets and nasal cavity were filled with opaque blobs. The blobs and spots appeared to be moving. Val got closer and realized that they *were* moving. They were moving and then jumping. It took a few seconds to realize that these were maggots and they were jumping *onto her*. She began to scream and then started swatting at herself to get rid of them. As she fiercely batted her arms at her head, Val pulled her mask and surgical cap off.

She inhaled the putrid odor of decomposition again. It was much more powerful this time without the protection of her mask and her knees buckled. Howie leaned over and grabbed her around the waist, trying to steady her. As soon as he put pressure on her stomach, she threw up all down the front of herself and him.

"Oh my God, I'm so sorry," she managed to get out before the next wave hit her and she vomited again.

Val attempted to run out of the room, but Howie had a firm hold on her. "Dr. Blythe is out there. You don't want him to see you like this."

At this point she didn't care who saw her or not, all she wanted to do was get to the door. "I have to get out of here. Now. Please," she whispered. This was far too embarrassing to endure. She felt the heave come to her throat, but it was dry. Noise only.

Howie put his arms around her. "I'll go with you." He helped her out, getting by Dr. Blythe undetected, before leading Val down the hallway to the woman's locker room. He instructed her to change and meet him back in the decomposition room. His tone was firm. It appeared that he would not succumb to any of her protests. "I want to see you back in ten minutes."

Val didn't answer and staggered into the locker room. She reeked of puke and noticed a big gob of it in her hair. Merely changing wouldn't be enough. She needed to shower too.

She stood under the water, grabbed the soap and began scrubbing her face. At first, she was just trying to get rid of the smell, but the rubbing grew more forceful as she tried to wash away the last year of her life. When that didn't work, she threw the bar of soap, and crumpled to the ground.

Hugging her knees to her chest, she sat and wept; cursing how she ended up here, broke, alone, and crying, naked, on the bathroom floor of the county morgue. How could fate be so cruel? She begged to be her old self again, a professional, someone in charge. Her patients trusted her because she knew how to take care of them. Right now, she couldn't even take care of herself.

The water made a loud gurgling sound as it swirled around the drain. The throaty echo caused her to look down. She watched for a minute. As the water circled, it distracted her from the misfortune that had become her life. She had a choice. Sit here and cry about the past or suck up her pride and get up and do something about her future. Val grabbed the faucet and pulled herself up, concentrating on everything she'd achieved. She had overcome obstacles before. She certainly wasn't a quitter. Everything she had in life, she earned, struggling to get to the top. She could do it again. And the way to do that was waiting for her back in the decomp room.

Val got out of the shower, grabbed a fresh set of scrubs and headed back to the morgue, dressing herself without instruction this time in a white jumpsuit. When she opened the door to the decomp room, the first thing she heard was the song, "Rolling on the River". Val saw Howie had the song playing from his cell phone.

"Don't you think that music is a little inappropriate?" she asked. "That poor man died in the river." As soon as she inhaled, her stomach grew queasy again. The mask filtered most of the odor, but not all of it.

"I play "Burning Down the House" when we have fire victims," Howie said matter-of-factly.

The sheer bluntness of the statement made Val laugh. She put her hand over her masked mouth, and looked at Howie, ashamed.

"It's okay. It's called morgue humor. That's how we cope with what we do. To some it might sound morbid, but it helps get us through this. There are days when it's easy and others where there's that one case you can't get rid of. It'll eat away at you if you let it. You'll get accustomed to most of this and it'll become routine. Now, you need to get to work." He handed her a box of X-ray film.

"Do you think he committed suicide?"

"Not sure, but this isn't the way I'd go. Drowning is painful. Plus, to be successful at it you have to secure weights to yourself before the plunge. Once you do that, you're at the point of no return. It's kind of like the person who jumps off the roof of a building. If you have a change of heart there's nothing you can do on the ride down."

Val moved around the body, getting all of the X-rays. Taking dental X-rays was something she knew how to do. She was uncomfortable with the maggots at first, but by the end she realized they would stay on top of her gloves.

"We already have a presumptive ID on this guy. His wallet was in his back pocket when he was found. That's what we call a clue." Howie raised one eyebrow in an exaggerated manner. "We already have X-rays from his dentist. These are called antemortem X-rays because they were taken before death."

They compared those to the victim's post-mortem X-rays. Each filling was the same. Even a gold cap on a molar and a root canal on the front tooth were identical. "It's a match!" Val exclaimed, proud of herself. "This is Mr. George Wolff."

"Congrats, Dr. Knight, you just made your first dental victim ID. It's a good feeling isn't it? You gave him a name and now he can be returned to his family. They can have closure."

At the end of her shift, Val was the happiest she'd been in a long time. On the drive home, she flipped through the radio channels, stopping at a station broadcasting the news. The toothless skull found in Chestnut Ridge Park was the top story. Why it remained in the medical examiner's office, still unidentified, was the focus of the segment. The announcer stressed that Dr. Blythe had been unavailable for comment. That his conclusions didn't seem to add up. Again.

4

It was a little before 5pm when Val swiped her ID card through the security pad at the employee entrance of the medical examiner's office. Her second day of work was the night shift, twelve hours from 5pm to 5am. Julia wasn't kidding when she said the shifts would be variable. With a large cup of coffee in one hand, keys and handbag in the other, Val struggled to open her office door.

Howie grabbed her before she had a chance to put her things down. "Don't get comfortable. We've been called to a death scene. We're leaving immediately."

Val followed Howie to the parking ramp, walking fast, trying to keep up. Her thoughts churned quickly, one rapid anxious hiccup to the other. She was nervous and excited at the same time. This would be her first real death scene investigation and she couldn't wait to be part of it, though she had no idea what to do once she got there.

When they arrived at the car Howie said, "The victim was found just like the other one. Her teeth were removed and left on the bedroom pillow. The rest of her is missing." He popped the trunk and placed several bags of equipment inside. "The apartment manager discovered her about an hour ago."

Val opened the door and slid onto the seat, her heart beating hard. This story was nonstop on the news. She couldn't believe it had happened again. *And this is where we are heading.* She took a deep breath and tried to hold her emotions together.

Howie got in behind the wheel, placed the key in the ignition, and quickly explained more. "At the first crime scene, there was an attempt to obliterate all physical evidence. Meticulous cleaning was performed. The killer wiped away not only fingerprints, but almost all visible signs of blood. Investigators had to use luminol to see where it was. And it was everywhere. Floors. Walls."

"Luminol?"

"It's a chemical that reacts with the iron component in blood. Even if it's cleaned with detergent and no longer visible, luminol will still detect it."

"I don't remember hearing about this on the news."

"That's because this information was never released to the press. There's no way this was a gang killing as they originally suggested. No member of any gang would have gone to that kind of trouble. From the preliminary report the cops sent to us, it looks like the same thing happened with this new victim. It's so ritualistic that this has to be a serial killer."

"The new victim, what's her name?" Val asked.

"Francine Donohue."

Howie made it to the Eastville Projects, one of the city's most run-down subsidized housing developments, in less than five minutes, but they were far from the first to arrive. Squad cars lined the street; reporters hustled and cameras were positioned.

Small groups of people stood outside the entrances to the adjacent buildings. They obviously lived here. Val shuddered at the thought of anyone having to live *here*. The tenements were ugly, bland, rectangular brick buildings. Nothing about them was the slightest bit appealing, or hospitable.

The Eastville Projects had a reputation that was established well before her own childhood. In these projects death came more frequently than the repo man. Gang fights, domestic disputes, drug deals all happened frequently. People shooting each other over cocaine or methamphetamine was common here. *But Jesus, what happened to Francine Donohue was anything but common, even for a crime haven like this.*

"Dr. Blythe will be here personally because of how important this case is. He'll be in charge and our job will be just to assist him," Howie said. "This is going to be really high profile."

Val looked around at the reporters and her pulse raced. "Oh my God. I think every news station is here. A second person killed liked this, someone else who had their teeth removed. This is huge."

"Huge is an understatement. Francine Donohue wasn't the only one to die here in Eastville. Jeanne Coleman, the first victim, was murdered here too."

Her head snapped towards Howie but he was already getting out of the car. Val reached for the door handle and quickly pulled it open. Adrenaline pumped through her system as they started to walk towards the building.

Howie stopped when a blue sedan pulled up. Two men got out. He explained that they were Mitchell Gavin and Alexander Warren, the detectives in charge of this case. He stressed that Gavin was the lead detective and pointed him out.

Val stood by Howie's side, staring as they came closer. She wouldn't have guessed Gavin to be a cop. He was a handsome man, moderately tall, slightly over six feet with a lean build. His light brown hair had small silver streaks throughout. Alexander Warren looked nothing like his partner. He stood several inches shorter, his head was shaved and he wore a goatee.

They came up to Howie and shook his hand. He introduced Val and then asked, "What do you know about the victim?"

"The suspected victim is Francine Donohue. The first responders found her driver's license in her handbag," Warren announced, then looked through his notes. "She was reported missing about six months ago by her sister. This sister hadn't spoken to her in almost twenty years but decided to pay her a visit. She went to Francine's previous residence, which was in Orchard Park, New York, but Francine was gone. Several people saw Francine heading to her car with suitcases a few days before this. No one saw her again after that. Get this. She was a dentist."

"Holy crap. What a way to kill a dentist." Howie quickly glanced over at Val.

She maintained her composure as best she could, though it did freak her out.

Gavin, who had been silent, finally spoke. "Do we know how long she's been living here?"

"According to the apartment manager's records, she's been here the last six months. Since she disappeared," Warren answered.

"So, she was living in Eastville at the time of the last murder." Gavin looked around at the layout of the apartment buildings. "This isn't even close to Jeanne Coleman's place. They're direct opposites in the complex. They couldn't be further apart."

"This may be a hunting ground," Warren said. "We could have a serial killer."

"No," Gavin said bluntly, and took the missing persons report from Warren, glancing at it before he spoke again. "Up until six months ago, Francine lived in an upper-class suburban neighborhood. She was a dentist and now she's dead in a slum? Killed like *this*? What in the hell was Francine Donohue doing *here* and for that length of time? Who was she hiding from? And what was her connection to Jeanne Coleman? This is what I want to know because there's no way this can be random. This is not the work of some serial killer. And damn it, this isn't some gang killing either."

The small group grew quiet after Gavin's rant.

"What was the first victim's occupation?" Val asked, her voice soft. Gavin stared at her. She was scrutinized as much as her question and wanted to crawl away, wishing that she'd never said anything at all.

"Jeanne Coleman didn't have one," he answered. "She was a recluse."

"Jesus, nothing in this case makes any sense," Howie said.

"Certainly not anymore," Gavin said, and entered the apartment.

Val followed the group in. Howie stopped to talk to a few people who were standing just inside the doorway. As she waited for him to finish, she watched the production unfolding. The experience seemed surreal as the number of people entering the small apartment grew larger by the second. Crime-scene technicians and uniformed officers hurried in, all discussing the course of action they were to take. They carried an array of equipment. Some had cameras around their necks. All wore jackets and name badges listing who they were and what they were there to do. Outside, commotion from reporters and bystanders created a steady hum in the background.

Howie walked away from the conversation and motioned towards Val to come too. She trailed after him down the hallway. She knew where they were going and what she was about to see. As they entered the bedroom, she held her breath and quickly looked around.

A team of technicians was busy collecting evidence and two more were photographing it. Gavin and Warren talked with several officers.

"So far we found one set of prints. They're on the ceiling in the closet over there," the one officer said. "The ceiling obviously had a repair. Water damage can be seen. The prints more than likely belonged to the person who fixed it."

Very few people were around the bed and when Howie moved closer to it, Val went too, now able to see what remained of Francine Donohue. On the pillow lay what appeared to be a complete set of human teeth. They had been ripped from the victim's jaws. This was obvious. Some had pieces of bone still attached while others possessed remnants of clinging tissue. All were covered in dried blood. Val winced at the sheer violence of it all. *God, I hope she was dead before any of this started.*

This was the only visible blood in the room. The pictures lying on the bed told a different story. They depicted Francine's murder and dismemberment. According to these, this room and the bathroom should have been a bloody mess.

The first photo was of Francine on the floor. Multiple stab wounds could be seen on her abdomen and chest. Blood spatter covered the wall behind the body. A furious attack must have occurred to cause that much spray. Though the scene in the photos was particularly violent, most notable was that Francine's mouth was bloody and sunken in. Val couldn't tell from the pictures if her teeth were removed before she was stabbed to death.

From what the rest of the photos showed, most of the dismemberment took place in the bathtub. Francine was cut up into several parts. Each arm and leg was sectioned in two, dissected at the knee and elbow. Her head was detached and her torso halved. The killer obviously wanted everyone to know what had occurred.

Val pulled on Howie's arm, trying to get his attention. After the third tug, he finally turned round. "Howie, I might be able to help if I examine the teeth."

"We can't touch anything until Dr. Blythe gets here. He's in charge and it's his call. If he wants you to examine them, he'll ask." Howie's tone was apologetic. "He should be here soon. We just have to sit tight for a little while."

Val tried hard to sit tight. This was an area in which she could shine and she wanted desperately to do that. She had lied to get this job. This was the opportunity to get past that—a chance to prove to everyone how valuable she could be as a strong member of this team. She turned her attention to what was going on in the room, the mesmerizing intensity drawing her in.

One of the technicians pulled out the alternate light source and began scouring around the bed, causing something to glimmer under it.

"Hey, I have something here," the technician called out. He reached for the object and pulled out a small, balled-up, foil chewing-gum wrapper. "Sorry, it's just garbage."

"Bag it anyway," Gavin ordered. He walked away from the officers and came towards the bed and began examining the photos of Francine.

Val stood within inches of him. She glanced at his face, and then at the pictures, trying to read his thoughts. He selected one image and narrowed his eyes. Then pointed to the pillow.

"The pillowcase is bloodied but the sheets are clean. They're also a different print than the ones in these photos," Gavin said, dropping the pictures down on the bed. "He did the same thing at Jeanne Coleman's crime scene. Why in the hell does he do this? Why change the sheets, but not the pillowcase? She wasn't killed on the bed and it looks like the teeth were placed on the pillow after the fact."

Val's gaze flew to the pillowcase. Gavin was right. She was so engrossed with the teeth that she hadn't even noticed the bedding didn't match.

Warren walked around the side of the bed. "The killer took them as a souvenir. This is what he needs to relive the event," he suggested.

"Kind of an odd souvenir," Howie said.

"A souvenir points to a serial case. This is not that," Mitchell Gavin said. He turned to a crime-scene technician. "Can you start getting pictures of all of this."

Another technician, who was busy searching the bedside table with a magnifying glass, eagerly motioned for Gavin to come over to her. She pointed out several small reddish-brown drops on the leg of the table.

"The size of these three drops is consistent with medium velocity spatter. It fits in with stabbing. And see, it's in this crevice. I think that's why it was missed. No matter how well they clean, something's always left behind. It's impossible to get it all. No one is that thorough," the technician said excitedly.

"Scour the room for more stains and then use luminol. If this is anything like the last one there's more to see when the lights go out," Gavin instructed.

"Detective Gavin, Dr. Blythe is here," Howie said.

Val watched Blythe come in and she smiled. She couldn't wait to examine the teeth. Show him how strong his newest employee was.

He entered the room breathlessly and pointed towards the bed. "Are they all photographed?"

"Yes, everything is documented," Warren responded.

"Just like the last ones. This killer doesn't leave much behind." Blythe hovered over the pillow, probing each tooth. It seemed like forever before he finally glanced over at Val.

Here it comes. He was going to ask for her help—her expertise. She grew ready to jump towards him.

His eyes lingered on her for a few seconds and Val's chest lurched with excitement. She stepped forward, her foot still in the air when Dr. Blythe looked away.

"I'll be finished in a couple of minutes," Blythe told the detectives.

Her leg felt like a lead weight. His words made her heart sink. It became fairly obvious that Blythe had no intention of requesting her opinion and she stared at him. She didn't like Dr. Blythe very much at this moment. Worse yet, after this snub, she felt he didn't respect her opinion, and she had no idea why. Other than maybe the obvious. *He suspects my connections to Oliver, the man who is supposed to have recommended me, are complete and utter crap.* The very thought of this made Val break out in a sweat.

Dr. Blythe picked up the teeth, placing each one into a separate evidence bag. "I'm done. You can go ahead with what you need to do." Blythe stayed for only a few more minutes and then thankfully for Val, he left.

The technicians began to spray the area with a liquid. Howie tapped Val on the arm. "That's luminol." He smiled at her, his face sympathetic. She feigned a smile back. He must have seen her reaction. "Once everything is covered, they'll turn out the room lights and use a UV light to see where the blood once was. Just wait. This should be pretty astonishing to see."

Once everything went dark, a blue light was shone on every surface. Howie was right. The room glowed like a Christmas tree. The horror of Francine Donohue's death was splattered on the walls and floor. The shocking, expansive patterns caused Val to forget being slighted by Dr. Blythe as she stared at the blood-streaked walls.

"Are you getting pictures of this?" Warren called to the photographer.

"My camera hasn't stopped," he replied.

"Who would take the time to clean this up? This would have taken hours," Warren remarked. "The crime scene from the other victim wasn't as bad as this."

"Someone was very comfortable in the house, knew they'd have time to do what they needed and that they wouldn't be interrupted," Gavin said.

Warren inhaled deeply several times. "You know, I've been trying to place that scent ever since we came in. It smells like Fresh 'n Clean." Warren sniffed the air again. Val did the same.

Gavin, who had been studying the patterns on the wall, seemed jarred by the comment from Warren. He stared at him.

"The laundry detergent. Fresh 'n Clean is a laundry detergent," Warren informed.

Gavin let out a deep breath. The lights came back on and he yelled out, "Who's checking the bathroom?"

A technician answered, "It looks like the bathroom was cleaned too. Everything in there has been bleached. The odor will knock you out."

"So, the bathroom was bleached, but not the bedroom? Why?"

"Could be a twisted expression of remorse," Howie stated. "I was at a forensic conference last month and they talked about killers who go to the trouble of cleaning up blood. They don't want to look at it after they committed the crime. It's kind of a way to distance themselves from what they've done."

"I don't think remorse was the issue here," Gavin said. "Bleach is one of the few things that will hinder the use of luminol, since it also reacts with it. If you're going to clean it up, why use something that will destroy the evidence in one room and not in the other?"

Val looked at Howie, searching for an answer.

He whispered, "Bleach makes luminol glow too. If the killer wiped the area down with it, the entire surface will be camouflaged and you can't see where the blood was anymore." He then turned towards Gavin. "Maybe he doesn't know how luminol works."

Val was thinking the same thing, she certainly didn't know before now.

"Oh, he knows all right. I'd bet *my* teeth on that one," Gavin said, and then glanced over at an officer who was standing in the bedroom doorway.

The officer had a container of laundry detergent in his hands. "Bleach wouldn't have removed the visible stains on the carpet. This did." He held up a bottle of Fresh 'n Clean. "It lists blood as one of the stains it's good at removing."

Val watched Warren and Gavin, waiting to see their reactions. Neither man spoke. Gavin finally said, "The fact that someone purposely removed the stains from the carpet, and didn't destroy them, is more important than what they used to do it with." Warren looked ready to respond but an officer came rushing in, grabbing everyone's attention.

"Whoever wiped down the apartment missed another set of prints. We just found them in the hall linen closet," the officer stated. "It also looks like a repair was made to the drywall but unlike the bedroom closet ceiling it doesn't have any signs of water damage."

"I don't want this information released," Gavin instructed. "Nothing like this was found in Jeanne Coleman's apartment. It's probably a dead end, but I want to keep it private for now."

"You got it," the officer responded. He turned to leave the room when a second officer hurried in and headed towards Gavin. A folder was in his hand.

"I think you need to take a look at this," he said to Gavin.

"What is it?"

"The victim's sister, the one that reported her missing, has a conviction record."

Gavin opened the folder, reading quickly, and then told Warren, "I want to see her first thing tomorrow. If she won't come in willingly, I want you to bring her in."

5

The next morning Gavin sat in his office staring at photos from the crime scenes of Jeanne Coleman and Francine Donohue. He flipped through each one, comparing them. He'd been going back and forth for over a half hour, completely ignoring Warren, who sat on the opposite side of the desk.

He reached into his desk drawer, pulled out a container of antacids, chewed on two and then took two more. The stress was burning a hole through his stomach. The media was all over this case and a gang-related killing was no longer suggested. Instead they had taken the liberty of announcing a serial killer on the prowl. The mere whisper of such a rumor had upped the game. *Damn it,* Gavin thought.

There was no doubt the same person was responsible for both crimes. They had the same signature, and it was something that was never released to the media. Only the murderer would know to remove the sheets but leave the pillowcase behind. But there was no way this was random. These victims were woven together on a tighter level than some bizarre fetish associated with teeth and a pillowcase.

Gavin initially thought Francine's sister, Samantha Ritcher, would be a prime person of interest because of her conviction record, but the more he checked out her past, the less optimistic he became.

Samantha had agreed to be interviewed and was due at any moment. As he waited for her to arrive, Gavin opened the case files, trying to see if there was any link between the victims.

Francine Donohue hadn't owned a private practice but had been employed part time for a large dental group. Seven months ago she'd quit her job and a month later had quickly and quietly disappeared, only to be discovered dead in the Eastville Projects. Why had she left suburbia to live in a slum shortly before her estranged sister went looking for her?

Jeanne Coleman had a nephew who described her as reclusive. The last time the nephew had seen her was nearly a year and a half ago, and that was by coincidence at a local supermarket. He stopped to talk to her, chatted with her briefly and was eager to get on his way.

Two deaths. Both included women who were trying to be almost invisible. What were they hiding from? Tossing the file aside, he picked up Samantha Ritcher's conviction record. He could feel Warren staring at him, and glanced up. Reading the expression on Warren's face, he answered, "I'm not discounting her, but she just doesn't fit the profile in this case." Though she had a dirty past Gavin just didn't think Samantha was the mastermind who executed these killings.

"That record doesn't convince you?"

"This record is *why* I'm not convinced," he answered plainly and handed the documents to Warren.

Warren read from the pages. "Samantha had three convictions before being committed to a state mental hospital at the age of seventeen—for involvement in a brutal killing. She was released several years back, but six months ago, decided to look up her sister—a sister that goes into hiding just before this reunion." He looked up at Gavin. "And Samantha doesn't fit a profile?"

Instead of arguing about Samantha's past, Gavin wanted to focus on the strategy they needed to take during the interview with her. "How do you want to do this?"

"She's not going to be easy to talk to. I'm expecting a struggle."

"I wouldn't imagine she'd sit calmly while being grilled about involvement in her sister's murder." Gavin's tone was biting, stress getting the better of him.

"Yeah, but it would make our job easier if she did," Warren said, equaling Gavin on the sarcasm. "By the way, how did you get a hold of that? Those are sealed. She was a juvenile then."

"I have my connections," Gavin said as his secretary poked her nose into the office.

"Samantha Ritcher's here," she said.

Warren got up first. Gavin followed him out of the office.

Samantha appeared much older than her years. Time in a facility and probably a drug addiction now had taken their toll. Gavin had seen the look of an addict enough to recognize it immediately. Her mousy brown hair was long and greasy, streaked with gray. Deep furrowed lines accentuated an ashen complexion and watery, bloodshot eyes. She was thin, almost too thin and held a cigarette through trembling fingers.

"Samantha, I'm Detective Gavin and this is my partner Detective Warren." He couldn't help but notice how on edge she seemed. "You're probably wondering why we've asked you to come in. We'd like to ask you some questions about your past, maybe find out a little more about you."

"I'm only here because I thought you were trying to find my sister's killer. I thought you had some news about it. What right do you have to question me?" she protested immediately, becoming defensive and angry.

"Your sister's been murdered. It's standard procedure to talk to everyone, especially family members. They get asked first. Your help allows us to rule you out and go after the monster who did this. We don't want to waste our time questioning you when the real person is out there, so the quicker we complete this, the quicker we can move on." Gavin reiterated, "It's standard procedure."

Samantha Ritcher nodded, seemingly accepting this explanation.

"What did you do time for?" Warren asked.

"How dare you dig this shit up!" she yelled. "What the hell does that have to do with Francine?" Samantha jumped up from the chair. "I don't have to listen to this."

"I'm afraid you do," Warren said sharply and unwaveringly, implying Samantha better sit back down.

Gavin wasn't surprised by her reaction. He also didn't expect her to be hard to neutralize. According to her record, she had spent a lot of time in the state hospital, and had a past abusive relationship. Submissiveness should be ingrained in Samantha. She would do as she was told to do. He just had to strategically coax the information out of her.

Gavin responded again with his rationale for questioning her. He encouraged her to continue talking. With his manipulation and Warren's dominance he knew someone like Samantha would eventually obey. This is why he thought Samantha was a poor suspect for the murders. She was too easily controlled. Someone who was in power committed these crimes, not someone who could be dominated.

It took a moment, but Samantha breathed deeply, and then stated her reason for conviction. "Possession." Her one-word answer was evasive.

"Of what?"

"Cocaine." Again one word.

"Drug possession was for your first two offenses, tell us about the third one, the one that ultimately landed you in the state hospital," Warren insisted.

Samantha remained quiet and just glared at the detectives.

"They don't put you in a mental institution for cocaine possession, Samantha. What else?" Warren grew impatient. So did Samantha.

She crushed her cigarette into an ashtray and fidgeted in the chair before speaking. "What the hell does this have to do with finding my sister's killer? Don't you bastards have a real suspect to go after? Is that what it is? Is your head so far up your ass you're questioning me? My record is all in the past. I was a kid back then," she said defensively. "Why are you asking me these stupid questions? This has nothing to do with finding Francine's killer."

"It has everything to do with it."

"Why don't you tell me then? Tell me about my record. You have it all right in front of you," she spat.

"Because I want to hear *your* story, *your* feelings of what happened. This report can't do that. This report lists what *they* said happened. Now Samantha, why don't you tell us about your stay in the state hospital? Why were you there? Tell us about it in your own words," Gavin said, his voice purposely calm and much more sympathetic than his partner's.

Samantha looked at the floor as she spoke, her foot tracing the outlines of the tiles. "I got mixed up with someone pretty bad. He had me do some things for him."

"What kind of things?" Gavin asked gently.

She shrugged her shoulders, avoiding a verbal answer. Her foot continued to trace the squares.

"You helped your ex-husband murder a young girl?" Warren

tossed crime-scene photos on the table from a case that happened almost two decades ago. Samantha looked up from the floor, showing no emotion as she glanced at the pictures.

"I didn't murder anyone. He did!" she said vehemently. "I'm the reason why he's sitting in jail. My testimony put him away. I told everyone what he did."

"After a plea bargain," Warren said unceremoniously.

"You're as much of an asshole as he was," Samantha hissed. "Christ, I was seventeen. I was a *young girl* myself. I was an abused child under the control of a bastard. I did what he told me to do."

"You could have let her go."

"I did what he told me to do," she repeated.

"You lured her in. She trusted you and then you sat back and did nothing while he did this to her." He pushed the pictures towards her again, this time she did not look.

"Do you still talk to Daniel Ritcher?" Gavin asked, referring to her ex-husband who was in jail serving a life sentence without the possibility of parole.

"I haven't seen him since the day I testified against him. I have no reason to talk to him."

"Does he try to contact you?"

"No."

"You wouldn't be lying to me, would you?" Warren said.

"I said no. What the hell more do you want?" Samantha's chest heaved and every muscle tensed.

Gavin knew if they pressed her too much on this issue, they might lose the ability to question her altogether. He softened his tone and asked a different question. "After all this time, you must still care about your sister very much."

"Yes, I do."

"How did you know Francine was missing?" he asked.

"I called and left messages," she said after a few seconds, seeming to relax a little.

"Did Francine return any of your calls?"

"No."

"Are you sure you had the right number?"

"I got her answering machine. The voice was Francine's." Samantha continued to relax.

"How many times did you try her?"

"I called her for about two weeks. Then I went to her apartment and asked around about her, but no one had seen her in a couple of days. What I heard is that she just took off but I didn't believe it."

"Any chance she took off because you were looking for her? Any reason she didn't want you to find her?" Warren questioned.

"Why the hell would she do that? I hadn't heard from her in almost twenty years. If she wanted nothing to do with me, well all she had to do was just say so. Why are you asking me all of these questions? Jesus Christ, you sound like I'm the reason why she took off."

"We need to know why she left," Gavin said.

"I don't know why."

"Did she ever come to visit you when you were in the hospital?"

"No. The last day I saw her was the day I was sentenced."

"Why look her up now, after all this time?"

"I'm getting my life together. Francine was the only family I had. I wanted to get to know her again."

Gavin looked at Warren. The interview was done as far as he was concerned. There was nothing more that they were going to get from her, at least not at this time. "I think that's all we need right now, Samantha."

She grabbed her purse, threw it over her shoulder and didn't bother to look back as she rushed out of the room. She did manage to mumble "bastards" on the way out.

"What do you think, Mitch? You have to at least be suspicious of her," Warren said.

"I don't know." Gavin shook his head. "She just doesn't fit the profile. If anything, the more likely scenario is that she's repeating a pattern by being an accomplice, not the one in charge. Did you find anything on her boyfriend? She listed his name and contact information as her own. It seems like she's living with him."

"I found nothing on the guy."

Gavin glanced down at his notepad, jotting down several points he didn't want to forget. He was so absorbed that he didn't even notice his secretary standing in the doorway.

She said, "I've been waiting for you to finish. Dr. Blythe called during your interview. The DNA results are in on that toothless skull that was found. He confirmed it belongs to Jeanne Coleman."

6

V al followed the Francine Donohue and Jeanne Coleman case nonstop. She gobbled any bits of this story from any source she could find. Three days had passed since the discovery of Francine's teeth and this story was still headline news. So was the claim that a serial killer was on the loose.

It was easy to feel the fear that gripped the city. The news repeated, *When will the next victim be found? Every single woman is now a potential victim.* It further stressed that people should make sure doors and windows were locked.

Though Val had heard from Detective Gavin's own mouth that a serial killer had not committed these crimes, she bought two new deadbolts anyway, one for each of her doors. If she had had the money, she would have gotten an alarm system too.

The one place where she heard nothing about these women who had their teeth removed by a depraved psychopath was at the medical examiner's office. There was no gossip, no talk at all. She began to wonder if Dr. Blythe had a gag order on the case. Even Candace was strangely tight-lipped. Then she thought of the likely reason for the silence. This was just another case to them and they had to be professional about such matters. The news sensationalized such things. The medical examiner's office did not.

Of course this is the reason why, she told herself. But damn it, I want to know what is going on. Val bit her fingernails and stared out of the car window.

"Val, are you ready? You're going in first. I'll jump in only when I think you might need me. Okay?" Howie said. "Okay?" he asked again.

Val snapped to attention. "Of course." Howie and Val sat together in their official death scene investigator van. The late afternoon sun streamed through the windshield and she put her hand up to her eyes, protecting them from the glare. They had parked a few minutes ago.

Howie grabbed the door handle. "Let's go," he said. "You've had enough time for any necessary pre-investigatory meditation."

Val was about to enter her first death scene as the lead investigator and was anxious as all hell. Dr. Blythe had decided to send her here today. From what she heard around the office, his newest investigator, one that Oliver highly recommended, should be ready to jump into action. Luckily, since the day she was hired, she had buried herself in Howie's death scene investigation textbooks, learning everything she could.

Julia had arranged for Howie to be with her on this assign-ment which made Val less nervous. Julia had also given her good advice: "Study basic technique. That's the most important thing right now. The rest you're going to learn as you go on. Mostly, know what to do when you first walk onto any death scene. Just act like you've been doing this for years and don't let the cops bully you."

Val looked at the house they were about to enter. There was

a dead man in there waiting for her to document the circumstances of his demise.

Oh my God, what if I screw this up?

She opened the car door, and stepped onto the pavement.

Howie came around to Val's side of the car and put his arm around her. "Just remember, you're here to do a job. Try not to get emotional and act confident."

Her assignment seemed straightforward. An elderly man had been found dead in his apartment by the visiting nurse. No foul play was suspected, but he was alone with his wife at the time of his death, and she failed to alert the authorities that the man had died.

As they walked to the front door, Howie read from his report and explained the circumstances the responding officer provided to them. "The wife had no idea where he was or what happened. The visiting nurse found him dead in the bedroom and called 911. She noticed some odd bruising on the man's head and was suspicious. Officer Reynolds responded to the call." Howie pointed to the uniformed man standing in the doorway. "That must be Officer Reynolds."

"We're not expecting foul play. They're both in their nineties," Reynolds said. "We're here mainly because no one can find the name of this guy's doctor to see what his pre-existing medical conditions were."

"He was in his nineties?" Val asked. "What pre-existing conditions *didn't* he have?"

The officer didn't respond, but sized Val up. He continued to look at her and she felt herself shrinking. She repeated Julia's advice to herself. *Don't be bullied. Stand up to them.*

"Where's the body?" she asked, her voice firm.

"He's in there." Reynolds pointed towards the bedroom.

Val walked into the room, then stopped suddenly. She expected the dead man to be lying on the bed or the floor, but that's not where he was. *Holy crap*, she thought, thankful that her thoughts didn't make it to the ears of others.

A portable commode sat in a tight space between the bed and a dresser. The man was still on the seat and would have slumped to the floor if the furniture hadn't supported him. His head leaned against the corner of the dresser. This could have easily accounted for the large bruise on the side of his head, the same side still in contact with the dresser. The visiting nurse who'd found him dead stood several feet from the body.

Val took a deep breath, walked up to the man and started her exam. Both the nurse and Officer Reynolds watched as she inspected him. She had been busy for about five minutes when Howie spoke. "By the condition of the body, he's been dead for how long?" he asked.

Val tried to remember what she read in the textbooks about rigor mortis, lividity and body cooling. All of these circum-stances of decomposition would help her estimate this.

As she tried to move the man's arms, it was obvious that they were starting to grow stiff. He was definitely in rigor. *So, he's been dead at least a few hours.*

Lividity is the settling of the blood in the body. When it stops circulating it causes dark purple patches on the skin where it comes to rest. The process starts anywhere from twenty minutes to three hours after death. There were no purple spots that she could see.

He was slightly cool to the touch. The body temperature decreases at a rate of about one to two degrees Fahrenheit per hour until the temperature of the surrounding environment is reached.

How did all of this pertain to how long this man's been dead? Why the hell was there no sign of lividity?

She tried hard to think of a response. The people standing around staring at her, quietly yet impatiently, waiting for her to say something, didn't help matters. If she didn't say anything soon, she'd look like an idiot. Val finally opened her mouth and spoke.

"It is awfully warm in here. When was the last time someone saw him alive? That would help narrow things down and be the best indication because the temperature of the room can have a big effect on decomposition." She was happy with the impromptu response. It seemed to work as the quiet crowd quickly started to discuss a possible answer.

"We don't have an exact time," the nurse said. "He lives here with his, well, I think his wife. I'm not sure. I'm not their usual nurse. Today's my first day with them. I've been trying to ask her questions but she's a little out of it, Alzheimer's maybe. I don't think she understands he's deceased."

Howie chimed in, "Val, why don't you try to get some information from the wife? She's probably the best one to answer your question since she was the last one to see him alive. Oh, and you'll probably also have to confirm she knows her husband's dead first, since the nurse seems to think she's not up to speed on that."

She shot him a worried look. He only responded with raised eyebrows and a nod of the head signaling a stern *Go to it.*

Death was her job now, and she knew she had to handle the circumstances associated with it, all of them, even the emotionally difficult ones, such as talking delicately with surviving family members to gain the information she needed.

The little old lady sat in the armchair. Her gaze was glued to the TV set and she didn't even turn her head when Val sheepishly approached her. She was so frail-looking, but, oddly, seemed at peace. Her face was serene, as if she didn't have a care in the world. Val wondered what would happen when she forced the harsh reality of death upon her.

Her small spindly fingers, shaking slightly, grasped the

blanket that covered her legs. Val noticed the woman wore purple fingernail polish and decided to start there. "I like your nail color."

The woman turned her head and smiled at Val. She let go of the blanket and held up her hands to show off all ten of her fingers. "It's called 'Orchid Frost'. Let me see yours." The voice was as rickety as the fingers.

"I'm afraid mine aren't as nice." Val held up her own hands to reveal digits that desperately needed a trip to the manicurist.

"Oh, Helen could fix that for you. That's my niece. She works in a beauty parlor."

Val took a deep breath, preparing to get the needed information. She placed her hand on the woman's arm in a sympathetic manner. "I'm sorry, ma'am, but your husband is..." She wasn't quite sure of what to say and hesitated.

The woman spoke first. "Husband? Who, Herbert? He's not my husband." The woman smiled again at Val and whispered, as if sharing a personal secret to a female friend. "He's my boyfriend."

Val swallowed hard, not sure if she could do this or not. She said a few things gingerly, trying to explain that Herbert was dead, but the woman didn't seem to comprehend what she was saying. She tried again.

"I'm sorry, ma'am, but Herbert has passed." Val raised her voice, making the obvious mistake of thinking if she talked louder the woman might understand better. She looked to the nurse for help but the nurse just shrugged her shoulders and backed away.

Confusion grew.

"Passed? What do you mean, *passed*?" the elderly woman asked.

"He's dead," Val finally shouted and then placed her hand over her mouth in repentance for saying such a blatant and insensitive thing. "*He died,*" she added quickly with a more sympathetic manner, but the damage was done. Everyone had been trying to treat the old woman like a coddled child being told of the death of a pet. Reality was out in the open now.

"Dead?" The woman turned her head and took the statement in. There was a moment of silence and everything seemed to move in slow motion, as Val prepared for her to break down. Howie moved towards her, ready to intercept.

Then the unexpected happened. The lady yelled, "I knew it! He was too quiet! Didn't bother me all day. It was the first time in two years he didn't bother me about something. I got to watch all of my shows today without one interruption. I was going to check on him after *Dr. Oz* but Ginny showed up before it was over." The woman pointed at the nurse when she said Ginny.

"I'm not Ginny," the nurse said. "Ginny's her regular nurse, I'm Susan." Susan thumbed through her notes. "From what I have in my file, her niece Helen visits regularly. Her phone number is listed in the file. I'll give her a call. This lady shouldn't stay here alone."

Val nodded her head in agreement and then went back into the room with the body. After the success with the old woman, her nerves eased and she could focus better. She couldn't see any lividity immediately. But since this man was sitting, and gravity pools blood downward in a dead person, she knew where she needed to look. Howie helped her ease the man from the commode down to the ground and she inspected the man's backside. Except the parts that touched the toilet seat, eggplant-colored splotches were on both cheeks. Val remembered another area where the blood would settle on a deceased individual found in a sitting position and pulled off his slippers. The soles of his feet matched the buttocks.

Core body temperature would be her next clue and she prepared to take a reading. She pulled an eight-inch thermometer from her bag. She'd have to make a small incision through which she would insert the thermometer directly into the liver. Feeling around the man's abdomen, Val took out a scalpel, located the right area and without hesitation, made a slice and pushed the thermometer through.

She cringed when she realized this motion had the same resistance as the time she used a meat probe to check a Thanksgiving turkey for doneness.

"I'd have to say he died about three to four hours ago," she informed Howie as she looked at the digital display on the thermometer. It read ninety-five degrees. "Everything is consistent with this time frame."

He nodded in agreement with her findings.

This man would have to have an autopsy of course, but it seemed like his death was due to natural causes. She'd heard of people having aneurisms on the toilet as they strained too hard to go. Many were found exactly as this man was found. Slumped over, still on the seat. This was thoroughly detailed in the natural deaths section of the death investigation textbook.

Val exhaled in relief, proud of her accomplishment. She was able to take care of the situation without much help from Howie. Things were a little rough at the beginning but she got through it. *What was I nervous about? I can do this.*

After getting the necessary information and collecting the medications in the bathroom cabinet, she released the body to go to the medical examiner's office. As she was doing so, Howie's cell phone went off. He spent several minutes talking, and when he hung up, he told Val the next order of business.

"You did so good here, why don't you take this one solo?" Howie offered. "It's a pretty simple one. Just skeletonized remains found at a landfill."

7

The sun was just beginning to set when Gavin and Warren arrived at the Lockland Landfill, twenty minutes south of the city of Buffalo.

The stench of garbage was foul and the sounds of the seagulls squawking overhead was deafening. Gavin, who had barely slept in the last twenty-four hours, thought the top of his head would explode from the unremitting noise. The events of today were only going to add to the unbearable stress he was under.

Just forty-eight hours after the discovery of Jeanne Coleman's skull, Francine Donohue's teeth are found. Several days after that, more human remains are discovered in this landfill. For two months there had been no clues, no additional body parts. Now they show up in rapid succession? Their discovery seemed planned, and from what was here, it appeared as if the killer's strategy was evolving. In addition to a skull, this time there was also an arm. The media was going to have a field day with this.

Warren pointed at a man coming towards them.

"You have to see it. It's just crazy. The arm's all dried up, like it's mummified. The skull has no skin on it. It's only bone," Todd

Spencer, the manager of the landfill, said. They walked with him to the location of the bones.

"Were they found together?" Warren asked.

"Yeah, both came out of the same pile. No other parts were with them. All the teeth were missing from the skull," Todd said.

Gavin stared at the remains. They'd been found together but looked entirely different. The color of the arm was brown and the skin resembled dried parchment. With its desiccated appearance it seemed brittle, as if it would crack at any moment. Its fingers were shriveled and curled inward. Gavin remembered that Jeanne Coleman's skull had also been stripped of its skin and desiccated. According to Dr. Blythe it was probably exposed to a heat source. He'd even gone so far as to imply that someone baked it.

This skull was completely skeletonized, but didn't look dried out, like the arm. There was no way this was an unintended find, though. Their states were so different that they couldn't have decomposed under the same conditions. Which means they had been deliberately placed here. They were meant to be found together; like this.

"We need this area taped off and a grid laid down for excavation," Gavin ordered with a sense of urgency to Warren.

Warren grabbed his phone and began to call for back up.

"Mr. Spencer, what time were these found?" Gavin asked.

"About 5pm."

"It's almost seven now. We're going to need some lights out here. It'll be dark soon and it's going to be a long night."

Val turned the car radio up as she drove towards the Lockland Landfill, hoping to catch the end of the show. She had been listening to *Crime in the City*. It was the radio counterpart to the cable television program of the same name. Howie told her about this series that portrayed true crime stories, and after listening once, she was addicted. Tonight's case had her hooked.

The episode was going to reveal how the renowned criminal investigator Thomas Hayden challenged a pathologist's findings about a murdered woman. She was becoming acquainted with Thomas Hayden through these broadcasts. Many high-profile cases had his name attached and he seemed to be a messiah to the criminally condemned. When compared to the other criminal investigators, he had almost a celebrity status.

In tonight's case, Mr. Hayden said the manner of death was suicide, corroborating the husband's defense strategy, when all of the evidence, including the pathology report, dictated that suicide was impossible. The husband said he heard a gunshot and when he walked into the bedroom, his wife lay dead with a self-inflicted wound to the stomach.

The only problem was that the firearm was a rifle. There was no way she could have reached the trigger for a self-inflicted wound. Plus, the entrance wound was in her back and the exit was the stomach. Not only that, there was confusion over powder burns and how close the gun was. It was suggested that she was shot from four to five feet away. There was no way that this was suicide. It was an open-and-shut case. The husband had been sitting in a jail cell for the last ten years when his case came up for an appeal.

Thomas Hayden, who had reviewed the case at the urging of the convicted husband's brother, saw the error. The entrance wound was mistaken for the exit wound.

On her back was the characteristic circumferential marginal abrasion so typical of an entering bullet while her chest bore torn jagged edges of a much larger wound exemplifying the bullet's exiting path. This finding needed interpretation and explanation because this case was indeed suicide, especially after Thomas reviewed the clothing the woman wore the night of her death.

The gun was held against the victim's chest, and as the bullet entered it was impeded by the zipper of her sweater and the underwire of her bra. The bullet pushed the metal objects ahead, ripping the skin as the bullet entered. Furthermore, the victim was sitting against a wall and as the bullet exited through her back the bullet hit the strap of her bra, where the skin was crushed, leaving a well-defined wound. An examination of the clothing proved it. Photos of the wound on the victim's back even showed the pattern of the sweater in her skin around the injury.

Thomas Hayden also determined that while holding the gun upside down, she had plenty of room to pull the trigger, especially if she was sitting down on the floor with the nozzle in her chest. This information helped the jury render an innocent verdict in the retrial and the accused was set free. The show went to commercial as Val drove through the gates of the landfill site. She immediately wondered if she was in the right place. She was only supposed to collect some skeletal remains but the place looked like a disaster zone.

Several other vehicles were in front of her, each taking a long time before either going through or being turned away by the officer who was blocking the entrance. She waited anxiously, drumming her fingers on the steering wheel.

What is going on? All of the local news vans were here. Cameras were set up and reporters with microphones scurried around. The landfill was lit up by the red flashing lights of squad cars and in the distance she could see an area of bright white illumination making that section glow as if it were daytime.

Slowly, she pulled her car up to the uniformed officer. He put his hand up, signaling for her to stop. She rolled down the window.

"Sorry ma'am. No admittance."

"I was sent from the Erie County Medical Examiner's Office. I'm a death investigator. I'm here to collect the skeletal remains found today."

The officer looked at her suspiciously for a moment, and then asked for ID.

Val's hung around her neck and she pulled it up so the officer could see it.

He stared at the badge, and then at her, and after a few seconds finally became convinced she was qualified to be here. "Sorry. Just have to make sure that you're not a reporter trying to sneak in. You're new. Haven't seen you around before."

"No. This is my first week."

"This is a hell of a way to start. It's crazy back there. You won't be able to drive much further. The cars are parking there." He pointed to a row of squad cars about fifty feet in front of her. "I can radio someone to help you if you have a lot to carry."

"Thanks, but I think that I can manage. What's going on?" she questioned eagerly. Something big had obviously happened here. This wasn't some simple collection of bones.

The officer seemed surprised that she didn't know. "They think the remains belong to one of those women who had their teeth pulled out. Detective Gavin's in charge. You'll find him about a quarter mile up the road."

Val couldn't believe what she'd just been told. *Big* was an understatement. It was huge. She parked the car, then fumbled through her bag, quickly pulling out her phone. She needed to call the office, call Howie. She needed to call someone. There was definitely some screw-up in sending her here. *Where was Dr. Blythe? Did he know about this?* She couldn't think straight as she tried to decide whom to call first.

With her fingers ready to press the numbers for Howie, Val stopped. What if this wasn't a mistake? What if Dr. Blythe was already with the remains and was waiting for his newest death investigator, the dentist, to show up? How incompetent would she look if she had to call for help before even getting out of the car?

She put the phone away, grabbed her supplies and started off into the landfill, heart pounding, wondering what on earth she was supposed to do when she arrived at her destination.

Bright lights showed the way. As she got closer, she found Gavin and Warren with a couple of other people. Blythe was not one of them. He was nowhere to be seen.

One man was talking and motioning at something on the ground. She walked up to the small group and stood silently, hoping to be noticed. When that didn't happen, she spoke timidly.

"Excuse me." Her voice barely audible.

They continued talking, unaware of her existence. She tried again, louder.

"Excuse me, sir!"

This time all the men turned round.

"I'm Dr. Valentina Knight."

"Doctor? I thought you were a death investigator, not a medical examiner," Gavin said.

"You're right. I'm the death investigator," Val immediately corrected. It was just habit for her to use the title Dr., one she was trying to break. Howie had told her not to do this because it would lead to confusion. As Val tried to explain, she felt the knot that was tied around her tongue tighten. "I'm a dentist with a change in profession."

Her awkward response fell like a lead weight on the intent crowd. She wanted to crawl into a hole. What an unprofessional thing to say at such an intense and serious moment. Here she was at an important death scene and she was blowing it, fast.

"This person is a dentist?" Gavin said to Warren. "Why the

hell didn't Blythe mention it?" He clearly sounded pissed off. "Honestly, I'm happy to have someone besides him examine this."

"I agree. But Blythe will rip you a new one if you do. He's in charge of the remains in this case," Warren said.

"As I see it, our medical examiner can't be reached. It's my decision now."

Rather than shooing her away, Gavin introduced Val to the men standing around them and then started to explain what was found.

She couldn't believe she was standing here, among police officers, hearing first-hand information about *this* case. This detective, the lead detective no less, was giving her information as if she was part of his team, more significantly, like she knew what she was doing. The more Gavin spoke, the more Val liked him. The fact that Dr. Blythe wasn't here was far from her mind. Right now, she was in charge.

"The skull is bone only. The arm appears to be mummified," Gavin explained. "All of the teeth are missing."

Val just nodded her head and glanced at the body parts from where she stood.

"You might want to take a look," Gavin suggested

Val moved forward slowly, anxious yet excited, like a teenager allowed to drive the family car for the first time. It took a few seconds before it sunk in that she was actually *supposed* to do this. Being a death investigator, she was privy to dismembered remains in front of her. She *could* touch them.

She put on a pair of latex gloves and picked up the skull, holding it upside down to get a good view at the empty tooth sockets, then flipped it back around, inspecting them from the side. All were fractured as if someone grabbed a hold with a pair of pliers and ripped the teeth out, breaking the front piece of bone holding them in.

She reached into her bag, pulled out a flashlight and shone the beam into the sockets. *That's odd.* She looked at the shape of the breaks and the amount of bone remaining around them.

Warren's voice made her jump. "Dr. Blythe is on his way. He told me to thank you and that he's sorry about the mix-up in sending you here. I'm to send you home."

Val just stared. The last thing in the world she wanted was to be pulled away now. "Okay, I'll finish documenting this first," she said hopefully. Maybe they would at least let her stay for that.

"I'm sorry, Dr. Knight. He told me to send you home now." Warren's voice was more apologetic than forceful. "He's in charge of the remains. It's his call."

Val noticed Gavin on his phone. He was yelling at someone, but Val couldn't make out what was going on. She put the skull down and started to gather her supplies. As she was doing so, Gavin walked over and handed her his business card, the phone still pressed to his ear.

"Call me if you know of anything that might help on this."

8

Val placed her keys in her jacket pocket and then tossed the jacket onto the back of her office chair. It barely caught the edge, holding on for a couple of seconds before falling to the floor. *It was going to be one of those days.* She picked it up, wiped off the dust, and set it on the counter this time. Then she quickly got situated. There was so much to do this morning and she really needed to get started.

Dr. Stedman was scheduled to perform the autopsy later today on the old man who died on the commode. Her report from the scene needed to be done before that. She opened the file from the case and sat down.

Val stared at the blank page, picked up a pen and began her documentation. After a few minutes she set the pen down, looked at the clock and then flipped through the remaining blank pages to see how many she needed to fill out. She let out a sigh and picked the pen back up, tapping it on the counter this time. It was no use. She couldn't concentrate.

All she could think about were the remains at the landfill and that made it hard to focus on anything else. Last night she was in charge of the evidence in this high-profile case. The lead detective wanted her professional opinion. God that felt good, to be a respected professional again, even if was only for a few minutes. Val pictured the skull, trying to remember the unusual breaks, then wondered what Jeanne Coleman's skull looked like. Did her teeth come out the same way?

Though Detective Gavin gave her his business card last night, she wasn't sure if she should call him. She wanted to tell him her thoughts, what she'd noticed. She just didn't know how important it was and didn't want to look foolish if it turned out to be nothing.

If only she could get another look at the skull she would be more certain. Inspecting it again would be impossible. Dr. Blythe would never allow it: everything she'd experienced so far told her that. He was excluding her. His entire demeanor towards her suggested he knew that she had lied to get this job.

But if that's the case, why not fire me right away? she wondered.

Julia. Julia was the only answer. Julia must be protecting her somehow. But what power did she have even over her own boss? Val was deep in thought when a knock on the door made her look up.

Howie poked his nose in. "Are you almost finished with the report from yesterday's case?"

Val glanced down at the three lines she had written. "Not quite."

"When you're done, two bodies just came in. They need dental IDs."

"Okay. This won't take long." She crinkled her nose and asked of the bodies, "How bad are they?"

"They're going to have to be done in the decomp room. You'll need to wear the jumpsuit. But on the bright side, I placed them in the cooler for now. The cold temperature makes the maggots move slower."

"Thanks." She feigned a smile.

"Anytime." He turned and walked away.

The report took longer to finish than Val anticipated. But, as she wrote it, she made a decision. She reached over to her bag and pulled out Gavin's business card. She grabbed the phone and dialed the number. He picked up after the third ring.

"I get off at five thirty," she said. "I can meet you at six."

"Why don't we meet somewhere closer to the medical examiner's office, so it's easier for you. Are you familiar with the Anchor Bar on Main Street?"

"Yes." She knew where the Anchor Bar was. Everyone from Buffalo did. It's where the deep-fried, hot-sauce coated, blue-cheese dipped, chicken wing originated—before becoming a *Buffalo wing* in every other city.

"Great. I'll see you later."

Val rushed out of her office and headed to the decomp room, dropping her report in Dr. Stedman's mailbox on her way.

At 5:40pm, Val ran into the locker room, and quickly showered. Another body had arrived late in the afternoon. It took forever to get Dr. Blythe's signature so that she could take the X-rays.

After two rounds of soap and shampoo, she put on her street clothes, wondering just how badly she still reeked of death. Not that she could tell. Spending the day in the decomp room had made her olfactory senses immune to the scent of decomposition.

She gave herself one last inspection in the mirror before walking out, narrowing her eyes in dissatisfaction, wishing that she could go home and change, but there wasn't enough time. She grabbed a barrette, and tied back her soggy hair. As she ran to her car she checked her watch. *Crap, I'm going to be late for Detective Gavin.*

When she finally got to her car, she reached into her pocket and felt nothing. Her hand fished around before inspecting the other pocket. That too, was empty.

"Damn!" She grabbed her bag and began rifling through it.

No car keys.

If they weren't in her pockets or purse where could they possibly be? She distinctly remembered putting them in her pocket. Val ran back to her office at full speed.

As soon as she opened her office door, she noticed them immediately. They were on the floor under the counter, plain as day. *How did I miss that?* The thought left her mind as soon as it entered.

Her attention was fully focused on trying to make her appointment with the detective. Val punched his number into her cell phone, but the voicemail came on. She quickly left a message and rushed back to her car. *Jesus, hopefully he'll pick this up and not leave before I get there.*

Val arrived at the Anchor Bar by 6:30. The place was full and she had to stand on her tiptoes to peer around as she searched for Gavin. She finally noticed him sitting at the bar. A half empty bottle of beer was in front of him. "Did you get my message?"

"Yes," he said. "I gave the hostess my name for a table. She said it could be a while. Looks like she was right. Have you eaten? The food here is pretty good."

"No. And I'm starving."

"Can I get you something to drink while we wait?"

"A Heineken would be great," she said, eyeing his bottle.

Gavin motioned for the bartender and ordered. The man sitting next to him stood up and offered Val his seat. As she sat down, the bartender brought over her drink.

"So, you were a dentist?" Gavin asked. "Are dead patients

treating you better than live ones? I can't imagine they would pay better."

Val looked down and started to play with the ends of the napkin that her beer sat on, nervously fidgeting and tearing at the corner. She hated this question, but tonight as she tore bits of paper, the answer wasn't difficult. Taking a deep breath she said bluntly, "I can't practice anymore. I had an accident."

Gavin immediately apologized, "I'm sorry, I didn't mean to—"

"There's no need for you to be sorry. Personally, I've spent too long feeling sorry about it." Her days as a dentist were a thing of the past, plain and simple. She had a new career. She dropped her fingers from the napkin and turned to face Gavin directly, ready to handle any more questions.

"Now I've done it," he said. "Sometimes I don't know when to keep my big mouth shut."

She smiled. "That's okay. In order to make up for it, I'll let you buy me dinner."

"Deal," he replied, grinning back at her. "So, what happened?"

"This." She held up her hand. The scar was clearly visible.

"That's pretty bad. Were you doing something dangerous?"

"Dangerous to the max," Val said, and rather than describing what happened, added, "I was trying to fight crime." She couldn't believe how therapeutic it felt to state it so simply. Her response made Gavin laugh.

"If that's what happened, you should probably leave crime fighting to the experts then," he said.

"Now that I'm one of the experts, I think I'll need pepper spray, Mace and a stun gun to avoid any more mishaps like this." Val took a sip of her beer and leaned forward. She had thought Gavin was a handsome man the first time she saw him. Here tonight, that opinion was reinforced.

"*You* might need a better weapon. Like something with bullets."

"I don't know how to shoot a gun. Is it hard to learn?" Val suddenly realized she was flirting and caught herself. This wasn't a date. It was a professional meeting with a detective, *on a high-profile murder case.* Her behavior was wrong on several levels. Apart from the professional issue, luck with men wasn't something Val could claim. She often made poor choices leading to doomed relationships that seemed to drag on longer than necessary. It was a cycle she couldn't seem to break. Her accident had closed the dating chapter of her life. Val hadn't gone out with anyone in over a year. Getting involved now, with this man in particular, was not an option.

Gavin smiled. "Not at all. I could teach you to shoot in a few afternoons." He was still smiling when the waitress interrupted their discussion, telling them the table was ready.

The two sat with menus and chatted comfortably about the food. It wasn't until the meal was ordered that they focused on the case. Though Val reassured herself that the more professional tone was for the best, she had to admit that she was also enjoying her evening with Detective Gavin on the personal level that she needed to avoid.

"What's your opinion of that skull? It seemed like you were looking at something last night," Gavin asked.

"There were several perfect rectangular shaped breaks around the sockets, like someone had used a set of pliers to get the teeth out."

"What's wrong with that?"

"None of the sockets had broken teeth in them. Getting a tooth out isn't easy and from the level of interseptal bone, that's the bone between the teeth, I would guess they were in pretty firmly. If you just grabbed them with pliers, chances are the crown of the tooth would snap off, leaving the roots in the socket."

"Is there any possibility of getting the teeth out without breaking them as you described?"

"Maybe. A good portion of the front part of the bone was gone where the pliers were placed, so I know the killer put the tool on the tooth and pulled forward. The bone was ripped out with it, so this could have helped to loosen it, making it come out intact. But this isn't the correct way to do an extraction so fracturing it still would have been an issue."

"Teeth do loosen in skeletal remains, it's not uncommon for them to just fall out," Gavin suggested. "Is it possible that if there were broken roots, they might have come out on their own?"

Val paused. For the front teeth where there's a single root, she might have agreed about this possibility, especially if this skull was being tossed around a landfill, but for back ones, with multiple roots, it was unlikely. She had to admit that she wasn't one hundred percent sure.

"I guess it's possible. But if it didn't happen this way, someone purposely removed the broken roots," she said.

"Any idea why?" he asked.

She shrugged her shoulders and tried hard to come up with answers. "They could have been used for an X-ray comparison, to get an ID."

She knew dental ID was an excellent way to identify someone. It was accurate, quick and inexpensive. With only the roots though, there wouldn't be much to go on. It would be a questionable ID. DNA would be indisputable. "The pulpal tissue, that's the nerve inside the tooth and roots, is a good source for DNA. Dr. Blythe is using DNA for the identifications. Right?"

"Yes." Gavin sat upright. "Is there any way to tell for sure if the roots were purposely removed?"

"The easiest way is to look at the victim's teeth and see if those are all intact. Were any of them broken?" she asked, trying to remember what she saw lying on Francine Donohue's pillow. Those teeth were covered in blood with bits of bone still attached, making it hard to tell what kind of shape they were in. She would need to inspect them more carefully to determine if any were fractured.

"I'll have to look at Julia's report. I can't remember if she noted that any of the teeth were broken or not."

"I thought Blythe was doing this case, not Julia," Val said, surprised.

"He is. He's in charge. Julia's assisting."

Both looked up from the conversation as the waitress came to the table with dishes. Dinner was here. Val's stomach growled. The grilled cheese sandwich she had eaten at lunchtime from the hospital cafeteria had long since dissipated. She took a few quick bites of her fish fry, and then asked another question, strategically. "I'm assuming this is a pretty big case?"

"Yes." Gavin set down his burger and wiped his mouth.

She trod carefully, hoping that maybe he would share some details with her. "You have to imagine that I would be interested in this because of the dental aspect. Is there anything more that you can tell me? Any way that I can help?"

He stared at her. Val waited to hear a *no* from him.

"I have two murdered women. One was a recluse. The other, a dentist, disappeared from an affluent community six months before she was found dead in the same low-income apartment complex as the recluse. They were both killed the same way. The same person committed both crimes. I have no leads for this case and the more we find, the more bizarre it gets."

"How so?" Val asked.

"The killer wants us to know what happened. This person is dropping clues very strategically. It all reeks of a serial killer but these can't be random murders. I think both Francine and

Jeanne were hiding from someone. So, any information that you can add, from a dental angle of course, may be important."

"I'll do what I can." She knew Blythe would never let her examine the teeth or the skulls. But she remained hopeful that she'd be able to help Gavin in some way.

The two talked nonstop as they finished their food, Val didn't even notice when the waitress placed the bill on the table. She had grown more attracted to Gavin as the evening wore on. She was about to ask him one last question about the case and then take a chance by proposing dinner again another time, but his cell phone rang. He checked who was calling.

"Can you excuse me? I have to take this one. It's my wife."

Gavin got up to answer the call. As soon as he said *wife* Val felt her heart sink. She sat at the table alone as he walked away. When he came back he laid two twenty-dollar bills on the check and thanked Val for her time. His demeanor was completely different. His face was taut, the smile that he had all evening completely gone. He seemed preoccupied and barely said goodbye before leaving.

Two hours after dinner with Val, Gavin sat at the desk in his study going over the crime scene photos again, drinking his third glass of wine. His limit was two, especially after a beer at dinner. The open bottle, a Saint-Émilion Grand Cru, was next to him, and tonight he intended to finish it. With each sip, he felt his frustrations easing.

Staring at the photos from Francine Donohue's and Jeanne Coleman's apartments, he knew something wasn't right. He just couldn't put his finger on it.

Though the wine was easing his stress, it was doing nothing for his ability to deduct anything and his thought process was getting more clouded by the second. He jotted down a few notes and as he did, his thoughts drifted to Val, and as quickly as she entered, he pushed her from his mind.

Gavin tossed the pictures aside and picked up the glass, swallowing hard what was left. A small amount of wine dribbled down the side. He set it down just as his wife walked in. She looked at him and then the glass, disgust radiating from her face.

"Put something under that, or you'll damage the desk," Melody Gavin snapped. She rushed over to him, lifted the glass, and stared at the ring on the wood. "Damn it, why can't you be more careful? Jesus Christ, this is ruined now!"

Melody grabbed the closest thing, which was Gavin's notepad, seeming to not care if anything important was written on it. She placed the glass on top of the center of the pad, covering a portion of what he had written. "This was my grand-father's desk. It's been in my family for over a hundred years and it only takes *you* one evening to destroy it."

"He did give it to *me*," Gavin said calmly. Melody's hair had fallen over her eyes. He reached up gently and pushed it back from her face. She swatted his hand.

He stood up, taking her wrist softly, and pulled her into him. Melody struggled, jerking away, but Gavin held on and drew her close to him. He lowered his lips to hers, kissing her deeply. For a second he felt her respond, her hands gripping him. Wanting him.

"You're beautiful when you're angry." He smiled and kissed her neck. "You like being angry with me, don't you?" He ran his fingers through her hair.

Suddenly her hands were on his shoulders, pushing him away. "Mitch! Stop it," Melody yelled. "You're tangling my hair."

"Forget about the hair." He ran his hand through again, purposely messing it. "It looks wild now. Let me see if I can drive *you* wild." He leaned into her, kissing her again, merely brushing her lips this time.

She shoved him, hard. "I said to stop it!"

He stood back from her. "I'm not even sure I remember the last time you let me touch you," he snapped. He was ready to say more but stopped.

Melody said nothing. For the first time she looked as if she was going to confess what Gavin suspected to be true. But she just simply walked out.

9

V al sat on the floor next to the dead woman, inspecting the emaciated body. She wasn't surprised this life was cut short. This person had obviously been a drug addict. As she glanced around at the room, she couldn't help but notice how poorly the victim lived—cheap, grimy furniture, threadbare, stained rugs—all of her money must have gone to support the habit; well almost all. There was a fifty-inch TV mounted on the wall.

A little more than two weeks had passed since Val had become a death investigator. Each time she examined a dead body, she surprised herself with how much she knew and was happy to be learning quickly. Today she was on her own and would be from now on. Her training wheels had been removed and Howie would no longer be at her side.

"So, what do you think?" Officer Perez asked.

One thing Val noted quickly: new death scene, new officer in charge. At the rate she was going, she'd get to know the whole force soon.

The deceased female lay on the living room carpet. Her lifeless eyes stared at the ceiling. Val thought for several minutes, evaluating the woman, carefully estimating time and preliminary cause of death. There was a slight amount of lividity starting on her back. Body temperature was about ninety-six. Rigor was just becoming apparent in the small muscles of the face. The rest of the body was still pliable.

"She probably died about two hours ago," she replied, confident of her answer. There was nothing to indicate the decedent had been dead any longer than that. She looked at the woman's arm then sat back from the body. All signs pointed to an overdose. Open, empty bottles of the prescription opioid pain narcotic Percocet were all over the apartment. She counted the bottles she'd noticed. There were at least five. Val reached out and turned the arm upwards, taking another look at the telltale sign of more than just prescription drug abuse.

On the inner surface of the arm was a small hole that resembled an injection site. It was a little raised, pinkish red and very recent. Val wondered where the heroin was because she hadn't seen any in the house. Nor could she find any needles. She glanced over at the victim's boyfriend who was being questioned by another police officer.

Val's attention returned to the body. Her preliminary account listed cause of death as overdose, this was obvious, but for some reason, the neck just didn't look right. It appeared swollen. So did the lips, and the skin seemed a little blotchy. She pulled the dead woman's mouth open and looked inside. The tongue was swollen too. She wasn't entirely sure if the edema was a consequence of how this woman died. It could just be a normal finding.

After several minutes Val decided to release the body for transport to the medical examiner's office so Dr. Blythe could figure it out. She had taken her part of the job as far as she could go. Only an autopsy could determine the rest. She stood up and addressed Officer Perez. "She's ready to go."

"Do you think it's drug related?" he asked.

"That won't be confirmed until the autopsy's done, but I think we can safely say yes." Val gestured to the victim's boyfriend. "Did he mention any other drugs she was taking?"

"He's not sure what she had today. He went out to shoot pool with a friend and when he returned, he found her dead. He says she wasn't an addict. Her pain pills were for a bad back."

"Not an addict, my ass." Val picked up two of the empty pill containers and read the date the prescriptions were filled. "Both of these were picked up just days ago. There should have been enough pills in each of these bottles to last for a couple of weeks not a couple of days. Did you find any other drugs in the house? Anything you would use a needle with?" Val asked, hoping the cops had found something she hadn't.

"Nope."

She pointed to the injection hole. "There has to be something more."

The officer just shrugged and nodded towards the boyfriend. "These people know how to get rid of the *right* things when the cops show up. Prescription meds won't get him into trouble: they're legit. That's why the bottles are all still here. But heroin would. Those drugs are usually missing along with the needles. We see it all the time."

Val couldn't help but feel she was missing something. "If it's okay I'm going to take one more look around," she said. "I'll be able to mention that I did so in my report."

"Be my guest."

In the bedroom, Val noticed two of the dresser drawers were slightly open and eyed them suspiciously. She opened each, quickly glancing through, moving clothing out of the way; feeling around, searching for any drugs. The first drawer had nothing but underwear and socks. The next, jeans and T-shirts. In the bottom drawer her hand hit something hard. Her fingers traced the rectangular outline. She pushed pajamas out of the way to see what the object was and noticed the vinyl cover. It was just a photo album. Val pulled it out anyway and flipped through the pages, making sure nothing was hidden in there, like the drugs she was searching for. She had heard how people cut out sections from books to hide objects. Why not use a photo album to stash some heroin.

This one was intact. The photos were old and appeared to be from the 1980s, probably from the victim's childhood. She shut the drawers, confident that if there were any drugs in the house, they were long gone by now. As she stepped out of the bedroom Val stopped and stared, shocked. Detective Gavin was standing right in front of her.

Her face felt flushed and her heart picked up a few beats. She addressed him quickly. "What brings you here? Homicide isn't keeping you busy enough? Are you handling vice too?" Though she hadn't seen him since that night at the Anchor Bar she had to admit that she had a hard time keeping him off her mind.

Gavin laughed. "I'm a jack of all trades."

Val didn't have a chance to respond. Officer Perez emerged from the living room and called Gavin over. She followed them as they walked back to the dead woman.

"Possible cause of death?" Gavin asked Val.

"Looks like an overdose. Can be either oral or intravenous. We won't know until the autopsy's done."

Gavin said a few words to the officer and then pulled out his phone. Val overheard him talking to Warren, telling him to get there as soon as possible, and then saying, "What the hell is going on?"

Val was confused. Why was Gavin so interested in this

victim? She glanced at her report to get the name of the deceased.

It read: Samantha Ritcher.

10

"Well, gentlemen, the remains from the Lockland Landfill are those of Francine Donohue," Julia announced. "*Both* the arm and the skull belong to her. We had the DNA double-checked. That's why it took so long."

Gavin couldn't believe it. *How could this be?* Warren raised his eyebrows, but said nothing. Blythe just had his arms crossed. The body parts sat on a small table in the private autopsy suite in the morgue. The fact that both pieces came from the same victim, and were discovered so quickly after her teeth were found, put this case in a different light.

Things were escalating.

"Did you roll her fingerprints? We'll need them to compare to the unknowns in her apartment," Gavin asked.

"Not yet," Julia answered.

"Do you think we'll get anything from these?" Warren asked. He pointed to the dried leathery fingers. They were shrunken and curled toward the palm as if trying to make a fist.

"We just have to soak them in warm water for a little while then inject saline in the fingertips and they'll be fine," Julia said.

"Why is the arm and skull so different?" Warren said.

"The skull was stripped of its tissue but not baked this time. The arm was though. He left the skin on the arm and then must have put it in an oven at a low temperature to get it to mummify like this. This time he cooked the arm but not the skull," Blythe said.

"Phil, slow down. You know this whole baking thing is speculation," Julia said.

"Only if you have no clue on how pathology works," he responded sharply.

Julia rolled her eyes and Gavin sensed a smoldering battle between these two. Jesus, he wished Julia was in charge of this case. Gavin glanced to his right at the lifeless body of Samantha Ritcher who lay not more than twenty feet from what remained of her sister. The Y-incision on Samantha wasn't closed yet and the skin gaped, exposing a body cavity devoid of organs. Those were placed on a specimen table awaiting tissue samples.

"When is the autopsy on Samantha Ritcher going to be finished?" Gavin asked. Though Samantha was a drug addict and there should be no surprise to see her on a steel slab at such an early age, he couldn't ignore the bizarre coincidence that she was sharing occupancy at the county morgue with her murdered sister.

Blythe said, "I've completed her autopsy. I'm just waiting for the preliminary lab reports before I decide if additional tissue samples are needed or not. Cause and manner of death will be ruled after that."

"I want you to call me as soon as it's done," Gavin said.

"I'll do that but she can't possibly be connected to your case," Blythe replied confidently. "This is completely different from the other two. I have no doubt the manner of death will be accidental."

Gavin tried hard to control his mounting irritation. It was so

like Blythe to be headstrong like this. So into his own precon-
ceived theories and so unwilling to let them go that he screws
up, makes wrong conclusions. Blythe had caused problems with
several other cases, though they were Blythe's errors, it was
Gavin who was made to look incompetent. He was in no hurry
to go down that route again. This case was far too important to
make even the slightest mistake with. "We can't afford to make
any hasty claims. This case is far too high profile for that. Any
wrong moves and we're all going to face a firing squad," Gavin
said.

Blythe's face reddened angrily after *hasty claims* and Gavin
knew he'd stepped over a line. He didn't care though. As far as
he was concerned the circumstances surrounding these remains
only complicated things. It didn't simplify them. "I don't want to
rule anything out. And you shouldn't either, Phil." Gavin tried to
maintain his composure, but his nerves were raw. "Samantha
Ritcher is lying dead in the morgue at the same time as her
sister. Ask yourself why."

"She hadn't spoken with her sister in what, almost twenty
years from what I've heard." Blythe laughed. "What you're
suggesting, given the scientific facts of death in front of me, is
absurd. And it's my neck on the line if I suggest otherwise. No
one helped this woman die but herself. Oh, and let me remind
you, Mitch, that it's your job to figure out *why* on any case. Not
mine. If you can't do your job, well then don't place blame on my
doorstep."

Gavin felt as if he was ready to explode at that last remark
but as Val walked into the room, everyone stopped talking.

11

V al quickly scanned the room, trying to tell what was going on. She immediately sensed she had walked in on an intense private conversation, especially for Gavin.

"I'm sorry, I thought you were working alone in here, Julia. I have the report you asked for. I didn't mean to interrupt." Val addressed Julia timidly, holding out the folder.

"Oh yes, thank you." Julia took the folder and stated with finality, "We're pretty much done in here."

Gavin looked at Val, and she realized she had been staring at him. She quickly averted her gaze.

He walked over to Val, his eyes still on her. "I'm going to need your report on Samantha Ritcher." His tone was direct and urgent. She noticed that Dr. Blythe had turned his back to everyone in the room, now looking through paperwork that sat on the counter.

"I'll get that to you ASAP." She searched for more words to say, but didn't find any. Though she tried to smother her attraction, she couldn't help what she was feeling. It was there, the sweaty palms, uneasy attitude, and an inability to sound intelligent when speaking. No matter how much she told herself she wasn't attracted to Gavin, that wasn't the case. What she needed to do now was just get over it.

"Thanks," Gavin said, lingering for a second, but as Warren walked past him and over to the door, he followed.

As the group disassembled, Val was about to leave too when Julia asked, "Could you stay and assist me with something? That's if you have nothing more pressing to do."

"Nothing that can't be finished later. I'd love to stay," Val said, thrilled. The only person Julia ever allowed to assist her usually was Howie.

Julia led her out of the private autopsy suite to the main morgue area and walked over to a gurney that held an elderly man who had been in a fire. She slipped on a pair of latex gloves and began examining the body externally. Val looked around. It was just the two of them in the morgue. She wasn't surprised. The autopsies were all done first thing in the morning, and no other late cases had come in.

"How has everything been working out? I'm so sorry that I haven't been able to spend more time with you." Julia talked as she worked, inspecting the burned skin of the old man.

"I understand. It's been crazy around here." Val had to look away. The man's legs resembled hot dogs that had been left on the grill too long. The charred skin had split to reveal pink underneath. The barbecue scent was sickeningly sweet. Meat would definitely be off her menu for the foreseeable future.

"Crazy doesn't even begin to describe it. We're all on edge right now. Sometimes I don't know how Phil handles it all."

"Dr. Blythe doesn't seem to want me around," Val said cautiously, hoping to get Julia's opinion on the matter.

"His problem is with me and not you. So, don't take what he says or does personally. If I took everything he said to me personally, I'd have a nervous breakdown. Truth is, Phil can be a nice guy. He's just under a lot of pressure right now. He gets nasty to be around with if things aren't running smoothly."

It was possible. Maybe this was just Blythe's personality. Still, Val couldn't help but think there was something else. Something Julia wasn't telling her.

Julia continued her exam, not saying anything more about Dr. Blythe. "Now look at this. This man set himself on fire while cooking dinner. The flames from the frying pan took hold of his sleeve and then traveled across his torso to his legs. He's burned over thirty percent of his body. For elderly people this is enough to cause death. They just can't recover from this type of tissue insult."

She pointed out the injuries. The man's arm was still bandaged in gauze, showing obvious attempts from the emergency room to stabilize his wounds. Muscle tissue, devoid of sound skin, was visible on the periphery of the bandages. His legs were in a much worse state and Val kept her eyes off them.

Julia worked silently for a few moments. "You've probably heard about my dilemma?" The words caught Val off guard.

Val tried to act like she had no idea what Julia was talking about even though she knew exactly what it was. Julia's dilemma was her lawsuit. She had performed a minor surgical procedure on a woman who, it turned out, was her husband's mistress. The woman had contracted a flesh-eating infection and had lost half her face.

"Stop being polite: everyone around here knows about it. Candace mentions it whenever she gets a chance," Julia said.

"You don't have to explain to me," Val said.

"I'd feel better if you knew the truth rather than listening to gossip." Julia looked Val straight in the eye, her face serious, and said plainly, "I didn't do it."

"I never thought that you did." Val really didn't.

"Thanks. It means a lot to hear you say that. A lot of people do think it and I can see why." Julia laughed wryly. "It would be a good way to get revenge on your husband's whore. But honestly, I didn't know she was having an affair with my husband." Julia took a deep breath. "I believe she knew I was his wife, though."

"What makes you say that?" Val asked.

"It's a long story," Julia said dismissively. "Basically, I was in love, stupid and blind to the obvious in front of my face. He played me for a fool—and so did she. She pretended to be my friend. We did lunches and shopping—and I fell for it all. It's as simple as that. It hurts but it's good for me to admit to it. At least that's what my lawyer says." Julia smiled bravely. "I don't have a shrink yet."

"They played you for a fool? How so?"

"I met him at a singles event. You know the kind of thing I'm talking about?"

Val didn't, and her expression must have said so because Julia laughed. "Maybe you don't. Maybe someone like you doesn't have to visit a prefab meeting event for the terminally un-hook-up-able," Julia said. "It's one of those things where an event is sponsored and everyone that shows up is single. It's supposed to be a safe way to meet strangers. Now that I think of what I ended up with, I probably would've been safer with some seedy internet site, and that's a scary thought. Colin—that's my soon-to-be ex-husband's name—wasn't there when I arrived. He showed up later in the evening. I had already met a nice guy, but he wasn't all that attractive. I was finding out all about his tax business, when I saw Colin come in." Julia hesitated in reliving the memory, her one-time romantic feelings toward Colin evident. "He took my breath away."

She looked at Val. Her face showed embarrassing admiration for the man who had once been her husband.

"As the tax guy spoke, I stared at Colin, thinking I could

never get someone like that. I was fixated on him and watched his every move. I'm not even sure whether or not the tax guy noticed I was checking out another man. Anyway, I didn't care."

Val let Julia continue. She wanted to interrupt, add some words of comfort, but couldn't find the right thing to say.

"*Tax guy*, isn't that horrible? I don't even remember the poor man's name." Julia shook her head at the memory. "Colin came in and went straight to the bar, ordered a drink and looked around. He saw me staring at him and smiled. I immediately turned away, embarrassed. I excused myself from the tax guy to go the lady's room."

Julia put her arms across her chest and leaned against the gurney and Val just watched her. With her head down and back slumped, Val couldn't help but notice how vulnerable Julia looked.

"Colin was outside the bathroom door when I came out. His first words to me were, 'Can I buy you a drink?' I couldn't believe that a guy like him was waiting for someone like me outside of a bathroom. He noticed me. He followed me. I told him that I was there with someone. He said, 'That guy at the bar? This is a singles event. He can't be your boyfriend.' I confessed I'd just met him earlier that night and he said, 'If it makes you uncomfortable to go back in and have a drink with me, then let's go somewhere else for one.'" Julia shrugged her shoulders. "I went."

Val searched again for comforting words, but Julia spoke first.

"I slept with him that night. Please don't think badly of me. I'm not easy. He hung around. He was still in my bed in the morning. I thought that was a good sign. I didn't care that he was more fascinated with my car, my house and my profession than he was with me. I was a plastic surgeon then, not a medical examiner," Julia explained. "I didn't have the looks to win him so

I thought I could impress him in other ways, so of course I bragged. And when Colin asked me to marry him four months after meeting him, I agreed. I know it sounds stupid now but I just wanted to believe that he loved me."

"That's not stupid," said Val. "That's something we all want; someone to love us." Val thought back to the day of her interview. Once Julia pressed her for the truth about her hand it was hard to hold back. The words tumbled out in relief as she unburdened herself. Julia was doing the same right now.

"Oh my, would you look at the time," Julia said, her voice cracking. "I have a lunch meeting today with my lawyer regarding this lawsuit and I can't be late, and the birthday party is probably already going on in the employee lounge. I have to make an appearance before I run."

"Birthday party?" Val questioned. She hadn't heard about a birthday party.

"Yeah, for Zoe Beauchamp, our toxicologist. Are you coming?"

"No, I don't think so."

"You really should, it's a great way to get to know the rest of the staff. I've heard you pretty much keep to yourself." Julia went to the sink and stripped off her gloves.

She was right. Val did keep to herself. There was good reason to do so. "I'm afraid someone will find out about Oliver, that I never knew him. Keeping a safe distance from everyone seems necessary."

"Phil is the only one you need to worry about and I can handle him," Julia said as she washed her hands. "Why don't you come over to my house tomorrow night? We'll have a low-key girls' night in. I'll cook," she suggested.

Val eagerly agreed. She hadn't had someone she could call a friend in a long time and was happy that Julia might fill that void.

"Let me warn you that I'm a bad cook. But I'll get a lot of wine, so we won't care."

"Sounds great to me," Val responded enthusiastically.

"I'm going to make pasta. It's the only dish I can make. I serve it every time I have company, along with a homemade loaf of bread. I'm a proud owner of a bread maker." She rolled her eyes at Val. "It was a wedding gift."

Julia rushed out of the room with Val sticking close behind. "I'm going to tell Phil that you need to be involved in the Jeanne Coleman and Francine Donohue case. With your dental background, you really ought to be."

Val stopped in her tracks. She couldn't believe what she'd just heard. She was so excited she almost hugged Julia. "You know, I noticed something unusual with Francine's skull and have been meaning to talk to you about it," she said.

"What did you find?" Julia asked eagerly.

Val explained her thoughts on how the teeth came out. "Did you happen to notice if any of the teeth were broken when you examined them?"

Julia thought for a second. "No. I don't think any of them were. But I'll have you take a look. Maybe I missed something."

Val asked what else was going on with the case. She wanted to know everything.

Julia gave her the details, then stressed the latest information. "Gavin seems to think Samantha Ritcher may be connected, but honestly, Phil's opinion is that it's a long shot. Gavin let us know that the last time Samantha talked to her sister was when she was a teenager. So, really, there's no link. It's probably just some bizarre coincidence."

Val remembered the woman with the overdose and grew confused. "Whose sister was she?"

"Francine Donohue's," Julia said as they walked into the employee lunchroom.

Val's legs froze. She took a moment to absorb what she'd just heard. *Francine's sister?* There was so much more that she wanted to know, but she didn't get a chance to ask. As soon as they entered, a woman pulled Julia away and started talking to her. Val had no idea who this person was. As she looked around she noticed several unfamiliar faces.

Small groups of people huddled together having work clique conversations. All were busy with their own chatter. Val stood alone. Drs. Phelps, Chang and Stedman were in the far corner near the refrigerator. In front of her, about ten feet away, a woman talked to Dr. Blythe and Howie. This was Zoe Beauchamp, the birthday girl. She would have joined Howie and Zoe if Dr. Blythe wasn't with them.

Her gaze continued to travel around the room and then it stopped, locked on a bulletin board that hung on the far wall. A good portion of the board was covered with employee photos, obviously pictures of the many parties that probably took place in this break room. It was more so the banner on the one side of the board that caught her attention. As she read it, her heart began to beat faster.

"To our good friend Oliver—gone but not forgotten."

It was a small tribute to Oliver Solaris. Val had no idea what this man even looked like, and here he was, captured on film, his image on the bulletin board. She had to see this. *Now, how to do this so no one notices?*

The refreshment table was next to the board. Val casually walked over and helped herself to a piece of cake, glancing at the pictures as she did. There were a handful of people in each shot. *Which one was Oliver?* She went with a process of elimination. He would be the one she had never seen before. Unfortunately, there were several people she didn't know in the photos.

Realizing that she was staring at the board for too long, she browsed through the assortment of soda and selected one, glancing back up as she poured. *One of those two must be him.* She jumped as someone reached past her for a bottle of diet Sprite. The person spoke.

"Val, did you manage to get the rest of that paperwork completed for me? I'm still waiting," Candace said.

"I'm sorry. It's done. I can run and grab it for you now." Val took a step backwards towards the door, hoping to get away.

Candace put her hand on Val's arm. "No need. You should stay and enjoy the party. Just get it to me later. So, how are you fitting in with our little family?"

"Things are going fine." The hand stayed on her arm.

"You know, just between me and you, I've heard some talk about you. It's probably nothing, so don't be worried."

Val immediately grew paranoid but thought for a second. Tact. She needed to be tactful. But that didn't happen. "What was said about me?" she blurted.

Candace maintained a cool and even tone. "Well, far be it from me to say, but it was about how you were hired."

Val could feel her face grow hot and her stomach flipped. "What was wrong with how I was hired?"

"Oh, nothing at all. Just some, and let me just say that I am not part of the *some...*" Candace put one hand on her chest and waved the other one in the air to emphasize insincere non-involvement in the gossip. "Well, these people are just a little concerned that you have no..." She whispered the last word, "*experience.*"

"They don't need to be worried about me. I can hold my own." Val's worst fears had come true. The fact that she had no experience was exposed. Julia had warned her to be ready for this.

"Oh I know. And I'm not judging. I just thought you *ought* to know about the things being said about you behind your back. Everyone is wondering why Oliver would recommend someone for this job who's never been a death investigator before." Candace took a sip of her soda and pointed to several pictures. "These are from the last party we had. Oliver was still alive then. Doesn't he look good? Who would have thought he'd drop dead two weeks later."

Val didn't know what to say. She felt as if she was being baited. The wrong answer would place the hook firmly in her mouth. There were two men in the pictures that she didn't know. One looked like he could run a marathon and the other seemed as if he needed a wheelchair. The wrong answer could get her fired. She opened her mouth to respond, but Julia quickly arrived by her side.

"I miss Oliver so much," she said, placing a finger on the image of the man who might have needed a wheelchair. She stroked it in a caring manner and then smiled at Val.

Candace stayed only a moment more before walking away. As soon as she was gone Julia said, "I have to run. My lawyer's waiting for me and I'm looking forward to meeting with him. I know what's going on, and I'm ready for it. There's no way Colin's going to win this." She touched Val's arm. "I think we'll need an extra bottle of wine to celebrate tomorrow."

12

W hen Julia arrived at The Towne Restaurant, she saw her lawyer, Bradley Underwood sitting at a table by the window. He was waving, trying to get her attention.

"Sorry I'm late. Things have just been hectic. More remains were found from that murder case. The ones with the teeth removed," she said, picking up the menu, glancing at the Greek choices.

"Are they getting any closer to catching this guy?"

"I don't think so." Julia talked about the case, describing nothing more than what had already been on the news. She stopped once the waitress came by to take their order.

As soon as the waitress left, Bradley spoke. "Julia, I had a meeting with Lauren's lawyer yesterday," he said optimistically. "She wants ten million dollars to settle this case. It's a good deal. Honestly, she might get much more if this goes to a jury. Your malpractice insurance is worth ten million. I think that's why they picked this amount. That'll cover it and you'll be done with this issue."

"I'm not going to settle. I'm not guilty," she said plainly. It was obvious that Bradley wasn't expecting this answer. His eyes opened wide and his mouth opened slightly. It stayed that way for a second or two before he answered.

"This isn't about you being guilty or not." His voice was firm. "That doesn't matter. The woman lost part of her face. She's disfigured. She'll easily get the sympathy of any jury. I think we should settle. In fact, I'm advising you to do so."

"My innocence does matter. It matters a lot. This is my life you're willing to give up. Maybe *that* doesn't matter to you, but it certainly does to me."

Bradley took a deep breath and calmly said, "Lauren lost portions of her nose, right cheek, lips and chin due to the infection that started just the day after you removed a mole for her. This strain of bacteria was aggressive, flesh-eating, and not responsive to any antibiotic therapy. The only way to save her life before septicemia set in was to cut the infected tissue off. How am I going to convince a jury that you, a plastic surgeon with a PhD in pathology, did not purposely do this in retaliation to your unemployed husband's mistress?" The tone of his voice trailed upward on the last few words. He took a deep breath. "It's your life I'm trying to salvage. Julia, think about the consequences."

"I've had the luxury of thinking about them every minute of every day since this happened. It's with me when I get up in the morning and when I go to bed at night and every waking moment in between. This is with me always. If I settle that means I admit to doing something I didn't do."

"I'm not saying you did anything wrong. This *is* about your life now. A jury decision could easily triple or quadruple that ten-million-dollar amount. How would you be able to pay that? After they garner your wages, a room at the Y might be all that you can afford. Do you want that? Just say the word and this nightmare ends now and you move on."

Julia didn't answer. She looked at the table, avoiding eye contact.

Bradley reached out and put his hand on her arm. "Settling this case is the smartest thing you could do."

"He wants a divorce, you know," she said, ignoring his previous comment. She shook her head, letting out a nervous laugh. "And that's not the worst part. Right after I married Colin, he asked me to prove my love to him by adding his name to the deed of my house and on my practice. I had the papers drawn up that included him as fifty percent owner of my assets."

Bradley looked at her sympathetically and held her arm tighter. "Julia, I'm so sorry."

"It's okay. I was stupid. I realize my mistakes now. I just wanted to believe he loved me. I guess I was wrong."

The lawyer had no response this time. Julia continued.

"He owns half of my defunct practice, half of my house and half of my investments. So not only do I lose my pride and malpractice money to his mistress, I lose half of everything else to him. Brad, all I have left is my dignity and professional name. I don't want to lose that too. I will not be broken down. You will fight this case for me or I'll get another lawyer."

"Julia, I don't know where to begin."

"They're at fault, start the case there. Ask the jury, why would my husband's mistress come to me to get a mole removed unless something else was going on, unless this was a set-up. It makes no sense otherwise. This was done on purpose, all of it. He planned it from the beginning. First, he got his hands on my assets and then he wanted more. So, he planned a way of taking my malpractice money, and she went along with it. They would get millions in the end."

Bradley just stared. "Julia, do you really think she literally cut off her nose to spite her face?"

"I believe he concocted this scam and didn't know what he

was doing. She ended up with a problem that got out of control. I think he infected her or had her do it to herself in the hopes of getting ten million dollars. All she had to do was get a bad infection, something that wasn't easily cured, something where there was a little pain and suffering and I would look incompetent. I think they just didn't plan on one that bad. They were just stupid."

"How would he have infected her? Where would he have gotten the bugs to do it? It's not the kind of thing you buy at a store." He couldn't hide the skepticism in his voice.

"After the mole was removed, there was an open wound. They just had to get something contaminated into it. Jesus Christ, they could have used feces and that would have done the trick. In this case, that contaminated material had some nasty, nasty unusual bacteria."

"This isn't going to be easy to prove. You have the greater knowledge about bacteria."

"If it was me, I could have used something that would have caused far worse damage than she received," Julia said plainly. "She has as much reason to set me up as I did to disfigure her. I know things now that I didn't back then. She befriended me on purpose. Keep that in mind. She befriended *me*!" Julia began raising her voice and a few people from neighboring tables looked over. Bradley motioned for her to keep her voice down, but Julia couldn't.

"I found out that she was already having the affair with him when she came up to me at the gym. She started talking to me every time I was there. She invited me to lunch and we started doing things together. I thought she was my friend. She asked me to remove that mole for her. This was all planned. I know it was."

"Julia, I'll do what I can."

13

Val glanced down the hall. The door to Julia's office was still shut. "Damn," she muttered. She needed Julia to sign some paperwork and had been looking for her all morning. Howie came around the corner and she grabbed him, asking, "Have you seen Julia anywhere?"

"She hasn't come in yet."

"Do you know when she'll be in?"

"No idea. I tried calling her but she's not answering her phone or returning my messages. She has a budget meeting this afternoon with Dr. Blythe and Candace so she'll eventually show up."

"Valentina, can I see you?" Dr. Blythe asked, though it was more of a demand. She hadn't even heard him walk up behind her.

Howie didn't reply. He simply waved and continued on his way.

"You're handling the Samantha Ritcher case, right?" Blythe asked.

"Yes, I am," she said.

"The cause of death was not drug overdose. She died from

anaphylaxis. That's a pretty severe allergic reaction." The tone was condescending and somewhat insulting.

Val knew very well what anaphylaxis was. She often prescribed medications when she was in practice and had to make sure she wasn't giving patients anything they were deathly allergic to.

It all made sense now. She couldn't help but picture Samantha Ritcher, on the floor with her swollen tongue and blotchy skin. A severe allergy would have easily produced these symptoms. She should have immediately suspected the possibility and listed it prominently in her report. The way Dr. Blythe was staring at her made her feel like an idiot for not doing so. But a drug *allergy* and not *overdose* as the cause of death for an addict like this? It almost seemed outlandish.

"I'm surprised someone with your dental background didn't pick up on the obvious signs," he scoffed. "Zoe's going to need a list of all the drugs Samantha Ritcher was taking."

"So, this was an accident?" she simply asked, preferring not to talk about her mistake.

Dr. Blythe crossed his arms. "Zoe should have the toxicology results finished. I want you to get them and follow up with the drugs that were in the house. I need to know which one she was allergic to." He handed her a copy of the autopsy report, and walked away briskly, not taking any time, or really seeming to care to hear if she had any thoughts on the matter.

Val watched Blythe's back as he moved down the hall. She was furious, thinking the whole time what a prick he was, making sure he schooled her on protocol. After she calmed down she glanced at the autopsy report, her new top priority chore for the day, and headed towards the toxicology lab. When she entered the room, Zoe was seated at her desk and looked up when the door opened.

"Hi, Zoe. I need the toxicology report for the Samantha

Ritcher case," Val said. Zoe's jet-black hair was cut into an angled bob with short bangs. It contrasted nicely with her watery blue eyes and pale skin. Several tattoos could be seen on her arms, peeking out of the ends of her T-shirt sleeves. Her right eyebrow was pierced, along with her left nostril.

"Yep, have it right here. I was just going through this earlier. The results were pretty strange." Zoe shuffled through several folders and picked up the one of interest. "Drug levels were high for pain medication Percocet, but not high enough to kill her."

"Dr. Blythe said the cause of death was anaphylaxis. Not a drug overdose."

"And he would be right. She definitely had an allergic reaction. Her post-mortem serum levels of the enzyme tryptase are elevated. This lets us know that histamine has been released. Histamine triggers the swelling that we see with cases of anaphylaxis. So, this test is a marker for the reaction. Her levels of the antibody IgE are also high. It's all telltale."

"She was allergic to the Percocet then?"

Zoe shook her head. "No, not to that. She had another drug in her system, but I haven't been able to determine what it is. Do you have a list of everything you found in her apartment?"

"What I found is listed in my report. I noted that she had a needle mark on her arm, but there were no traces of any other drugs in the apartment."

"Dr. Blythe documented the injection site too. My guess is that whatever this is, this is what she was allergic to. Standard tests aren't giving me any answers as to what it is, but so far I only tested for routine street drugs. It doesn't appear to be anything typically used for recreational purposes. I'm going to have to do a bit of detective work to figure out what it is."

"Do you think you'll be able to do it?" she asked hopefully, feeling that Dr. Blythe would probably hold her responsible for this even though it was Zoe's job to figure it out.

"I'll try. Her post-mortem serum can be tested for several weeks yet. I'll let you know what I find."

Val thought for a minute. No other drugs were found in the house. No needles either. Someone had obviously gotten rid of them. Though Samantha died from an allergic reaction, she couldn't have done it on her own. She needed to talk to Gavin ASAP. He needed to know about this.

14

I t was just after 6pm and despite leaving messages about the Samantha Ritcher case all afternoon for Gavin to call her, Val had yet to hear from him. But she really wasn't all that concerned with Samantha Ritcher's death right now. Samantha could wait. Something else was bothering her more.

Julia hadn't come into work that day and no one could reach her by phone.

Val was supposed to meet her for dinner tonight and planned on keeping that date, if for nothing more than to see if Julia was all right. She pulled into Julia's driveway and looked around before getting out of the car.

The houses in the development were huge. Manicured lawns and neatly-trimmed shrubs lined the walkways and front garden beds. A woman with a straw hat and pink gloves stood along the flagstones carefully tending to her bushes, trimming ends with a pair of shears. She looked up at Val, studying her briefly. Then returned to her pruning. Moments later she glanced up at her a second time.

The evening was warm and voices and music carried

through the open windows. Several teenagers were outside bouncing a basketball around a hoop.

Val looked to her right and left, watching what was going on. Nothing seemed out of place in this affluent community. People went about their everyday lives. With the door shut and windows closed, Julia's house had an odd stillness to it. Val couldn't shake the feeling that something wasn't right. She'd feel better once Julia answered the door.

She rang the bell and waited.

No answer.

She rang again, waited several more seconds, and then tried knocking. She was about to knock again when a woman's voice made her jump. Startled, she turned around quickly and stared at the lady with the hat from next door.

"I'm Marnie Horvath, Julia's neighbor. Are you a friend of hers?"

"I work with her," Val said, her answer abrupt. She was worried about Julia and really didn't care to be interrogated by her neighbor right now. But the more she looked at Marnie it became apparent that she was worried too. That's why she was here.

"I'm sorry. I don't mean to bother you. It's just that I've been trying to call Julia all day," Marnie said.

"She was home today?" Val asked.

"I thought she was. I didn't see her leave this morning. I usually do."

In a matter of seconds Val's worried feeling began to churn. Her chest tightened and a sinking unease ratcheted in the pit of her stomach. She immediately went around the side of the house and started looking in the windows. Something definitely wasn't right. Where the hell was Julia? She wasn't at work and she wasn't at home. Marnie was at her side, trying to peer inside too.

"Last night the lights were on for a really long time. They were still on when I went to bed and that was after midnight. Julia's never up that late," Marnie said. "I wouldn't be so concerned but she had an awful fight with her husband yesterday evening."

"Her husband was here?" Val questioned quickly. Julia had mentioned a meeting with her lawyer but said nothing about her husband.

"Yes," Marnie said. "They were loud. It was hard not to hear."

Val peered through each window, putting her hand above her eyes to shield the glare on the glass. From what she could see, nothing seemed out of place in the house and nothing was amiss outside. That was, until she arrived at the back door, which was unlocked and easily swung open.

"That's not like Julia to leave her door unlocked. The alarm system must be off too, otherwise we'd be hearing it right now," Marnie said.

Val's heart pounded and her legs felt rubbery as she cautiously stepped inside. Marnie followed her.

The two women walked through a utility room and entered the kitchen. Val called to Julia. Her voice echoed in the large room. There was no response.

"Do you think we should be doing this?" Marnie asked, putting a hand on Val's arm, trying to pull her back. "I think we should call the police."

Common sense told Val to leave Julia's house and call Gavin, but she felt compelled to keep going. It was the food on the countertop that made her move forward.

On the counter sat a box of spaghetti and a jar of sauce. Two bottles of Merlot were next to the jar. A bread maker looked poised and ready for action. Everything was there to make the dinner Julia was supposed to cook. She couldn't be far with dinner ingredients left on the counter. The only thing missing was Julia.

She yelled Julia's name several more times.

Again, there was no response.

"We should call the police," Marnie said, tugging on Val's arm harder this time.

"Let me try calling her once more," she said, struggling with a decision on what to do now. "I wouldn't want to call the police if she just went to the store for something."

Val pulled out her cell phone, punched in the numbers and waited. In the distance, in another room, she heard ringing. Confused, she pulled the phone from her ear. A ring could clearly be heard on her cell followed by an immediate ring coming from down the hallway.

"It's coming from inside the house," Marnie said, her eyes wide.

Julia's voicemail came on and the ringing stopped.

"Where is that coming from?" Val asked frantically.

"I don't know. It sounded like it came from upstairs."

"I thought it was down the hallway." Val immediately hit redial and the ringing started again. Every time the voicemail came on, she hit redial. Following the sound, the two went up the stairs, where it began to grow louder.

"It's coming from in there." Marnie pointed to a door, which was ajar.

Val took the handle and pushed the door open just as the voicemail came on. The women walked into what appeared to be Julia's bedroom. The bed was at the far end of the room, but the dresser on which Julia's cell phone rested was close to the door. Val picked it up.

"What's that smell?" Marnie choked. "It's burning my throat."

Val agreed and began to cough. "Smells like strong laundry

detergent. Something must have spilled. Does Julia have a washer and dryer up here?"

"I'm not sure if she has a second-floor laundry."

Val looked around the room, her gaze lingering on the bed. *What is that?* She walked closer, focusing on the pillow now. Then she stopped just a couple of feet from the bed. It couldn't be real. *Was this some type of joke?*

Then she saw one of the photos.

Marnie looked too and shrieked loudly before running out of the room.

On the pillow were numerous human teeth. All were covered in blood.

Horrified, Val wanted to scream but no sound would come. Breathing in panic-stricken gulps, she dropped to her knees. Her gaze remained glued on the pillow.

15

By the time Gavin and Warren arrived at Julia's house it was surrounded by the media. Every neighbor on the block must have been outside too, all huddled in groups, staring at Julia's house. Val stood in Julia's hallway, trying not to look at them. Once she heard Gavin's voice she turned her head, relieved he was finally here.

He went up to her as soon as he entered and put his hand on her shoulder. "I need to ask you some questions, but I need to talk to the neighbor first. Okay?"

Val nodded, her response automatic. She felt as if she were standing somewhere outside of herself. *How could this be happening?* Nausea overwhelmed her as the images on Julia's bed seared into her mind. No matter how hard she tried, she couldn't stop replaying them.

Gavin quickly returned and called her over and instructed her to sit in one of the chairs in the living room. Marnie was already seated on the couch.

"I have questions for both of you, but Mrs. Horvath, I'd like to start with you first. Can you tell me what happened last night when Julia's husband arrived?"

"I was working outside in the garden and I could hear them arguing. It got loud. She screamed at one point," Marnie told Gavin stoically.

"Did you call the police?"

"No. He left right after that, within minutes. I went over after I saw him drive away. I asked her if there was anything I could do. She said that she was all right. I could tell that she was embarrassed about the fight. I didn't press her much more after that."

"Did they fight frequently?"

"The last couple of months that he lived here, it was bad. Then Julia found out that he was cheating on her and it got worse. He moved out shortly after that. This was the first time that I've seen him back."

Gavin wrote a few things down. "Let's get back to last night. You can confirm that she was alive after he left?"

"Yes," Marnie said. "Well, after he left the first time."

Gavin looked up from his notepad, his eyes wide. Val stared at Marnie too. "You mean he came back?"

"Yes, he came back about a half hour later."

"Did they argue again?"

"If they did, it wasn't anything loud enough that I could hear."

"How long did he stay the second time?"

"I'm not sure." Marnie hesitated for a moment, recalling. "My son played soccer yesterday evening. We left for his game shortly after Colin arrived."

"How long were you gone for?"

"About three hours."

"Was Colin still here when you got home?"

"I don't know. He pulled into the garage when he came back. Lights were on in the house when we returned. They were still on when we went to bed. I didn't see or hear the garage door open."

"You didn't call or check on her the second time?"

"No. It was quiet over here. There was nothing to be alarmed about." Marnie wrung her hands together. "Julia looked so embarrassed when I checked on her earlier. There was no reason to do that to her again, not last night. If I thought something was wrong, of course I would have done something." She stopped talking. Tears streamed down her face. "I was planning on seeing how she was doing today. I called several times."

"Thank you, Mrs. Horvath. I'm going to give you my card, could you call me if you remember anything else. We might like to ask you questions again, at another time, if we need to."

"Of course," she said before getting up to leave.

Val watched Marnie walk to the door, the whole movement seeming to go in slow motion.

"Are you okay?" Gavin asked.

"No, I'm not okay," Val said bluntly. "I just spoke to Julia yesterday. Jesus, I was coming here for dinner tonight. What she planned to make is sitting on the kitchen countertop. I should be having a drink with her instead of standing here answering questions about her..." Val choked. "Oh, my God, she's dead!"

"We can do this another time," Gavin said gently.

"No, I want to do it now," Val said. Gavin looked at her doubtfully. "Really, I can do this. She was my friend. I want to help her in any way that I might be able to."

"Did she ever say anything to you about her husband? Anything personal. I know some things about him but that's mostly gossip."

"She was kind of private about that. But you're right. There was a lot of office gossip. She did open up to me yesterday. He sounded like a real bastard. She was happy. She said she'd figured it all out and he wasn't going to win."

"Figured what out? He wasn't going to win in what way?"

"I don't know. She was running out of work, to see her lawyer."

"I'm going to bring her husband in. With the neighbor's statement and what you told us about him, we have enough to do that. I also need to track down this lawyer. Why don't you go home and get some rest. I'll call you if I think of anything else I need."

"No, I want to stay. I want to know what happened to her."

"Val, this isn't a good idea. In fact, it's a really bad one. Your memories of Julia should be of her alive. If you see what's in that bedroom, that's what you'll see whenever you think of her."

"Too late. I've already seen what's in the bedroom. I've moved on from that. I want to help catch her killer." She looked straight at him, her decision firmly made.

Gavin got up. Val rose too and went with him to the bedroom. Blythe was on his way and Val knew that as soon as he arrived, she would be asked to leave. Now, this moment, was her chance to help Julia. But Val knew it couldn't end here. She wouldn't stop until Julia's killer was caught.

Val walked up to the bed. Julia's teeth lay on the pillow, just like Francine Donohue's had. Suddenly her legs felt weak. She glanced around, looking anywhere but the pillow, trying to collect herself. Her gaze stopped on a lamp that sat on the nightstand next to the bed. It was a pretty shade of aquamarine accented with brass fixtures and a wide butter-colored shade. She concentrated on the lamp, managing to distract herself. Then she saw something reddish brown on the ceramic surface and her jaw dropped as she realized what it was. Blood spatter was streaked across the front of the lamp. Julia was ripped apart and part of her was on this lamp. Val took a few steps back, and steadied herself by leaning on the wall. Gavin came towards her, but she waved him away. "I'm fine," she said and straightened herself up. Glancing back at the teeth now, she leaned over, getting closer, looking carefully. She had no gloves with her and couldn't touch them. She'd contaminate the evidence if she did. But she didn't need gloves to see that not one root was broken. Her gaze shifted a few inches and she noticed the pattern of the pillowcase. It was different from the sheets.

"Do you think this is a copy?" Warren asked Gavin. "Colin might have just seen the TV reports and made this murder look like the others. It's nearly identical. The only difference is that this one is not as clean. Some bloody fingerprints were found downstairs on the kitchen cabinet. With the dark wood, it's hard to see. Could be why he missed them in a cleanup attempt."

"It can't be a copy. He changed the sheets. He left the pillowcase and changed the sheets. We never released that information to the media. How would he have known to do that?" Gavin asked.

"Julia was working on the case with Blythe. She might have told Colin about certain parts of it."

"It's possible but unlikely. This would hardly be a conversation to have when you're trying to win back your husband."

Gavin's cell phone went off and he answered the call. When he hung up he announced, "Colin Turner's been located. He's being brought in as we speak."

Mitchell Gavin was in his office when the phone rang again. He felt like pulling the cord from the wall. Since Colin Turner's arrest last week, he had been pelted with calls from the media. Nonetheless his spirits were high. He was looking at a promotion for making the arrest in the most high-profile murder case that Buffalo had seen in the last twenty years.

The evidence found in Julia's house was indisputable. DNA

confirmed the teeth and portions of the jawbone clinging to them belonged to Julia. Blood at the scene belonged to Julia. And Colin left his fingerprints in her blood on the kitchen cabinet door; this was better than a confession. Other evidence was being uncovered that connected him to the murders of both Francine Donohue and Samantha Ritcher, but the department was keeping it quiet for now.

Gavin finally picked up the receiver and though he hadn't spoken to the person on the other end in quite a while, he recognized the voice immediately. "Well, Thomas Hayden, how have you been?"

"I couldn't be better," Thomas answered.

"How are things in Boston? Are you keeping the crime rates down?"

"I'm doing what I can."

Gavin couldn't read the tone—if Thomas was joking or sarcastic he didn't know. But he did know Thomas's background and reputation. Thomas Hayden had spent years as a criminalist working in various roles for the State of Massachusetts, and was very highly regarded. After his retirement, he branched out and was now a high-profile expert usually hired by the defense. He was well known for being able to turn the odds around, especially with hopeless situations. This is what he was famous for. Christ, there were radio and television shows depicting his cases.

Thomas Hayden was also arrogant and rightly so. Gavin decided to stroke that ego, if only to find out what this call was about, though he had his suspicions. "So, are you working on anything unusual? I just heard about your latest triumph on that show, *Crime in the City*. It's such a good case that they keep repeating it."

"That was a challenge. The one I have right now is boring.

It's a suspected arsenic poisoning death. The family is requesting a second autopsy to test the victim for it."

"Do you think they'll find any?"

"Oh, I don't doubt that arsenic will be found in the body. I'm having samples tested as we speak."

"So, you're suspicious that someone killed him?"

"No. I'm covering my ass. There's an old well that used to supply the drinking water for the house on the property. It's only several hundred yards from the Aberjona River in Woburn, Massachusetts. There used to be a lot of tanneries along the banks and tanneries used arsenic in their processing. The soil and water are probably still thoroughly contaminated. This is where I think the arsenic came from. For nostalgic reasons, the victim used to drink from the well. I just have to make sure the water and soil samples are consistent with anything they find in the body."

"Thomas. That's ingenious on your part. Who are you getting off the hook for murder?"

"No one. I was hired by the children of the victim to find proof that the stepmother did it."

"Finding a killer. This is prosecutorial not defense. It doesn't sound like your kind of thing."

"It's not. I'm not taking the case, but not for that reason. I have another one that just popped up. It interests me much more. This one is, as you just described, 'my kind of thing.'"

"I'm assuming that's the reason for this phone call?" Gavin clenched the phone tighter. He knew what was coming next.

"Yes, it is. What can you tell me about a Colin Turner?"

Thomas had made his career from taking cases like this, but this one was beyond hope and Gavin was prepared to set Thomas straight. "Colin Turner is a guilty, egotistical, arrogant bastard who murdered his wife over money. It's the oldest reason in the book. You don't want to get mixed up with him. You have better things to do with your time."

"I disagree. That's just the type I like to inspect. I'm thinking of coming to look at things."

"Save yourself a trip. There's really no reason. The evidence against him is overwhelming."

"I've seen the report. His lawyer sent it to me. What's his excuse for not killing his wife? Is it a good one?"

"His defense is about as lame as they come. He said, and I quote..." Gavin picked up the notes from his interrogation with Colin and read, "'After I came back, she tried to commit suicide. She was bleeding. She was holding a bloody towel on her wrist. I grabbed the towel to help her. But she pulled away. I had blood on my hands when I opened the cabinet. That must be how my fingerprint got on it.'"

"That's actually not bad. I've heard worse," Thomas responded. "Anyway, I hear, mostly from the news, that there have been other murders committed in the same way. Is he a suspect in those too?"

"The prime suspect."

"You know, Mitch, this *is* my specialty."

Gavin heard the enthusiastic tone in Thomas's voice and responded strongly. "The evidence is airtight against him. He left his fingerprints with his wife's blood at the scene. There is no debating it. He just created some story to try to explain it away."

"I think I would like to be the judge of that."

"Suit yourself." Gavin tried to sound cordial. "By the way, where did Colin get the cash to hire someone like you?"

"Mitchell, you know I can't disclose my potential client's finances. Anyway, we're just finishing up the arsenic testing for that case I mentioned earlier. Oh, I almost forgot. I've been working with a partner for the last few years now. His name is Jack Styles. We should be in Buffalo by next week."

16

S ince Julia's death, Val had experienced mixed emotions. She felt sorrow at losing Julia. She felt vengeful because she wanted to catch her killer. And she feared what her fate at the medical examiner's office might be. With Julia gone, and Julia's support and protection gone, her future was unknown. *Hell, my entire career at the medical examiner's office could come and go in little more than a month,* she thought.

But today, she didn't feel the dread. Even the irritating ride into work she was experiencing couldn't drag her spirits down.

Traffic was heavy on the thruway, making a slow drive into the city. Steady downpours, which now tapered to drizzle, had slicked the roads all morning, and everyone was driving in an unnecessarily cautious manner. Cars were going at less than 20 mph, stopping and starting, creating gridlock. A solid mass of dark clouds filled the sky, threatening more precipitation, and as Val arrived for work, the rain started to pick up in intensity again.

She pulled into the parking ramp and went up two levels to her designated parking spot, thankful she wouldn't have to walk outside. It was a long hike to the entrance from where she parked her car, but at least this was indoors. The spot was clearly labeled: "# 232. *Reserved for Death Investigator*". Today, however, another car was parked in her place. It wasn't the first time. Doctors from the hospital took any open spot, regardless of who it belonged to.

Pissed, she circled around, winding up one level at a time. There was only one level left, the top. Uncovered. No roof. As she emerged back into daylight from the darkness of the ramp, drops speckled the windshield. By the time she had parked the car the rain was pounding.

"Damn, damn, damn!" Val muttered, realizing she didn't have an umbrella. She made a mad dash for the entrance, running as fast as she could, but it was no use: she was soaked by the time she arrived at the door.

Dripping wet, Val sloshed through the corridors heading towards her office, thankful she could grab a pair of scrubs to change into. She was not thankful when she bumped into Candace.

"What happened to you?" Candace asked.

Val began to wonder how bad she really looked. "You might be surprised to hear it's raining outside." She didn't bother to hide how irritated she was.

"Don't you keep an umbrella in your car? I keep one in my car *and* in my purse. My hair just takes on a mind of its own if the rain gets at it."

"Thanks for the advice. I'll try to remember it for next time." She turned to walk away when Candace spoke again.

"Oh, I have a surprise for you. I left her in your office."

Val stopped and turned towards Candace, staring at her impatiently, expecting to hear what she was talking about, but Candace merely crossed her arms and said nothing.

"Who is it?" Val was curt. She was in no mood for Candace's games. All she wanted to do was change out of her wet clothing.

The morgue was always kept fairly cool and she was already feeling uncomfortable.

"I'll let her introduce herself. I wouldn't want to spoil the surprise."

Val hurried to her office, nervous. *Who in the hell could this be?* When she arrived, there was a red-headed woman standing in it. "Can I help you?" she asked.

The woman was busy unloading items from a large cardboard box. She stopped once she heard Val. "You must be Valentina Knight," the woman said, staring at Val's dripping hair.

Val immediately felt self-conscious about her appearance and began to explain, "I was caught in the rain." She reached a hand to her hair, pushing soggy strands from her face.

"The administrator, Candace, told me to wait for you here. Sorry I seem a little disorganized. Today's my first day of work."

"Oh, you must be one of the new public relations people." Val relaxed and sized this woman up. She was attractive, with curly auburn hair. She stood about five foot nine inches and had to be in her late thirties or early forties. Yes, she belonged in a public relations department. All of the people working there were pretty. They looked good in news interviews. She had heard about the new PR people who had been hired mostly to take care of the media frenzy surrounding Julia's murder and the arrest of her husband Colin. Val was told she would be interviewed by one. This is probably what Candace was so happy about. Maybe Val's background would be revealed during the inquisition.

The stranger laughed. "Public relations? No, I'm here to work with you. I'm your new fellow death investigator." She extended her hand. "I'm Gwen. Gwen Carmondy."

Val stood still for a moment, not moving. Then she mechanically held out her hand. Gwen shook it and then let go. Val felt her body go limp, as if the wind had been knocked out of her. She heard what the woman was saying but somehow it wasn't registering. This couldn't be true. She was suddenly standing in the middle of a very bad dream. Then reality hit hard as she stared at the person she'd stolen the job from.

"Are you okay?" Gwen questioned. "Maybe you should sit down. You don't look well." She pulled a chair over and tried to coax Val into it.

"I'm fine." She waved away the chair.

"Anyway, Dr. Blythe hired me yesterday and asked me to start today. He said the office was pretty busy."

Val had wondered how much time was left before her days at the medical examiner's office were over. With Gwen Carmondy standing in front of her, the end might be sooner than she thought. Choosing her words carefully, Val asked, "How did you find out about the position? I mean, how did you know there was an opening?"

"Oh, I was good friends with Oliver Solaris. He used to be one of the head death investigators here. I heard you knew him too. I can't believe he's gone. Wasn't he awesome?"

"He was the best." Val placed a hand on the counter to steady herself. Oliver Solaris could have been an ax murderer for all she knew of him. The room suddenly became hot and she felt dizzy.

"Are you sure you don't want to sit?" Gwen patted the chair.

Val just shook her head.

"This is such a funny story. I was actually supposed to be interviewed about a month ago. After Oliver died, they decided to hire someone else he knew. That must have been you."

Val nodded. She felt the lie was written all across her face and waited for Gwen to ask something that would make it all too obvious that she'd never met this man. She held her breath, as Gwen continued.

"I called out of the blue and spoke to Dr. Blythe. I told him who I was and asked if he could keep my résumé on file in case a position should open up. He offered me the job on the spot. He said with the death of the deputy medical examiner, he needed help. I can't believe what happened to her. I hear her husband did it, that he's a serial killer. He's killed more people, right?"

"That's what they say." Val spoke automatically. Her thoughts started to run wild as she waited for more discussion about Oliver. She pictured another futile job search, losing her house. Living on the street. Her anxiety now ratcheted up to epic proportions. Wavering, she finally took hold of the chair and managed to sit down, before she fell down.

"Valentina—that's a pretty name. Is it Italian? You look Italian," Gwen said.

Val just nodded.

"You know, I don't know anyone in this area. We'll have to get a drink after work one night and you can let me in on all of the gossip around here."

Val nodded again. Though she had managed a smile, feigning some enthusiasm towards Gwen's suggestion, she was horrified at the thought. The last thing in the world Val wanted to do was be alone with Gwen for any length of time. How on earth would she handle any questions about their *mutual friend Oliver*? She barely knew what the man looked like.

"If you'll excuse me, I have some work to do, plus I really need to change out of these wet clothes. Nice to meet you," Val said in an effort to get away.

"Nice to meet you too."

As Val got up to leave, Gwen said, "Isn't it great they give us our own parking spot? Mine's in a bad location. It's in a corner on the second level of the ramp. Candace assigned me #232. Where do you get to park? I'm sure it's better than that."

17

Thomas Hayden and his partner Jack Styles sat in Gavin's office, waiting for the detective. They had arrived in Buffalo from Boston a little more than an hour ago. After checking into their hotel room, they had come straight to the police station. Neither took time to unpack.

Jack glanced at his watch and frowned at Thomas. "We've been sitting here almost a half hour," he said. "Maybe you should call him."

"Be patient. Detective Gavin is working a murder case. He's trying to find some solid evidence against our potential client. I'm sure he wants to influence us with something very good. Why else would he make us wait?" He checked his own watch. Then peered at the clock hanging on the wall.

They both turned towards the door as Gavin finally appeared. He had several folders in his hands and a confident smile on his face. He shifted the folders, extending a free hand to Thomas first and then was introduced to Jack.

"How was your flight?" Gavin asked.

"Horrible," Thomas said. "The only positive thing was that I did get through Colin's case file. I have to say you were right, Mitch, it's pretty damning. He left a trail in his wife's blood."

"It's gotten worse since we spoke last week. I think you'd better have a look before going much further with this." Gavin opened one of the folders and handed Thomas the report, pointing to the last part. "That evidence was found just this morning."

Thomas read slowly, letting the information sink in.

Jack read over his shoulder and then asked, "Is this confirmed?"

"Yes. It's concrete. Up until now we only had circumstantial evidence linking Colin with Francine Donohue and Samantha Ritcher. This is a little more substantial."

"Well then, it looks like the odds have taken a turn for the worse." Thomas closed the folder.

"I wouldn't want to play against these odds," Gavin said abruptly.

"When can I see Colin?" Thomas asked, unaffected by Gavin's comment.

Gavin sat back in his chair, his eyebrows raised. "Thomas, I'm surprised you still want to go forward with this. You can see him now. Colin doesn't know about the last part in that report. We only received that minutes before you arrived."

"Good, I'll get to see his honest reaction to it. Let me talk to Colin and then I'll make my decision about this case."

Gavin met up with Warren in the hallway and the two led Thomas and Jack through the building and into the section that housed the county jail. They went through the necessary security checks before being placed face to face with Colin Turner in the interrogation room. His lawyer sat beside him.

Wearing an orange jailhouse jumpsuit, Colin relaxed in the chair. He possessed an air of arrogance, even in this situation.

Thomas noticed that Colin's hands were damp with sweat when the two exchanged greetings.

The lawyer barked at Gavin as soon as they were seated. "You'd better not be jerking us around again. If you have something, say what it is."

"There's no time like the present, then." Gavin opened his folder and started. "Colin, did you know a Francine Donohue?"

"Who?"

Gavin repeated the name.

"No."

"What about a Samantha Ritcher?"

"No."

"Never met anyone with those names? Think carefully."

"No! I said I never heard of either of them before."

"Then can you explain to me why a Samantha Ritcher called you?"

"I never had a call from her. I don't know anyone by that name." Colin didn't even bother to look at the detective as he spoke.

"I have Samantha's phone records. There are three calls to your cell phone."

Colin responded dismissively, "It's probably a wrong number, I get them all the time. Who the hell cares anyway?"

"She died recently and may have a connection to your wife's case."

"Jesus Christ! What does this have to do with me? I don't know any Samantha Ritcher."

"Why would she be calling you?" This time the question was posed more forcefully.

"I don't know. I don't know her. I told you, maybe it was a wrong number."

Warren spoke up. "The first call lasted two minutes and thirty-six seconds, the second, four minutes and thirteen seconds, the last one was almost five minutes. Most of my wrong numbers are over and done with in less than ten seconds. Why so long on the phone, and more than once? Were you helping her place the correct call each time?"

"Yeah, I'm the goddamn information hotline."

"Cute. You'd better hold onto that sense of humor. It'll win you friends when you're locked away for the rest of your life for murder," Warren said.

"I didn't kill anyone!"

"Sure you didn't. Your name just happens to be linked to several dead women, but you had no role in their death?" Gavin said.

"What do you mean *several* dead women?" Colin's lawyer asked.

Gavin continued questioning Colin, ignoring his lawyer. "Have you ever been to the Eastville Projects, specifically the residence belonging to a Francine Donohue?"

"I told you I have no idea who that is."

"She was victim number two. Jeanne Coleman was number one, Samantha Ritcher number three, and your wife was the fourth in the string of murders. Three of those women were dismembered and their teeth removed."

"I still don't know who she is."

"Can you tell me why a gum wrapper with your DNA was found under this dead woman's bed?"

Colin stared in disbelief, not answering the question. Gavin was unwavering. "Colin, were you having an affair with Francine Donohue?"

No answer again.

Gavin continued. "Did you murder Francine Donohue?"

This time Colin jumped up from the chair and began pounding on the table; wildly hitting his fists on the wood. "I'm not listening to this bullshit anymore!" Colin yelled. His lawyer grabbed him by the arm and pulled him back down in his seat.

"This is all circumstantial evidence. It doesn't prove my client murdered these women. So, he talked to someone who called *him*. So, a gum wrapper was found. It's garbage, literally. I can give you a million different explanations for all of this. Do you have anything else against my client?" the lawyer calmly asked.

"Not *yet*," Gavin said.

Colin smiled smugly, composure regained at the *not yet* statement. "You have nothing real on me, or you would have done something more by now, something other than this fishing crap. I told you I didn't know who those women were." He turned his focus toward Thomas. "With my lawyer and you I should be out of here in time for dinner."

"That's all well and good but I need more information before I decide if I will take your case," Thomas said plainly. His cool response was a sharp contrast to the heated tension in the room.

"What the hell do you mean 'decide to take my case?' I didn't fly you here from Boston to shoot the shit."

"I said I would meet with you. I didn't agree to anything beyond that."

"I'm offering you a lot of money. You'll take my case," Colin said. He sat back in the chair and folded his arms.

"Listen carefully, Colin. Don't be cocky with me. I know what your financial situation really is. I didn't get on the plane without finding *that* out." The words were icy and sharp, and meant to pierce straight through Colin and put him in his place. "Now, *I* will speak and *I* will tell you what *I* will or will not do. But first I will start this conversation off with what will happen to *you*. You will not only be charged with the murder of your wife but perhaps a couple of other people too. The DNA evidence against you is damning. Honestly, Detective Gavin doesn't need more proof. What he already has against you is not trivial by any means, no matter what your lawyer says."

"It's all circumstantial," the lawyer stressed.

"It's also all damn concerning. Don't you think?" He turned to Colin, addressing him pointedly. "New York declared the death penalty unconstitutional in 2004. And though you will not die by order of this state you will never walk out of one of its prisons alive if convicted of these crimes. As a presumed serial killer, with DNA evidence implicating you, I would think that someone in your predicament would be a little less... how shall I say this... *ass-like*."

Thomas's words, "serial killer", hit Colin hard. His face became ashen. He grabbed his head and pressed his fingers to his skull, growing increasingly despondent. The more Thomas talked the more real the situation seemed to become. Colin was finally taking this seriously.

"Colin, I'm a busy man. I know the logistics of this case. I know full well the extent of the evidence against you. What I don't know is, how is it possible that you're innocent when everything points to the fact that you are not. I'll know within the first two minutes of your answer to my question if I will take your case. So, don't waste my time, and yours, on inconsequential or stupid matters," Thomas said.

Thomas Hayden had a lifetime of experience reading people. The speech, mannerisms and body language of those questioned usually let him know immediately if he believed someone or not. "Convince me as to why you are innocent. I don't care that the judicial system likes it the other way around. To me, you're guilty until I get some type of proof that shows otherwise. This is what I want to know right now and if you choose to waste my time with anything less, I'll walk out of here taking any hope you have with me."

Colin spoke, his voice cracking, "I didn't kill her or anyone else because I don't kill people. What in the hell would that do for me?" He looked Thomas straight in the eye and didn't move. "What would I have to gain from her death or anyone else's? You want me to say it? I'll say it. I'm a player. I use women and I get money from them. If they're dead, I get nothing. That's why I'm innocent."

Thomas placed his elbows on the table and leaned forward. He absorbed what Colin said and deliberated the decision to move further with this interview or not. He sat back in his chair, put his hand to his face and rubbed his chin. The room was silent, waiting for Thomas to say something. He finally spoke. "Okay. Now, tell me what you did the evening your wife was murdered."

"She had it all planned to ruin me financially. The house was in foreclosure and her surgery practice was worthless. She owed about five million. As her husband, I get half of what she owns. And owes. I'm also responsible for her debt. I was in for about 2.5 million, is what she told me," Colin said. "She set this up. She wasn't poor. She must have withdrawn the money from the account somehow, hidden it somewhere and then messed around with everything else. The mortgage, her practice... she wanted to make them worthless. She also said that she cancelled her malpractice insurance, that I was getting nothing from that either, but I didn't believe her. Julia's lawyer had just met with Lauren and they discussed settling the case."

"You said that the property was worthless. Is there any possibility that she was tricking you with this? That maybe she just wanted to scare you?" Thomas asked.

"She showed me the bills. Collectors were sending her notices. That was real. That's how she was going to get revenge on me. But she had the money hidden. I know she did."

"Didn't *that* make you angry?" Jack asked.

"Of course, I was angry, but I was also screwed at the moment, so I was worried."

"What happened next?" Thomas asked.

"We talked. She was calm. I lied to her. I told her that I wanted to give our relationship another chance. I was hoping to string her along. If she thought I still loved her, she'd back off."

"How long did you stay with her?" Thomas asked.

"About two hours, maybe a little more. I wasn't looking at the clock. She was alive after I left. I swear she was alive when I left."

"There's a partial of your fingerprint in her blood on the cabinet in the kitchen. If she was alive when you left, why was she bleeding while you were there?" Jack said.

Colin looked down, studying his hands, locking and unlocking his fingers before he answered. "She cut herself. I was trying to help her. That's how her blood got on me."

"How on earth did she cut *herself* badly enough to get her blood on you?" Jack's tone didn't hide the fact that he was skeptical.

"I don't know. It's all such a blur. I was trying to get her into bed, you know, trying to get her to think I wanted her back. It almost worked. We were just about there when she pushed me away and freaked out. She said I was only acting and I really didn't love her."

"At least she was perceptive," Jack said. "Let's get back to the blood. I asked you how she came to be bleeding."

"She ran into the kitchen saying what a fool she was. She was crying by the sink. I wasn't paying attention to what she was doing. All I could think about was what to say to calm her down. I didn't even see her do it."

"Do what?"

"She slit her wrist." Colin paused. He placed his hand on his forehead, pulling back his hair.

"Please continue," Thomas prompted. His full attention on Colin.

Colin took a deep breath. "She grabbed a towel to try to stop the bleeding. I didn't even notice what she did until I saw the bloody towel. I tried to look at it but she wouldn't let me. I reached for her arm but she pulled away. Blood was dripping everywhere. When I opened the drawer to get another towel, she ran into the bathroom and locked the door. I followed her, pounding for her to open up. After a few minutes she answered calmly, saying that she was okay and the cut wasn't bad. When she came out of the bathroom her wrist was bandaged."

"Did you take a look at it?" Jack asked.

"No."

"Why not?"

"She was a doctor, a surgeon. You want me to question her about how to put a bandage on? I stayed for a while after that. She calmed down and promised to see me the next day to talk more about this. She was alive when I left."

"You said that you stayed for at least two hours. You had to have done something else. What you described doesn't account for two hours."

"Like I said, I wasn't checking the clock."

"Do you know anyone who would want to harm your wife?" Thomas asked.

Colin took his time, thinking for a minute. "She worked with some lunatics, but was mostly worried about her boss, Dr. Phillip Blythe. Julia was reviewing his cases and she found a lot of mistakes. She confronted him one time and he didn't take it too well."

"What kind of mistakes did she find?" Thomas asked. Gavin's full attention was on the conversation.

"I don't know. I left her right after that and didn't talk to her anymore about it."

． ． ．

Thomas Hayden walked out of the prison not completely convinced of Colin's innocence but intrigued enough to want to investigate further. He hadn't had a media-worthy case in a while, and if nothing else, this would certainly give him a challenge.

Jack questioned him on the way out of the jailhouse. "That's very convenient, isn't it? It's a fairly easy explanation for how her blood got on him. Who can argue it? The only other witness is dead."

"Yes, too convenient. We'll have to look into that. I think we also need to get a copy of Dr. DeHaviland's financial records and her autopsy files—the ones that detail her review of her boss's work."

"So, I'm assuming that we are going to take this case on?"

"Yes, Jack, I am. It's quite fascinating."

"Shouldn't we go back in and let Colin know?"

"No, let him sweat for a while. It'll be good for him."

"Right, then. Where should we start?"

"We need to talk to the people who knew Julia. Her murder is the center of all of this. She's tied to Colin, the accused. We need to start here. And that's going to be with Dr. Phillip Blythe."

18

V al read Dr. Stedman's autopsy notes and Howie's report from the investigation at the scene.

White male, age 25-35. Cause of death: Cerebral Hemorrhage. Manner of death: Accident. A broken bottle of Jack Daniels was found next to where he fell. And shortly thereafter, died. Blood Alcohol content was 0.22.

So, the idiot fell and hit his head on the pavement after downing a staggering amount of liquor. How could someone be so stupid and end their life like this?

She noticed the dead man had abrasions on his hands. It looked like he tried to stop his fall at least. What this person needed now was a name and this would be done through his dental records.

Val had to remove the upper and lower jaws so she could perform the dental ID properly. On the table next to her sat an open textbook depicting the necessary steps on how to do this. She had no choice but to use the book. Hell, she never had to remove a set of jaws before. Howie's help was rare these days. In fact, she hardly saw much of him at all. Dr. Blythe was continually assigning duties for him that never coincided with her schedule. Without Howie, she was at a disadvantage. How was she supposed to keep pace with Gwen Carmondy without his help and guidance? The simple fact was that she couldn't.

After Gwen's arrival, only a few days ago, Val had been pretty much confined to the morgue to identify people by their teeth when no other means were available. Her job consisted of everything smelly, rotting, and labor intensive. As Howie predicted, she'd grown mostly accustomed to the odor and sights of decomposition and was now unaffected by even the worst decaying corpses. The maggots though, were still hard to handle. Luckily, this victim was pretty fresh and there was no need to worry about bugs. Today Val wore scrubs only, seeing no need for a Tyvek suit. She did have to work in the decomp room though, because this is where the dental equipment was kept.

Periodically, Val glanced up at the door, hoping no one would come in and see her referring to a book. That's all she needed right now, to look inexperienced and grossly incompetent, to the point of performing her duties on a *learn as you* go basis with a step-by-step guide in a textbook for a forensic *dental* procedure. According to her lie, Oliver Solaris recommend her for this job. Now, more than ever, she needed to be Gwen Carmondy's equal, not some second-rate idiot.

Val picked up a scalpel and made an incision from the corner of the dead man's mouth towards his ear. She repeated this on the other side. The victim had been dead for about 18 hours and was in full rigor. She couldn't even open his mouth enough to separate his upper and lower teeth, let alone get X-ray film in there. His face might as well have been made out of concrete for all of the movement she was able to get out of the jaws. Removing them from the body was the only way to get the X-rays.

Now that the slices were made, she placed her scalpel in the vestibule, the area inside the mouth between the gum tissue and the lip. She cut across, separating the bone from the lips and cheek. Val took another look at the open textbook. So far so good, her progress corresponded to the diagram.

Next, she picked up a large pair of long-handled garden loppers. God, it was six weeks ago when she saw Dr. Chen using the same instrument on a decedent's ribs. She'd never have thought a pruning tool would have so many uses in a morgue, let alone be the instrument of choice for cutting the bones. Val placed the blade into the area just under the nose on the upper jaw, the maxilla.

Awkwardly, she stretched out her small arms as far as they would go, attempting to maneuver the large instrument. Gripping the handles and arms widely extended, she didn't have enough strength to bring the ends of the loppers together. *Jesus, Dr. Chen had made it look so easy with the ribs.*

Sweat started to form on her brow from the exertion and her arms began to ache from the pulling. Val glanced at the book again to make sure that she had the technique right. She jumped when the doors opened and Gwen came in. She stopped and stared.

"You need to bring the handles closer together," Gwen said. "Here, let me show you an easier way."

"I'm doing just fine. I can manage." Val gritted her teeth and pulled again, desperate to hear the bone snap, desperate to accomplish this in front of Gwen. She grunted and pulled on the ends as hard as she could. After trying several times, she finally let the loppers drop, mostly out of sheer exhaustion.

Gwen reached for the tool. She placed the long handles close together, only opening the blades wide enough to get them around the jaw. With a quick push, they snapped through the bone. "If the handles are too far apart, you won't get any lever-age." She held the instrument in place and moved out of the way. "Here, give it try."

Val did exactly as Gwen showed her and was amazed at how much easier it was. She quickly moved the instrument around the upper jaw and on the last snip, it detached from the man's body.

"That's a good trick. I never tried it that way before," Val said, smiling to herself. This technically wasn't a lie, since she'd really never tried it in any way before.

"If you can break away for a second, there's an investigator here to see you. That's what I came to tell you," Gwen said.

"An investigator? Is it Detective Gavin?" Val's interest perked up at the possibility.

"No, it's someone else. He wanted to speak to Dr. Blythe, but Blythe's unavailable. The man wants to know if he can talk to you in the meantime."

"What does he want to see me for?" she said, disappointed it wasn't Gavin.

"He's here about Julia DeHaviland's murder."

"Why? Her husband did it. What on earth can he be investigating?" Val began to lose interest and looked back at the dead man on the table, his face oddly contorted now that he was missing his upper jaw.

"I don't know. He didn't say. Can you talk to him now or should I tell him to come back later?"

"I might as well do it now and get it over with." She pointed to the jawless man. "He can wait." Val went to the sink, pulled off her gloves and washed her hands. That was about as far as her cleaning up was going to go. She glanced in the mirror hanging over the sink, thinking how disheveled she looked with her hair pulled back in a messy ponytail and no makeup on. Her scrubs had several stains on them, making her wonder not only how they got there, but also what they were.

Gwen walked over to the side of the sink and stood against the wall. "There's a great band playing downtown tomorrow night at this bar in Allentown called Nietzsche's. We should go. Howie's on call and we're both off. The music's kind of alternative but I read good reviews about them. The bar's supposed to be a good place to meet men too. Good music and men. The way I see it, it's a win-win situation. You are single, right?"

Val just nodded, hoping Gwen would move on to a different topic. Val really liked the idea of going to Nietzsche's. She hadn't been there in years and ached to get back into socializing, seeing a band. Seeing people. But knew she had to say no to Gwen. Again.

This wasn't the first time Gwen asked to do something outside of work. In just the last couple of days, she had been bombarded with offers. Val came up with excuse after excuse not to go anywhere with her and quite frankly, was running out of good-sounding reasons. The last thing she wanted to do was socialize with Gwen Carmondy. Val had to admit that she liked her. So, nothing personal. Val simply shuddered at the thought of possibly being asked the one question she dreaded the most, the one that could get her fired... "*So how did you know Oliver Solaris?*"

Thankfully, Gwen did move on. "Oh, by the way, the detective is British. Love his accent, but his face..."

"What's wrong with his face?" Val asked as she wiped her hands.

"Well, it's just that..." Gwen hesitated. "It's just that he might have been in an accident, so don't stare at him."

Val threw the paper towel in the garbage and reached for a second one, wiping them vigorously another time, not even realizing her hands were dry as she quickly grew irritated by Gwen's remark.

"I don't stare at people," Val said abruptly, then thought, *What kind of person does she think I am? Does she really think I would be rude enough to stare at some disfigured man? Maybe I'm not a seasoned death investigation professional, but I'm certainly not an uncouth baboon.*

"Just warning you, that's all. Sometimes it's hard not to stare no matter how many times you tell yourself not to. I just don't want you to be surprised."

Val said nothing further and walked out of the decomp room. For some reason Gwen was on her heels, following her down the hallway. A feeling of superiority wafted over Val. She sensed Gwen wanted to find out why the detective was asking to see her and was trying to be included in the interview. She had no problem with Gwen tagging along. This detective was here to talk to her about one of the most high-profile cases in Buffalo's history, a case she had been part of. *Let Gwen sink her teeth into that.*

When they arrived at the office, a man was sitting in the tiny space, reclining in the chair. His back was to the door.

"Don't stare," Gwen instructed in a hushed tone in Val's ear as the two went inside. Val reached a hand behind her, swatting at Gwen, trying to keep her at an acceptable distance, and quiet.

The man turned round, stood up, and smiled. "I'm Jack Styles. I'm investigating the murder of Julia DeHaviland and was hoping that I could ask you some questions."

Val did stare, and her mouth opened but no words came out. She was speechless.

He was tall, his frame outlined by broad shoulders that tapered to a narrow waist. Chiseled cheekbones and a strong jaw were accompanied by dark hair and dark eyes. Everything about him looked good, but it was mostly his eyes. He had devilish eyes, the kind of eyes that grabbed women's souls instantly and held them indefinitely.

"You must be Dr. Knight." Jack continued to smile.

"Yes. How can I help you, Detective...?" Val hesitated. She was staring at him so intently she forgot who he said he was. Out of the corner of her eye she could see Gwen cover her mouth to hide the satisfaction of fooling her. Her cheeks grew hot as she became self-conscious.

"Styles. Jack Styles." He held out his hand, still smiling but now in a pretentious manner. He hadn't taken his gaze off her and seemed to be aware that she was distracted.

Val immediately disliked him, growing increasingly annoyed by the pompous grinning. He was an attractive man and he knew it. She hated this type. Worse yet, the realization of how unkempt she looked was embarrassing to say the least. It put her at an immediate disadvantage in dealing with him. It would be hard to put him in his place when she looked like something even the cat wouldn't drag in.

"Well, Detective Styles..." Her words still went nowhere. She was so irritated that she had lost her train of thought.

"Let me explain." He crossed his arms and looked right into Val's eyes. "My partner and I have been privately hired by Colin Turner. I tried earlier to talk with Dr. Blythe but he's unavailable and says he will be for the rest of the day. I bumped into Ms. Carmondy and she told me that you knew Julia DeHaviland quite well. I was hoping to ask you some questions about her."

Val had been at the medical examiner's offices long enough to know that when Blythe was *unavailable* he didn't want to, nor did he need to, speak with you. This meant that this investigator wasn't anyone important. Blythe didn't need to be polite with him. Nor did she. And she didn't want to be polite. This jackass was working for Julia's husband, her killer.

"Privately hired? Oh, so you're not a *real* detective," she said.

Jack looked down at his arm and pinched himself in an exaggerated, affected manner. "I think of myself as very real. Though I'm not normally referred to as 'detective.' Mr. Styles or Jack will do just fine."

Val's irritation soared. "How can you work for that murderer?" she snapped.

"Who says he's a murderer?" Jack asked calmly.

"Everyone," she snapped again.

"So, he's tried, convicted and sentenced all without ever stepping into a courtroom?" He had an air of superiority that Val couldn't stomach. Every word she lashed at him, he replied with a smart retort.

She tried again. "Does he need to waste the taxpayer's money?"

"I'm not paid by your taxpayers."

"No, Colin's paying you with Julia's money."

Jack just grinned.

Touché, Val thought. She was about to ask him to leave when he spoke up.

"So, what can you tell me about Dr. DeHaviland? I have Colin's version, which I will admit is not the most flattering. She really couldn't have been *that* bad," he said.

Val hissed, "He was a lousy two-timing bastard. How *dare* he badmouth her?" She lingered on the *dare* as if she herself would call Colin out.

"Please continue." Jack sat back down and crossed his arms, letting Val rant. She went on, the events from her last conversation with Julia erupting. "The last thing she said to me is that he wouldn't win."

"How so?" Jack stood up from the chair, his demeanor serious now. "Did she ever mention anything to you?"

"No." Val looked away. "I was supposed to have dinner with her. She was going to tell me more then, but I found her dead instead."

"What can you tell me about the other murders? Francine Donohue and Jeanne Coleman. Did Colin have any connections to these other women?" Jack said, his tone softened.

"I don't know very much about them. If Julia suspected Colin knew them, she never mentioned it to me. Anyway, Dr. Blythe is working on those. You should talk to him." All Val wanted at this point was to be rid of Jack Styles.

"If I give you my card, do you think that you could give me a call if you remember anything else?" He held the card out to her.

Val took it, and as soon as he was out of the room she tossed it into the trash.

"I told you not to stare. You could have caught flies with how wide your mouth was open," Gwen said. She was clearly amused with the joke. "You have to admit a guy who looks like that doesn't walk through the door every day."

"I wouldn't have stared if you didn't set me up," Val said, fuming.

"I'm sorry. I thought you would think it was funny."

"Maybe it would have been if he wasn't such an egotistical bastard."

"True, but he is good-looking. Just remember I saw him first!" Gwen said. "Anyway, the band starts at nine tomorrow night. I'll pick you up at six and we'll get something to eat. I'm not taking no for an answer."

19

Gwen was true to her word. She picked Val up at six the next night.

Avoiding an evening out with Gwen was something Val couldn't do anymore. Gwen was friendly, personable and liked by many of her coworkers, something Val couldn't claim. If Val outright blew her off one more time she'd look like a bitch, and then risk becoming labeled as a bitch in office gossip. Val tried to be as anonymous as possible in the medical examiner's office. Having Gwen hate her, turning into an enemy, would be far worse and definitely much more dangerous than hanging out and socializing for a few hours. An enemy wouldn't hesitate to get her fired—a friend maybe not.

Val concocted and stowed a plausible excuse for how she knew Oliver Solaris just in case. If she needed to resort to this, it was ready to go.

Luckily for Val, Gwen kept the conversation light and airy, venturing no further than run-of-the-mill chitchat as they drove to the restaurant. The conversation continued, minus Oliver thankfully, as the two were seated at Cole's restaurant on Elmwood Avenue in the north section of the Elmwood Village.

A collection of trendy restaurants and shops peppered each side of the street but this one was the only one with an outside patio.

With the weather being warm, Val and Gwen jumped at the opportunity to get the last open table. Once their glasses of wine had been delivered Gwen asked Val about her background and her family.

Val took a deep breath. She knew it would only be a matter of time before the conversation took a dangerous turn. She responded plainly. "I'm an only child. My parents died a long time ago. I was in my late teens when it happened. My father went first with a heart attack and my mother followed one year later in a car accident. When she died, my family was gone."

Val often described her parents' death candidly. It wasn't that she was callous. It was a protective mechanism. It was the only way she could answer the question without falling apart, though it had been almost twenty years. She was a grown woman, yet at times she still felt like a lost child.

"You don't beat around the bush at all now, do you?"

"It is what it is," Val said. "So, what's your story?"

"It's kind of boring. Better order some coffee to keep you awake if you're going to sit through my saga."

"I'll get a cup if I need it."

"Just remember, you asked for it," Gwen said. "I got married when I was seventeen. Dropped out of high school to do it. He was twenty-seven. God, was I stupid back then. My parents disowned me. They said if I was going to throw my life away, then they wanted nothing to do with me. I haven't talked to them since that day."

"I thought you said this story was going to be boring?" Val said.

"It is to me."

Val took a sip of her wine. "What happened to your husband? It's obvious that you don't have one anymore."

"I divorced him five years after I married him. After I caught him cheating on me for the third time. You know, I wasn't even mad when I caught him. I guess I had just grown used to it."

"What a bastard."

"You got that right. He wasn't much of a husband. I'm far better off without him."

"That must have been tough. The divorce, I mean. You were what? Twenty-two? Did you have anyone to help you through it?"

"No. I had to learn to take care of myself, which I did. I grew up fast. It took a couple of years to get back on my feet after my divorce. Then, I got my General Education Diploma and went to college and became a registered nurse."

As Gwen spoke, Val couldn't help but think how similar their lives have been. Both lost parents while still teenagers and they had to struggle to make something of themselves. She felt close to Gwen, perhaps a bond through similar hard life experiences. Val felt comfortable discussing more of her own story, telling Gwen things she never told anyone. "In order to make ends meet while I was in school, I worked nights and weekends as a waitress and still had a hard time. How did you do it, moneywise?"

"I worked full time at a shoe store in the local mall while going to school. There was no extra money to buy anything. Christ, I had to buy clothes at the thrift store. Nowadays, I don't wear anything without a label..." Gwen laughed. "And never anything previously worn by someone else!"

Val shook her head and smiled as she reminisced: her own story was so much the same. "I still remember one particularly rough year when I went into a drug store and couldn't spend the three dollars it cost to buy red fingernail polish. Do you know what was the first thing I bought when I starting making money as a dentist?"

"Designer nail polish?"

"No. I bought a Mercedes that was almost the same color red as that nail polish I wanted to buy."

Gwen burst out laughing and lifted her glass in a toast.

"Keep laughing. I drive a ten-year-old Honda now! It *is* red." Val laughed so hard that it hurt. She couldn't believe how good it felt. She liked Gwen and wanted to know more about her and asked another question even though it was risky and might possibly bring up Oliver Solaris. She wished at that moment the Oliver Solaris issue didn't exist. Unfortunately, it did. Val wondered how quickly this new friend would hate her if she knew the truth about her. "You said you were a registered nurse. How did you wind up as a death investigator?"

"Well, I worked as a nurse for a while, but was bored with it. A friend of mine pointed me in the direction of the morgue and death investigation. It was love at first sight and I knew immediately this is what I wanted to do."

Val took a deep breath: that friend must have been Oliver. She waited for the obvious question now and thought to the excuse she had concocted as to how she knew this man, ready to use it.

"So, how did you get into death investigation? It's a far cry from what you used to do," Gwen asked.

Here it comes. But at least there was no mention of Oliver, yet. Val picked up her glass and swirled the contents. Then took a healthy gulp. This question was easy and she decided to answer it truthfully. She told Gwen about her encounter with Mr. Tate. There was no reason to hide it. It was because of him that she became a death investigator.

"You know, I felt my life was over when I couldn't practice anymore. I had no idea what I was going to do. There was nothing else I wanted to do, so I thought. I liked dentistry—hell the money I made was great—but I was never excited about it. Something was missing. Truthfully, many days were dull. I was bored at the office and couldn't wait to leave. So, I understand perfectly how you felt when you were a nurse."

She looked at Gwen and continued, answering from her soul.

"When I was hired at the medical examiner's office, it was basically to fulfill a need and that need was to pay my mortgage. It was a paycheck. But, now, life *is* exciting. My job *is* exciting. It certainly is anything but mundane. It's kind of odd to say, but working with the dead has made me feel more alive than anything else I've done before." She held up her hand to reveal her scar. "To think, without this, I would never be sitting here today. My life would never have taken this bizarre turn."

"It's funny where life takes you sometimes, isn't it? To be doing something that makes you feel excited is a rare thing to find. I know what that's like."

Val realized that she dangerously exposed herself and then quickly added, "Yes, without Mr. Tate and Oliver I might not be here today." She took one last gulp of her wine, finishing what was left, ready with her excuse for how she knew this man. It had to be coming next.

"So, I didn't notice a wedding band on that Jack Styles' finger. Do you think he's single?" Gwen asked.

Val was stunned and she stared at Gwen. This question, she wasn't expecting. Though she was surprised, she exhaled in relief and answered, "I could care less. He's an egotistical bastard. In fact, that's my new name for him. Egotistical Bastard. I'll call him EB for short."

"He has every right to be an egotistical bastard. Did you hear who he works with?"

"Who?"

"It's someone big. The criminalist, Thomas Hayden!"

"*The* Thomas Hayden?" Val nearly dropped her empty glass.

20

Val paced back and forth in the decomp room, biting her nails. She stood beside a burn victim who had not only been torched, but also had a large irregular injury over his eyes, probably due to some type of firearm.

The new digital X-ray equipment was positioned next to the gurney, equipment Julia had wanted to get for the office. Val grew sad at the thought of Julia, but it was short-lived. Val missed her a little less each day, mostly due to her friendship with Gwen Carmondy. Her relationship with Gwen was taking a turn she would have never expected. Since their evening out, several days ago, the two began spending more time together. Val really liked her. Now, the issue of Oliver Solaris had taken another costly twist. Not only would she lose her job, she could lose her friend if this secret got out.

But after today's mishap she might not need the help of the Oliver Solaris lie to lose her job.

She was so mad she could spit and she wanted to strangle Dr. Blythe for doing this to her.

Though he didn't say it directly, he was testing her with this victim. She was convinced of it. He had instructed her to get dental X-rays and provide a complete preliminary report of her findings about this individual. Except for the X-rays, this was an unusual request since this victim was already at the morgue. Everything else she would have performed at the crime scene. The only reason Blythe would ask her to do this now was so that he could evaluate her skills as a death investigator. He had every right to use any poor performance as grounds for firing her.

Val looked at the dead man on the table, trying to figure out how to fix the problem, cursing herself for not taking more time to understand the equipment. But in all honesty, taking dental X-rays was something she could do in her sleep.

Seeing as she thought it would be the easiest part of the examination she decided to get these first. This was a digital system however, and the part that went into the mouth was an electronic sensor, which was quite a bit thicker than typical dental film. Getting it positioned so that she could take the pictures was something she thought she'd learn by trial and error. Unfortunately, today's experience had been entirely error.

Though she'd been as careful as possible, while trying to put the sensor in, she broke off four of the lower front teeth.

She had several textbooks open and quickly glanced through the chapters that dealt with burn victims, trying to find out what to do. But this body didn't look like any of the ones in the pictures. Skin shrinks when it's burned. She knew that, and the photos showed the typical appearance of charred flesh around the oral cavity as the tissue pulls back from the teeth, exposing what's left, and what was left in the photos wasn't much. According to the book this person should be devoid of front teeth: they should have disintegrated in the fire. This wasn't what had happened here.

The left side of his face appeared unaffected, and the lips were mostly closed. All of the front teeth had been there before she touched them. Now, the fractured pieces rested on the man's tongue.

She read further, panicking. The next few paragraphs in one book did warn to be careful in the circumstances where the teeth seemed to be intact, stating they may be fragile and breakage was a possibility.

"Great, it's a little too late to see this now." She slammed all of the books closed and was still assessing the situation when the door opened and Jack Styles casually walked in.

Val stared in disbelief and then quickly jumped, grabbing a few stray paper towels that were lying on the countertop, hiding the textbooks as best she could with them.

"Who let you in?" She spoke with authority. This certainly wasn't the time to be anything less than assertive. With a catastrophe on her hands the last person in the world she wanted to be standing with her was Jack Styles. Surely he'd see how inexperienced she was. Plus, what would he think of her if he noticed that she, a dentist, couldn't take X-rays without screwing up? She cringed at the thought of Jack Styles telling the renowned Thomas Hayden that they hire idiots at the Erie County Medical Examiner's Office.

"I was told I could find you here." He waved his visitor ID at her. "See, I even have permission."

"Dr. Blythe's in autopsy room one. You'll want to speak to *him*." Val resumed her work. Maybe he would just let her be and leave quickly if she didn't engage him in conversation. She couldn't risk him staying in the room long enough to notice anything wrong.

"He's busy. I was hoping you'd keep me company while I wait."

"I'm busy too," she said, knowing that Blythe must have blown Jack off again. She continued working, though really not doing much.

Jack made no motion towards the door. He wasn't leaving. Val took a deep breath, trying to focus, but it didn't help with him in the room. She couldn't think of what she needed to do next.

He watched her as she busied herself doing absolutely nothing at all. She had a partially written report in front of her and could see Jack trying to read what was on the paper. Val picked up a pen and added new findings to her report, but each time she wrote something, she quickly crossed it off. She let out a frustrated sigh and attempted to write something again. The pen stopped mid-sentence.

"So, what happened here?" Jack asked of the charred body.

"He was found in the trunk of a burning car." Her words were clipped, hoping to not give him any latitude to venture into a discussion that would make it obvious that she had no idea what to do with burn victims. Her heart began to pound when Jack circled around the body, quietly examining what lay on the table.

"Why they use fire is beyond me," he stated.

"Excuse me?" Val asked, struggling to keep her tone even and uninterested as she broke out in a nervous sweat.

"It's just that it doesn't work. Or I should say, rarely works. Some criminals do manage to be successful, but I think that's more out of luck than skill. Don't you feel the same way about this tactic?"

"Uh huh." Val held her breath and purposely didn't lift her head to look at him as she feigned focus in her report. She had no idea what to say and prayed Jack wouldn't keep asking questions.

"If you wanted to hide something about your crime, wouldn't you use something that did a better job?"

"Honestly, Mr. Styles, fire can work well if it burns up the evidence," she said, her eyes still on the report, convinced that he was pressing her intentionally. Her nerves were already worn thin and she didn't know how much more she could take if he kept tugging at them.

"Please, call me Jack," he said and then pointed to the victim. "Did fire work well here?" The tone suggested that he already knew the answer to the question.

Perspiration rolled down Val's neck, but she was determined to be unaffected by this attack. She put down the pen, looked up and locked eyes with him. "That depends. If the cause and manner of death are incorrectly determined then yes. But as you can see, I'm not finished with my examination. So, Jack, I don't have any answers yet."

He nodded in agreement. It was a fair answer and Val felt relieved. The relief lasted only a few minutes.

Her eyes opened wide as Jack reached into the box of latex gloves, grabbed two and put them on. He placed a finger over the jagged opening on the forehead. "Now, where did you come from?" He spoke to the injury. Then turned towards Val and pointed out the obvious wound on the forehead, grinning as he did so. "This was caused by a bullet, not a fire."

"I know that already!" Val snapped, "I didn't need to have it pointed out to see he died from a gunshot wound to the forehead. The big hole kind of gives that away."

"Not a gunshot wound to the *forehead*, Dr. Knight." He picked up the man's head, inspecting the back of it. This time the joking nature was gone when he spoke. "The hole on the forehead is an exit wound. Obviously, we would expect to see an entrance wound somewhere else, and this is it." He pointed out a small opening at the base of the man's skull and then explained further as Val just stared, mortified at making such an error. This examination had just gone from bad to worse.

"You see, this well-defined marginal abrasion is characteristic of an entrance wound, while the irregular larger injury on the forehead is the exit wound. The *manner* of death is homicide, but I think you already knew that, especially with the way this body was burned." Jack's tone was serious. He spoke as if he were discussing possibilities with a colleague, not pointing out that colleague's deficiencies. There was no sarcasm in his voice.

Val did have homicide written down. Obviously, the man didn't shoot himself in the head, get into the trunk of a car, and then set himself on fire, but she would have gotten the direction of the bullet wrong. She was too worried about the broken teeth to even think of looking anywhere else.

Jack set the head back down. Next, he reached for the victim's mouth and pulled back the lips. Val became light-headed and for a second she thought she was going to pass out. *Here it comes, he's going to see my other error; the broken teeth.*

"Most people think fire will destroy the evidence. It doesn't. Look at this poor soul's teeth. Except for these on the right side, they look in good shape. My guess is he was lying face down in the car."

Val was surprised that Jack said nothing about the broken incisors. "That's a very nice theory," she managed to say.

"Not a theory, Dr. Knight. You see, this man was shot in the back of the head, execution style. Then someone tried to cover up the crime by setting a fire. A drug deal gone wrong, he owed someone money... a scorned lover? Those are theories. Why he was shot is a theory. Why he was killed, at this point, is speculation. *How* he died is not." Again, Jack had no derisive tone in his voice.

"Of course, it's not speculation. He was shot, that's how he died," Val said.

"Now, we shouldn't jump to conclusions with the *cause* of death. Just because he was shot doesn't mean that's what killed him. He could have survived the bullet to his head and then died from the fire. The only way to tell is with an autopsy where you would expect to see soot in the mouth, esophagus and lungs, since he would have been breathing when the fire started, plus carbon monoxide would be in his blood. But I will confirm that he was face down in the car, left side down to be exact. Everything we need to decipher that is right before us."

Val said nothing. Everything about this examination, she either managed to do wrong or get wrong. If Jack didn't point out her errors, she would have failed Dr. Blythe's test miserably. She made rapid mental notes, preparing to add Jack's facts to her report as soon as she could.

"His face is barely damaged by the fire on the left, so he must have been face down with his head turned to the right, exposing the right side to the flames. I told you just a few minutes ago that fire is a very poor way to cover a crime. Do you know why?" He lingered on the words temptingly.

She took the bait. "Why?"

"It draws attention to what you've just done. Someone commits a crime, pours a flammable liquid all over the scene. Then puts a match to it and what happens next? Smoke. Smoke goes up in the air and alerts everyone within miles to what has just occurred. Very good citizens that see the smoke call the fire department and the firemen come and put the fire out. So, your crime scene doesn't get the opportunity to burn long enough to destroy everything. The victims are usually still in great shape for dental ID since the lips and the cheeks protect the teeth, especially the back ones. The parts of the body in contact with the floor or some other surface are also protected from the flames and have little damage, that's why his face looks pretty good on the left side but not on the right."

Jack let out a heavy sigh. "Now if they had just put the body up on something, got it off of the ground, that would have given a whole lot more oomph to the burn process. It would have gotten some oxygen underneath it. If you're going to use fire, you really should learn some mechanics of how it all works. Face down in a trunk of a car is fairly amateurish."

Val had to admit she was impressed with his knowledge. And Dr. Blythe would be impressed with her report. She needed to write down everything Jack said before she forgot the details, and had to get him out of the room so she could do so. "Well, Jack, this visit has been interesting, but I really must get back to work."

"As you wish." He stripped off his gloves, washed his hands and walked towards the door. "By the way, charred teeth break easily because they're so fragile. It would almost be expected if anyone tried to X-ray them."

Val shot him a look, but said nothing about his remark. He didn't seem to be going any further on this issue, and at this point, neither would she. Instead, she decided to ask another question, one she wanted the answer to. "You said face down in a car is amateurish, what did you mean by that?"

"There's just no way to hide the fact that a crime was committed. It's obvious. The dead person is in the trunk of a car. Really, I can think off the top of my head several effective ways to get rid of a body that would be considerably better. Plus, one ought to be mindful when using fire, the hydrocarbons that tend to be used in these circumstances are so easy to detect with lab tests. It all just screams *set-up*," Jack said.

Val stood silent for a moment, thinking.

"Oh, I'm sorry if you don't understand. People that set fires like to use gasoline," he said, smiling smugly. "Gasoline is a hydrocarbon."

"I know what a hydrocarbon is, Mr. Styles!" Val shot back at him. "Since you seem to know it all what do you suggest then?"

"Something that burns clean and then disappears. A strong vodka would do the trick." He smiled broader and then stared at her. "It tackles many problems. Perhaps I can interest you in one."

Jack's invitation still lingered in the air. No response came from Val as Gwen burst into the decomposition room and shouted, "They found another skull!" Her eyes opened wide as she focused on Jack.

"Holy crap." Then Val held her tongue. Not saying more out loud. *What in the hell is going on? Did they find Julia's skull?*

"Perhaps I can interest you both in a drink, and possibly dinner? Tomorrow night?" Jack offered. "I think we ought to compare notes. Because, ladies, you need to hear my side of the story. What I know. This latest discovery doesn't make me surprised. It makes me concerned."

"We'd love to join you," Gwen responded.

Val didn't say a word.

"I don't see what the problem is," said Gwen.

"It'll get us fired for a start," exclaimed Val. She wanted to kill Gwen. Talking with Jack outside their professional capacity of the medical examiner's office was grounds for immediate firing. "Thomas and Jack aren't official investigators. Discussing details with either of them is no better than talking to the media when we've been told not to."

Though Val would do anything to put Julia's killer behind bars, she couldn't afford to rock the boat with Dr. Blythe. He was out to get her, that was obvious, but Val didn't want that lynching to happen as early as tomorrow. If he was going to fire her, he'd need just cause to do so. Her inappropriate involvement in this high-profile murder case would be all the cause he needed. The way she saw it, if she talked to Jack outside of work, she'd only be giving Blythe the rope to hang her with. And if Val was fired, there was no way she'd be able to help Julia. She needed her position at the medical examiner's office for that.

Gwen was adamant that they were doing the right thing and after Val finished lecturing, got the opportunity to explain why —Dr. Blythe might need to have the boat rocked.

"They found another skull, but he didn't seem interested in it at all. In fact, he was being really dismissive about the whole thing," Gwen said.

"How do you know this?"

"I overheard him talking about it. I don't know Val, something isn't right. The teeth were all missing and he didn't seem concerned." Gwen added, "*I* was concerned and *I* have nothing to do with this investigation."

"Then you should talk to Detective Gavin, and not Jack Styles. Another victim could have a big impact on this case."

"Detective Gavin knows about it. That's who I overheard Blythe speaking to."

Val heard the words but they didn't make sense. "What did he say?" she asked. "He must have challenged Blythe."

"No. He didn't. In fact, he agreed with him. Dr. Blythe was so convincing that I'm not surprised."

"You must have misunderstood."

Gwen shook her head. "The post-mortem interval on this skull is well over a year. This person died long before the murders of Jeanne Coleman, Francine Donohue and Julia DeHaviland; too long to be part of this case. He thinks it's not connected."

"I can't believe this! What about the possibility of an earlier victim?" Val could barely contain herself. So much in this entire case didn't add together. This was just one more thing.

"This is what I heard from Blythe. Due to where the skull was found, Blythe was confident that the extensive injuries came from that source. There was more trauma than just the missing teeth, which is unlike the other victims. Plus, with Colin already in jail, and all the ironclad evidence against him, why speculate about another victim until there's reason to believe there is one? It would be a different matter if they'd found another set of teeth. The media attack with this type of information could be nightmarish at best, and quite damaging to already strong evidence against Colin." Gwen added, "See what I mean, it all *sounds* convincing."

"Why wouldn't Gavin investigate this? Who cares if Blythe sounds convincing?"

Gwen paced back and forth. "Blythe also told Gavin that if the media gave the public reason to believe Colin might be innocent and that the wrong steps were taken for the arrest in this case, the lead detective would look like an asshole and probably get demoted or at very worst, fired. That lead detective is Gavin."

Val was stunned by what she heard and her thoughts ran wild.

"Val, I'm not a medical examiner and I'll be the first to admit Blythe has knowledge and experience way beyond what I could ever hope to have. But I'm not sure how he came to those conclusions. I saw him go into the autopsy room with the skull and I also saw him come out. He was in that room for all of five minutes. He didn't go back in there until his meeting with Gavin. How do you reach those detailed conclusions in five minutes?"

"You can't," Val said.

"Something isn't right. Gavin didn't challenge Blythe. Unless another set of teeth are found, this is going to be swept under the rug and then it's going to disappear. Detective Gavin's happy that Colin has been arrested and he's not going to do anything to screw that up. The only way to have someone look into it is to have Jack Styles and Thomas Hayden do it."

Gwen was right, but, what to do? If Blythe was hiding information from Gavin, if he was purposely trying to sway the case in the wrong direction, then Blythe's mixed up in it somehow. Any way she looked at it, Blythe's odd behavior needed to be investigated.

Val became wedged between a rock and a hard place. She wanted to help find who really murdered Julia. Julia had saved her by giving her this job—she would always be indebted to her. But if she embarked on this journey, she could lose the job Julia gave her *and* the ability to look into her murder. Blythe would have every reason to fire her if he found out that she had got involved in this case with Jack and Thomas. Plus, what *else* might Blythe do if he discovered that she was also searching for evidence?

"Val, you're the only person I trust right now and if something isn't right, and I'm not just being paranoid, I don't want to be the next person who has my teeth ripped out and gets chopped into bits. If Blythe has something to do with this, then the murderer is still out there." Gwen appeared scared, making it obvious she shared at least one of the same worries as Val. "He knows I overheard his discussion with Gavin. You should have seen the way he looked at me when he noticed. And Val, you should be concerned too. Because, how do I say this... he just doesn't like you."

21

The restaurant was not only small, it was crowded. Fortunately, Val, Gwen and Jack were seated at a table in the far corner that offered some privacy. Dinner menus, three glasses of water and a basket of papadums, with a dish of chutney, sat on the table. Val reached into the basket and pulled one out. She picked this place because she thought Jack, with his British background, would appreciate curry. The Taj Mahal served authentic Indian cuisine. And it did so superbly.

Gwen didn't waste any time and quickly began explaining about Dr. Blythe's odd behavior with the newest skull. Jack listened closely, showing little emotion. No more than a disgusted shake of the head. When she was finished he shared his own information.

Though there were three victims, Julia was the one they were focusing on. It was her death that led to Colin's arrest and the police to conclude he was involved in the other murders. But all the people in Julia's life needed to be ruled in or out as suspects. "Your Dr. Blythe is quickly springing to the top of list," said Jack. "His uncooperative behavior, with outright refusal to speak to either of us, has raised a few red flags." But, Jack explained, it was mostly his supposed relationship with Julia that was the concern. A number of her reports described the re-examination of Blythe's autopsies. If he knew about these, and what she'd written about him, this could certainly be a motive to kill her.

"Her conclusion was that Dr. Blythe should be relieved of his duties," Jack said. "There was also suggestion that he was possibly involved in fraud. The report was scathing, but Julia's superiors wanted more evidence before taking any disciplinary actions against Dr. Blythe. What Julia had found was circumstantial only. It looks like she was just about to embark on this task."

Val was shocked by what she heard. She knew Blythe had a problem with Julia but she had no idea that it was something like this. The conversation stopped as the waiter came by and asked about drinks—Jack ordered Cobra beer. Val and Gwen did the same.

As soon as the waiter left, Jack said, "With your information Gwen, it only adds to our suspicions about Dr. Blythe, but I'll be honest, that's all it is at this point, a suspicion. There was no proof, nothing tangible at all to link him to these crimes."

"So, what are you going to do?" Val asked, scared, her stomach tightening. If Blythe was guilty, she wanted him behind bars. Not roaming the same halls that she did, let alone loose on the streets of the city. Val knew she was on his shit list already, and had been for some time. She felt the target on her back getting bigger.

"If he's involved, he must have screwed up somewhere. We just have to find out where. We have to keep going at him. This is how it's done. Sometimes it's persistence that pays off in the end," Jack said. He took a papadum and scooped some chutney onto it. "Which brings me to the reason for our meeting tonight. With your positions at the medical examiner's office, you are the best people to get information, anything on Blythe. With the medical examiner refusing to speak to us, this investigation is about to stall. We need information quickly. Ladies, Thomas and I need your help."

"What if Dr. Blythe finds out? This could be dangerous," Val said, fidgeting uncomfortably in her chair. It creaked as she moved. She looked at Gwen. Working on this case with someone like Thomas Hayden should be a dream come true. This dream, though, could quickly become a nightmare. "Two things could possibly happen. If he's guilty, he could kill us. If he's not guilty he could fire us. We lose either way."

"I don't think either of you has to worry that Dr. Blythe will take out your teeth and dismember you," Jack said. "If he is guilty, the last thing he would do is to murder someone in the same way, especially with Colin sitting in jail for crimes like this. I've seen stupid criminals before, but never one daft enough to do something like that."

"What about firing us?" Val asked, though her mind was still focused on the getting killed part.

"How would he know you were involved? I have no intention of telling him. The only way he would know is if he was arrested and you had to testify against him. And honestly, at that point, he wouldn't have the capacity to do anything to you. He'd be behind bars."

Val wanted to do this. She wanted it badly. If Blythe was guilty, she wanted to help catch him. But it was such a risk. For some reason tonight, she loved the idea of taking a chance. She looked at her hand, at the scar. The images of the attack were far away as she studied the odd pattern that would be forever on her palm and thumb. This had made her an insecure victim just as much as her dental career molded a confident professional.

She had taken a big risk lying to get this job, a job that she was enjoying tremendously, more so than dentistry. Val knew it was time to take another risk. Plus, to work on a case with Thomas Hayden was a once-in-a-lifetime opportunity, one that was either going to make her, or destroy her. She could see the desire in Gwen's eyes. Gwen wanted the same thing.

The waiter came by, set a bottle of beer down in front of each of them and asked if they were ready to order. Jack, Gwen and Val had been so preoccupied they hadn't even looked at the menu. After a moment, Val flipped it over to the last page and pointed to a series of choices which offered a range of smaller dishes for a set number of people. "Let's just have this one to save choosing. We can share."

"Good call," said Jack. "It all looks great."

Gwen nodded in agreement. "All of my favorites are there."

Val pointed to the menu. "We'll have this one for three people."

The waiter nodded his head in approval. "Excellent choice. Naan for the table?"

"Of course," Val said.

The waiter hurried off to put the order through.

The conversation quickly moved to the latest skull.

"Where was it discovered?" Jack asked.

"Dr. Blythe thinks it belongs to someone who went over Niagara Falls. It was caught on some rocks four miles downstream along the shoreline of the Lower Niagara River. It's the part that runs next to the trail in Devil's Hole Park. In his opinion, that's where the damage came from," Gwen said. "It did have good sized breaks in it."

"What's the area like?" Jack asked, "I'm not familiar with it."

Val tried to explain what she knew of Niagara Falls. She had purposely prepared for the meeting with Jack tonight, hoping to sound knowledgeable on this issue, especially after her less than stellar performance that afternoon.

"There are three waterfalls, the Horseshoe, American and

Bridal Veil. People planning to go over the falls for suicide or a daredevil act tend to jump into the Horseshoe, because it's the largest, but this one is mostly in Canada. Those who want to jump into the water in America do so with the American Falls." Val paused, lining up her facts. "As the Niagara River approaches the American Falls, the water is going about sixty miles an hour. Then it drops about 110 feet onto large boulders."

"I can certainly understand how that could cause some damage. With the speed, large drop, not to mention the rocks, someone's head could easily have been shattered," Jack said. "But the skull was found several miles away."

"Yes, and more damage could have come from the next part of the trip," Gwen added. "That's what Blythe thinks."

Val continued with her list of facts. "Once over the drop, the river becomes known as the Lower Niagara. As it enters the Niagara Gorge it calms slightly. That's because the gorge widens but then the water travels through a narrow part and quickly picks up a lot of speed and turbulence, forming the Whirlpool Rapids. These are class six rapids, the most dangerous kind and considered nearly impossible to travel on."

"Why is it called *Whirlpool* Rapids?" Jack asked.

"There's a ninety-degree bend in the river. At the elbow of the bend there's a basin that the water's forced into. The water circles slowly here forming a whirlpool," said Val.

Gwen remarked, "Actually, the whirlpool is on the Canadian side of the river. It's a common spot where bodies wash up. They get caught up in the swirl of the water."

"What happens after this spot?" Jack asked. "This skull wasn't found there. Evidently it missed this prime congregation area for human remains."

"After the whirlpool, the gorge widens again and the water slows again. It picks up speed once more at Devil's Hole, forming the Lower Whirlpool Rapids. After Devil's Hole, it calms one last time and remains like that all the way to Lake Ontario."

"So, there are several places where the water calms or slows down."

"Yes," Val answered.

"And a place where bodies typically wash up. The Canadian side of the whirlpool."

"Yes."

"So why didn't this skull wash up in these areas? Or a body for that matter?"

"The water's pretty strong. It could have moved it along," Val said, unsure of Jack's point.

"Only where the water's strong. But there are places where it's somewhat calm."

"Then it simply floated down the river."

"That all sounds very reasonable—the only problem is that human bones usually don't float. Their density is greater than water so they sink. Oh, let me correct that, they might float for a couple of reasons. One is if the victim has osteoporosis which makes the bone less dense than they ordinarily would be. The other is when bones become dry, also making them less dense. And we do have a drying issue in this case, from what I've heard."

Val's eyes went wide as she finally understood where Jack was heading. "So, it's incredibly unlikely that someone went over Niagara Falls and an ordinary decomposed skull washed ashore as it did, where it did," she said.

"Exactly," Jack answered. "This raises far more questions than it answers. How did it get there? Why didn't it end up in one of the more likely spots? And where is the rest of the body?"

At that moment, the food arrived. The conversation paused awkwardly as the waiters loaded small, fragrant dishes onto the table along with a basket of naan and a bowl of rice.

Once they were free to talk again, Gwen asked, "That skull—do you think it was deliberately placed there?" She spooned some dhal onto her plate. "The remains from the other victims were purposely put out where they'd be found. The first was in a park, the second in a landfill, now this one is in a river."

Jack thoughtfully tore off a piece of naan before responding. "A good way to begin to answer that, and some of these other questions, is to look at the area where the skull was discovered but more importantly, examine the skull itself." He turned towards Val. "Is this a possibility?"

"You *are* joking, right?" she said, fork in mid-air.

Jack laughed. "No, I don't suppose the good doctor Blythe would let me see it. He won't even say hello to me so I don't think he would let me examine key evidence." He thought for a moment then said, "Francine Donohue was the only victim to have another body part found, something other than a skull."

"Yes," Val said. "Her arm."

Jack stared straight ahead for a moment. "So why are we finding more remains of Francine than any other victim?"

"She was also the only one in a landfill. Thrown out like she was garbage," Val said eagerly. She could see where Jack was heading with this.

Jack appeared to be grappling with possibilities and he said, "Maybe we're looking in the wrong direction. Julia should be the focal point since her death resulted in the arrest of Colin. But, what if we're wrong? What if the focal point was elsewhere? What if this case centered on Francine and not Julia?"

Val thought the exact same thing, and agreed with strong nods of her head.

"Francine's sister was also found dead," Gwen remarked, nudging Val. "Tell Jack about that."

Val explained what she knew about Samantha Ritcher. "She had high drug levels of the pain medicine Percocet in her system, but was injected with something and died from anaphylaxis."

"Do you think someone purposely killed her?" Gwen asked.

"If you wanted to kill her, 'why kill her *this way*?' is the more important question," said Jack, "Especially if she was impaired because of a drug like Percocet. It makes no sense. Push her down a flight of stairs or hit her on the head with a heavy object. This is far easier than to inject her with something she's allergic to. Who would have even known what Samantha's allergies were?"

"Maybe her ex-husband? He's getting even with her for putting him away?" Val suggested. The newspaper had the story of Samantha and her ex-husband all over the front page. "He could have made a deal from prison and hired someone to do it for him."

"Again, by injecting her with something she's allergic to? A hired killer would have been an executioner. This person would have done it in the easiest way possible." Jack smiled at Val. "She would have been shot in the back of the head."

She felt her face grow hot as she remembered the victim from this afternoon.

He continued to smile and his eyes never left hers, until he winked and said, "No, to inject Samantha with a drug means something entirely different, if she's connected."

They continued their conversation and as Val watched Jack describe his suspicions, she grew more excited about the case.

The dishes were mostly empty when Jack announced, "I'd like for the two of you to meet Thomas. We're going to re-examine the evidence found in Julia's bedroom, that's if Detective Gavin allows it. If you're free the day after tomorrow, you should join us."

22

Julia's bedroom had an unsettling feeling to it. When Val first entered, she relived the shocking reality of being in a place where such horror occurred to her friend. She tried hard not to think about how much terror and pain Julia must have suffered. Instead, she focused on why she herself was here. It helped. She needed to find the bastard who was responsible for this.

Gavin agreed to let Thomas and Jack examine the crime scene. All of the evidence had been collected and photographed, so technically, this scene was cleared. But still, he and Warren stood close by, watching everything. Val sensed that this was more out of want than need. If anything was found that hinted at Colin being innocent, Gavin was going to be here for it.

As soon as she saw him, Val begged him not to tell Dr. Blythe or anybody else that she was here today. He reluctantly agreed, lecturing her on how inappropriate it was, but Val shot back that she needed to do this. "Julia was my friend. This is important to me." She was pleasantly surprised when he agreed to keep things quiet, and allowed her to stay.

For the medical examiner's office, she had a great excuse as to why she needed to be away. Part of the job of death scene investigation involved getting out of the office to re-examine scenes for evidence, or talk with family members of victims, getting information that would be helpful for the medical examiner. She was still following up on Samantha's medical records, all which were dead ends so far. Samantha had been prescribed high doses of Percocet for her back pain. According to her doctors, she received nothing else. Val used this as her reason to get out of the office today. Following up on leads. No one questioned her.

Gwen didn't need an excuse. Her shift didn't start until tonight.

Thomas Hayden walked up to Val and handed her a spool of white kitchen string. The string would aid in determining angle of impact and point of origin of the blood, giving them an idea of where Julia was when she was being attacked. Since the killer removed almost all of the visible blood during the cleanup attempt, they were using the crime scene photos showing the luminol reaction as a guide in positioning the string. Some of the patterns weren't making sense until now. They had been in the bedroom for nearly two hours taping pieces of the string from the blood spatter patterns that were once on the wall, to those once on the carpet. There were only a few more left to do and he suggested that Val and Gwen give it a try.

Thomas was an excellent teacher, explaining each process as they performed it. Val was nervous at first, but he quickly put her at ease. She found him friendly and approachable. He was attractive for an older man, neatly styled and polished. She guessed him to be in his mid to late sixties and couldn't help but think that he resembled a more mature version of Jack.

Gwen held up the photos depicting how Julia died. Though Val didn't want to look at them, she had no choice. She had to see where to put her end of the string.

The carpet had two sections of pooled blood on the left side of the bed, presumably where Julia had been lying when she was attacked. One was smaller than the other. It was thought that she was first stabbed in the location of the smaller one and then managed to move a short way before she was assaulted again, creating the larger area as she bled out and was subsequently dismembered.

The walls to the left and right side of the bed had been sprayed with blood spatter, and as Val finished placing the last piece of string, Thomas stood back inspecting the projections and asked Jack, pointing at the wall, "Do you see what's wrong there?" Val quickly glanced at Jack, waiting for his response. She couldn't tell what Thomas was referring to and wanted to know the answer.

Jack walked closer to the left side of the bed, inspecting the string, then glanced at the photos. He pointed to the same section of the wall Thomas did. "The cast-off spatter pattern, right there. That's what's wrong."

Thomas signaled for Val and Gwen to stand next to him. "Ladies, do you see the problem?" he asked them.

Val narrowed her eyes in confusion. "I'm not sure I understand what you mean." She had crammed all night with her textbooks to learn as much as she could about spatter analysis. The size of the droplets on a surface will tell the speed in which blood travels from the victim. These were about one to four millimeters, exactly the size they should be for this type of attack, which was stabbing. They were also teardrop shaped with an elongated tail on the pointy end of the tear. The tail end shows the direction it was traveling.

The shape of the drop gets longer as the angle of impact gets smaller. The angle from the floor to the wall wasn't that big, indicating the person had been attacked on the ground. The string confirmed this.

Val continued, "These photos show a large area of medium velocity spatter, which is consistent with someone being stabbed. The angle is also consistent with the victim being on the floor and Julia was stabbed on the floor. Everything looks okay."

Gwen nodded in agreement. "I don't see anything wrong with it either."

"That's an excellent observation and you're correct, but it's not the size or angle of the droplets that's the problem," Jack said.

Val just stared. "What do you mean?"

"It's the fact that they're even there that's the issue." Jack put his finger on the photo and pointed out the aquamarine-colored lamp that sat on top of the nightstand. "This is why."

Val looked at the lamp in the image, and experienced the sickening feeling she had felt the first time she saw it. It caught her eye the day she'd found Julia dead. The sight of the blood on the ceramic surface had made her knees buckle then, and it did so now. The noticeable reddish-brown stains in the image were glaring. It was one of the few things in the room that did have visible blood, obviously missed by the killer in the cleanup attempt—after he took Julia apart.

"The spatter shouldn't be on that specific part of the wall because this lamp is in the way. There's spatter on the lamp and there's spatter behind the lamp," Jack said. "When blood is traveling from the victim and spraying on an object, it will be blocked from depositing on any surface behind the object. There should be a blank spot on the wall if this lamp was there during the attack. There is no void."

"We noticed the issue of the lamp, but really it's insignificant," Warren said. "Colin spent quite a while cleaning the room and he obviously must have moved it there at some point after he murdered his wife."

Thomas chimed in. "Oh, it was moved from somewhere, Detective Warren, you're right about that. It wasn't on this nightstand to begin with. That's why there isn't a blank spot on the wall. This lamp was placed here after the attack was completed. It couldn't have been anywhere on this table while Julia was being stabbed. Not only is there no blank spot on the wall, the spatter pattern on the lamp is going in the *opposite* direction than on the wall. That, gentlemen, is also impossible if the lamp was here during the attack. So, it's not the blood on that part of the wall that's the problem. It's this misplaced lamp. My question is why put it here?"

Val felt her jaw drop open slightly. She wanted to ask questions, learn more, but she just listened, amazed by what she'd just heard. Thomas Hayden was impressive on *Crime in the City*, but he was even more so in person. Jack was brilliant too and she began to wonder why he was never featured on any of Thomas's broadcasts.

"Maybe Colin needed some light while he was cleaning the blood?" Gavin said sarcastically.

"If the lamp was moved, if the killer had his hand on it then it should have been cleaned too. The blood on this lamp is obvious. It couldn't have possibly been overlooked. Why leave the blood here when such meticulous cleaning occurred in this room?" Thomas added sharply. "Someone would have had to be blind to miss this. That fact makes me think this lamp was placed here, *purposely*."

Thomas then went back to the pictures and asked Gavin this time. "What *is* wrong with the blood on *that* part of the wall?" He pointed to the right side of the bed, to the other area of spatter.

Gavin said nothing and waved Thomas away, dismissively.

"How did that occur?" Thomas questioned again, not affected by Gavin's attempts to ignore the findings. "The angle depicted by those droplets indicates that our killer and Julia had to have been closer to that part of the wall, but there's nothing to show movement to get over there."

Gavin again, failed to engage in discussion on this.

Thomas said, "How did they move from right here without leaving a bloody trail? Based on these large pools of blood on the carpet, Julia would have bleeding profusely. How did she get to that side of the bed and leave no blood on the carpet if she was stabbed again over there? This is impossible. The blood on that part of the wall also didn't occur during the attack. It couldn't have landed there, at that angle, from this point."

Thomas walked around to the right side of the bed and studied the angle of the droplets shown in the photographs. "This had to have happened somewhere around here, on this side of the bed, not that side. It's as if someone took the bloody instrument and splashed it here to make the spatter look more expansive."

"Maybe this was the point of origin of the attack, Thomas," Gavin said. "He stabbed her here and she managed to run to the other side of the bed where he finished her off. That would make this spatter pattern isolated from that one."

"Even if this is where it started, some type of blood trail would be seen from here to there. Julia would have been bleeding. The killer would have had an instrument that was dripping. There is no trail. There is no blood on the floor here or anywhere to show movement from one side of the bed to the other. Not a drop. How do you do that?" Thomas challenged.

For the third time Gavin didn't respond.

"There are obvious signs of staging here," Jack said. "It's made to look like something other than what it really is. You have to at least admit that, Detective Gavin."

"Why clean it then if that's the case? Why clean any of the crime scenes?" Gavin finally asked, his tone challenging. "If there's blood on the walls and floor, we can spray luminol and know where it all once was. So why bother getting rid of it? Why go through the trouble staging the blood and then removing it?"

"Excellent point. Why clean it? That's what we need to find out," Thomas said, hesitating for a second before continuing. "But this is a staged crime scene. The lamp and that impossible blood pattern confirm it."

"All the more reason for Colin to be guilty," Gavin said. "Only killers with a connection to the victim would bother to create a crime scene that makes it seem like something happened that really didn't. They would want to throw the investigation in the wrong direction. That's what staging's all about. He wanted his wife's death to look like it was connected to the others."

"But why would he do that? Mitch, as you know, the most common type of staging is usually when someone tries to disguise a murder as suicide or accident, hiding the fact that the manner of death is really homicide. The guilty person wants to *avoid* apprehension. Here, they are masquerading in a completely different way. Someone wants us to know a murder occurred, a violent murder no less," Thomas said. "And the circumstances practically point to who's responsible."

Gavin shrugged his shoulders. He didn't seem to care.

"The pillowcase was the same but the sheets were changed. It's the signature. Only the killer would know to do this. The murderer of Jeanne Coleman and Francine Donohue committed this crime. Why would he need or want to stage this crime scene —unless he was implicating someone else?" Thomas asked. He took a deep breath, adding, "I think the killer intentionally made this crime scene look like his others."

Jack joined in. "If Colin were the killer why would he stage a crime scene in a way that would only incriminate himself for multiple murders? He would be the prime suspect. This is his wife. They were going through a nasty, complicated divorce and he was the last one to see her alive."

Both Warren and Gavin stared, having no quick reply. Gwen grabbed Val's arm and mouthed, "Oh my God."

"It doesn't make any sense," Thomas said. "It tells us that Colin's either incredibly stupid as a murderer or he's been set up. And the person committing these crimes is anything but stupid. So, this makes me believe that the killer not only knew these women, this killer knows Colin and has an agenda because the staging focuses the investigation on him."

Gavin's cell phone began to ring. He glanced at who was calling. "I have to take this," he said and then walked out of the room.

He was gone for only a few minutes before he hurried back in. A smile was on his face and Val wondered what the phone call was all about.

"Well, gentlemen. I hate to spoil your theory. That was the crime lab calling with the DNA results from Colin's clothing. I must admit that your idea sounded *interesting*, that Colin was set up, but we have more against him now. It's overwhelming. The district attorney is going forward with murder charges for Julia *and* Francine Donohue. The inclusion of Samantha Ritcher is pending the final results of the toxicology report."

"You can't be serious," Jack said, stunned. "The link you have to Francine Donohue is weak. A gum wrapper under her bed? It's circumstantial. Hell, talk about staging."

"There's more evidence. This is a little more concrete. We found DNA on his clothing."

"I would expect Julia's DNA to be on it. He said that her blood got on him. There was never any question we would find her DNA on his clothes."

"It's not Julia's DNA we're concerned about. Francine Donohue's DNA was detected on his pants, quite a bit of it actually. He knew this woman."

Val heard the words, but she couldn't believe it. She watched Jack's eyes open wide, the surprise evident. Thomas just pursed his lips together before he said, "This makes no sense. DNA from both women got on the same pair of pants?"

"Killers can be very ritualistic, even down to wearing the same clothing for each murder," Gavin said. "You should know that, Thomas."

"So, you're also not concerned that this scene is staged in a way that makes no sense if Colin is guilty?" Thomas insisted.

"Colin *is* guilty. You have to accept that. All of the evidence points to him."

"It also points away from him too. The staging tells us that."

"Tell me how Francine Donohue's DNA got on his clothing then. How do you stage that Thomas?"

23

J ack stopped the car. Thomas sat next to him. Val and Gwen were in the backseat. Good crime investigation focused on following leads, re-examining evidence— going after every shred of evidence until all was exhausted. New day. New perspective. Something may jump out at you. This is what Thomas and Jack told Val as she looked at the apartment that belonged to Stanley Wallace, the manager of the Eastville Projects. Francine Donohue's place was vacant and he'd agreed to let the group see it again.

Though she had originally liked the thought, that she'd be seeing this place again, that Jack and Thomas wanted her opinion, Val began to wonder if she should be here or not.

Her doubts had been brought on by Gavin, who had had a talk with her about getting involved in this case. The detective had stressed the huge risk she was taking by being around Jack and Thomas. "If Blythe finds out, you'll lose your job," he said seriously. Gavin had agreed to keep it quiet that she had been to Julia's house. "But," he'd added, "there is only so much I can do if you persist with this. I'm giving you my honest opinion here: Thomas and Jack are taking this case in an absurd direction. It's insane to think that Colin could be innocent."

She wondered what Gavin would say if he knew where she was and what she was about to do right now. *I'm not going to worry about that,* she thought. She didn't need to. He wouldn't be coming for the visit to the apartment today. There was no reason for it. Like Julia's place, this apartment was not a crime scene anymore. Plus, Gavin had lost interest in any *musings* these two privately hired detectives might come up with, and elaborate on. DNA had sealed Colin's fate. It was ironclad.

Val looked around at the shabby, government-subsidized buildings. Their depressing appearance told a story of poverty and Gavin's warnings about being fired intensified. The twinge in her gut strengthened to a wrenching twist. She was one paycheck away from an existence like this.

But Val couldn't ignore the possibility that Colin might have been set up. And she couldn't ignore the suspicions she had about Dr. Blythe. Something just wasn't right. And then there was the prominent role of Francine Donohue. More of Francine had been found than of any other victim. And now her DNA had been discovered on Colin's clothing. What was her link with these other dead women—apart from the similarities in the killings?

Though Francine's murder seemed to be strongly connected to Julia's, Val had some doubts about what might be gained from visiting her apartment today. She finally broke the silence in the car by saying, "I told you that the fingerprints on the back of the linen closet and on the ceiling in the bedroom closet both belong to Francine Donohue. Both places had small repairs to the drywall and she probably did it herself. I'm not sure why you want to see this in person."

A good set of usable prints had been obtained from the mummified remains of Francine's hand. Gavin had told her that they had compared these prints with those found in her residence.

"Because that," Jack said, "is something interesting."

The group got out of the car and went up the walkway. Thomas knocked on Stanley Wallace's door. It took a few moments for him to appear, and after some hesitation, to let them in. Val could see why he wasn't eager to have guests. The place was nasty.

It was as shabby on the inside as it was on the outside. Val couldn't help but notice that Stanley himself didn't seem right standing in the dingy space. He invited the group to sit down. Once positioned on the couch, carefully trying to touch only what was absolutely necessary, Val took a closer look at Stanley, studying him as he answered Thomas's and Jack's questions.

Each time he lounged back in his chair he placed his hands behind his head and the arms of his shirt pulled up to expose a gold watch on his left wrist. Everything he wore appeared too expensive, something he couldn't afford. Val wondered where he got the money to pay for it. She looked at the watch again. Her own gold watch, a Rolex, was the first thing she pawned when she needed money for a new furnace last fall.

"I don't know much about Francine Donohue," Stanley said. "She was quiet. Paid her rent on time. I don't bother with the quiet people who keep to themselves. I have too many people in this complex always complaining about something. They make me run around, doing everything short of wiping their asses, and are still never happy because they want me to do more."

"What about Jeanne Coleman?" Thomas asked.

"That woman was a nutcase who rarely came out of the house. What do they call that? A recluse?"

"Is her apartment also vacant?" Jack inquired.

"Yeah, hers is too." There was something in Stanley's voice that suggested that letting an apartment in which a psychopathic lunatic had viciously murdered a woman would be an impossible task, even in these projects where people didn't bat an eyelid over other types of death. Drug or gang-related was socially acceptable; rumored serial killer was not.

"Can we see her place too?" Thomas asked.

Stanley shrugged his shoulders. "Sure."

Gwen and Val chatted quietly on the walk to Jeanne's apartment, mostly remarking on Stanley. Thomas and Jack were a few steps ahead of them. Val commented on how Stanley was opening up, letting his guard down. When they neared Jeanne's building, he was speaking a little more freely about Francine. "I think he had a crush on her," Gwen said.

When they finally arrived at the entrance, Val's heart raced as Stanley opened the door to the residence that once belonged to Jeanne Coleman. There was a faint smell of paint in the air. Someone had attempted to erase what happened here. Nothing could bring this place back to life. As they entered Val noticed the place was desolate. Not a piece of furniture remained. No rugs covered the floors. As the group walked the floorboards creaked loudly and their voices echoed in the empty rooms.

Thomas started to make his way down the corridor. "Why is the bedroom door closed?" he asked Stanley.

The manager inhaled deeply before responding. "I shut it last time I was here. Kind of gave me the creeps thinking about what happened in there."

Stanley's simple explanation sent chills down Val's spine as she pictured what occurred behind that closed door. She tried hard not to think about it as the group moved forward. When Thomas turned the handle and pushed the door open, she wasn't sure what to expect and anxiously looked in. The room was empty and clean, as if nothing had ever happened there. The air of innocence was unsettling.

"You were the one who found her, am I right?" Thomas asked Stanley.

"Yeah." He looked at the floor when he spoke.

"How did that come about?" Thomas asked.

"The pipe under her kitchen sink was busted. When I came by to fix it, she didn't answer. I thought I'd just let myself in to get it done and that's when I found her." His eyes lingered on the floor.

"If you came to fix the sink, what made you decide to look in the bedroom?" Jack asked. Val was thinking the same thing.

Stanley's eyes shot up and stared at Jack. "I called for Jeanne when I let myself in. I expected her to be here. She didn't go out of the house at all. I thought I heard a noise in the bedroom. So, I checked in there. You know, to see if she was all right."

Thomas circled around the empty room, his footsteps loud in the small space. He looked out the window and turned back to face the four people staring at him. No one spoke and the room became eerily quiet.

"Stanley, didn't you find Francine too?" Thomas asked.

"Yeah. Her mail was piling up. A lot of people who live here just take off with no warning. I thought Francine might have done that. So I checked."

Thomas raised his eyebrows and said, "I've seen all I need to here. Let's move on."

Francine's place was on the other side the complex. Thomas and Jack again kept Stanley engaged in conversation on the long walk. Val and Gwen followed close behind.

When the apartment door opened, Val felt as if she'd stepped back in time. Her heart began to bang nervously. The apprehension that she felt in Jeanne's place was amplified at least a thousand times. It looked very much like it did the night she was last here. Remnants of fingerprint powder still covered the walls, light fixtures, doorknobs, and anywhere else someone would have made hand contact. Much of the furniture was still present too. Val wondered why keep it the same when Jeanne's was emptied and painted.

"No one came for her things?" she asked Stanley.

"Can't find anyone to give them to. I have nowhere to store this stuff, so I just keep it here. No one's beating down the door to rent this place, so it really doesn't matter."

"Didn't Francine's sister come for her belongings?" Thomas asked.

"She was supposed to. That's why I waited. She called and told me she would, but she never showed up. I need the furniture gone to get this place cleaned up. Can't do much with it here."

Thomas didn't mention that Samantha was now dead. And Stanley didn't seem to know. "Who took Jeanne's belongings?"

"Her nephew," Stanley said.

After a quick glance in the living room and kitchen, they headed to the bedroom. Val hesitated in the doorway, taking a deep breath. She jumped when she felt someone grab her arm.

It was Gwen.

"We should go in," Gwen said. Val nodded.

Thomas and Jack were standing in the closet. As Val and Gwen walked across the room to join the men, Val's gaze lingered on Francine's bed. It was a bare mattress only. Bloody teeth on the pillow flashed through her mind. As quickly as the memory entered, she pushed it aside for now. Though she was most interested in the teeth, what was in the closet is what brought them all to Eastville today and she hurried to see it.

On the ceiling, faint traces of fingerprints could still be detected around a piece of drywall, obviously added as a patch. It seemed fairly new. "Did you do this?" Jack asked Stanley.

"I never fixed that," Stanley said. "Francine must have done it herself."

"Why would Francine be doing it? Why would *she* be placing drywall?" Thomas asked this time.

Stanley shrugged his shoulders. "Beats me. She never said anything about it needing to be fixed."

"It's a very small piece, probably no more than a foot. You don't need to be a carpenter to manage that. It looks like it was replaced because of water damage." Val pointed out parts of the ceiling around the patch that had brownish yellow discoloration. "I've done this type of work myself before. It's not that hard to do." She had no choice but to do some of her own home repairs. With no money to spend on a handyman, she had become knowledgeable on home maintenance. It's amazing what can be learned on the internet.

"But still, why do it herself when she has Stanley here to do it for her?" Thomas said.

He led the pack out of the bedroom and down the hall to the linen closet. Once he opened the door, Val could easily see the area in question. A part of the wall had been altered. Not once but twice.

A small section had been cut out and replaced with new drywall. And then later it had been cut again and patched a second time. This second patch was obvious. The two pieces had a slightly different color. One was darker, suggesting a time span between alterations.

"This one's different." Val pointed to the lighter section. "It's newer."

Jack felt around the edges of the second patch. "There was water damage in the bedroom closet, but there's nothing wrong here. Why repair it more than once? For that matter, why repair it at all?"

"Good question." Thomas reached in and pushed on the piece. "It's solidly in place." He quickly walked away from the linen closet and headed back towards the bedroom. Jack and

Stanley followed him. But Val stayed behind. Something caught her eye. Gwen remained with her.

"What are you looking at?" Gwen asked.

"Those," Val said, pointing to the top shelf that held a few medication bottles. She was interested in two prescription containers partially hidden behind a bottle of cough syrup.

Gwen reached up and pulled the prescription containers down. One was empty and the other only had a few pills left. She read the label. "They're for doxycycline."

"Doxycycline is an antibiotic," Val said, disappointed. Francine's sister Samantha had many bottles of the prescription pain medication Percocet found at her place and Val thought maybe she could find a connection with the same type of drug. No such luck. Gwen put the bottles back on the shelf and they left to join the men in the bedroom.

When they returned, Jack was in the closet standing on a chair, feeling around the added section of drywall. "The repair in the hall closet was better than this. This one isn't adapted well at all. It looks like it was done rather quickly."

He applied a little more force to the area and the added piece slipped up as it separated from the rest of the ceiling. He pressed harder to complete the detachment. With one hand in the hole he felt around. "There's something up here."

When he jumped down off the chair he had a large envelope in his hands.

Inside the envelope were personal documents. A few concerned someone named Lorelei Sebastian. An address for her was listed on one of the papers. But most of the papers belonged to Jeanne Coleman.

"Jesus Christ. Francine Donohue and Jeanne Coleman did know each other," Val said.

24

"It can't be a dead end," Gwen said to Val. The two sat in their tiny room at the medical examiner's office whispering, but Gwen started to raise her voice. "Where the hell could that woman be?"

"Shh," Val scolded. "It's not *that* dead of an end, and please, close the door before someone hears you. This is private information. Gavin told me this morning that they're not releasing this."

Gwen got up and did what she was told, then quickly sat back down. "What do you mean?"

"Gavin and Warren went yesterday evening with crime scene technicians and searched the address that was listed for Lorelei Sebastian. No teeth were found there so there's a good chance she's still alive. The problem is, no one was even sure she was ever at that address. The landlord basically had no records of any use and couldn't tell who'd lived there in the last several years."

"What about the neighbors?" Gwen's eyes were wide. "Someone must have known *something* about this woman."

"It's not the type of neighborhood where people know

each other. Most of the houses are rental properties and the tenants turn over pretty quickly. If she was hiding out there, like Francine and Jeanne seemed to do in the Eastville Projects, she got what she wanted because she certainly wasn't noticed."

"You would think they'd remember someone named Lorelei. It's a pretty uncommon name."

"She might not have used her real name." Val sighed. "This woman might as well have been a ghost."

"Bottom line is, there's no trace of Lorelei Sebastian."

"At least this gives Gavin probable cause to start an investigation on her," Val said. "Plus, there's a little more to it. There was a life insurance policy found with Jeanne Coleman's documents hidden in Francine's ceiling. The beneficiary was Lorelei. So far, no one has tried to claim the money."

Gwen stood up from the stool and paced a few feet in one direction and then turned and went in the other. In the tiny room she had nowhere to go, and simply leaned against the counter and sighed. "And Jeanne Coleman herself? What do those papers say about her?"

"She's why the trail is still hot. A lot of her personal information was found, but much of it was out of date. An expired driver's license, several bank statements for accounts that were closed about a year ago, but a recent application for a passport was there."

Gwen's eyes opened wide. "Why in the hell would a recluse have an application for a passport?"

"That's exactly the point." Val stopped short here. She didn't want to tell Gwen about Gavin's reaction. He had hit the roof when Val told him that she and Gwen were involved with the investigation at Francine's apartment. She had cringed as he lectured her on acceptable and unacceptable professional behavior. He didn't hold back on his opinion, letting her know how dangerous her involvement was with Jack and Thomas. "They're going to get you fired," he insisted.

"Did they check behind the section of drywall in the linen closet?" Gwen asked.

"Yes, nothing was there. They think that was the original hiding place and the documents were eventually moved to the ceiling in the bedroom closet. That's why that section of wall was replaced twice."

A knock on the door caused both Val and Gwen to jump. "Come in," Val tried to say nonchalantly. It still sounded guilty.

"I hope I'm not disturbing anything," Howie said.

"Just girl talk," Gwen said. "What's up?"

"I've been asked to find Val."

"I'm all yours," Val said, trying to sound cheery. She really wanted to continue her discussion with Gwen and the last thing she wanted right now was to be pulled away. She rose from her chair and smiled, hoping this wouldn't take long.

"Candace is looking for you," Howie warned. "She asked if I could find you and send you to her."

The smile immediately fell from her face and she stared at Howie, trying to read from his expression what this could possibly be about. "Why?" she asked cautiously.

"I'm sorry but she didn't tell me what she wanted you for. She just asked me to get you."

"Was she in a good mood?" Val tried to joke, knowing Candace was only in a good mood when she was screwing with people.

"She looked cranky, so I think you're safe." Howie was upbeat, trying to make her laugh. It didn't work.

Did Gavin tell Blythe about her involvement at Francine's apartment? Was she fired? Val headed towards Candace's office. Her heart was in her throat as she knocked on the open door. Candace motioned for her to come in and sit down. She had a piece of paper on her desk and flipped it around so that Val could read what it said.

"Consider this your first written warning. After one more, you *will* be terminated," Candace said bluntly. Val wondered why Dr. Blythe didn't reprimand her himself. He was clearly behind this attack. Candace was merely carrying out his orders. But Val had to admit that she was somewhat relieved. Candace didn't mention anything about her escapade yesterday. That's not what this was about.

"I wrote in my report that the teeth were damaged and extremely fragile due to the fire. It would have been impossible to do my job without breaking them," Val said, surprised at the accusation as Candace questioned her competence with the fire victim. "Dr. Blythe even complimented me on how well I wrote the report."

"Yes. It *is* a well-written report. However, that doesn't excuse the fact that you *did* break the teeth. We've overlooked some of your other errors and frankly, Dr. Blythe can't do it anymore."

Val looked into her eyes and saw Candace was enjoying every minute of this. Candace couldn't have cared less why the teeth broke. What Val had feared for some time was becoming painfully obvious. Her days at the medical examiner's office were numbered. It was only a matter of time before they fired her. Candace was now simply building the ammunition needed for a proper termination.

"What other errors?" Val asked.

"Since we have no written documentation of them, it would not be in the best interest of this office for me to discuss anything considered exploratory."

"If I've done things wrong, I have the right to know what they are." Val knew there were no such errors.

Candace gave a sympathetic look. "Yes, of course you do. That's why we're starting here. Everything else is just water under the bridge." She pushed the paperwork across the desk towards Val. A pen lay on top and she pointed to a blank line at the bottom of the page. "I need your signature here to document that I've given you this written warning."

Val picked up the pen and signed her name in large letters. "Is there anything else?" she asked as she got up from the desk.

"I just would be more careful if I were you. And, I do mean that in a constructive way," Candace warned.

Val exited the office and walked down the corridor, not completely sure where she was going. Her mind couldn't grasp a single thought. At first she was seething, she wanted to scream, "Screw it all!" and walk out. They were going to eventually fire her, she was sure of it. The next time she did anything even slightly wrong, she was going to be let go. The broken teeth were beyond her control. If they were going to fault her for that, then they were looking with a searchlight for any reason to get rid of her.

She knew that this wasn't because of her involvement with Thomas and Jack. It couldn't have been. She would have been terminated immediately for that. Dr. Blythe wouldn't need to be going through this in such a roundabout way.

Without even realizing it, Val had circled around the building and was now standing in front of the door leading to the loading bay, where the dead were dropped off and picked up. Several hearses were parked and undertakers were busy wheeling bodies into the back of them. Suddenly her anger was replaced with a worse emotion, dread, and the reality of the situation hit hard. She was going to be unemployed again. No job. No money. No life.

No life. The thought caught her as she watched one mortician slam the back door of the hearse. She was so busy being mad that she hadn't even thought about this additional problem. If Blythe was involved with the murders, if he found out what she was up to, that she was trying to prove he was guilty, he wouldn't want to just fire her, he'd want to do much worse.

"Oh my God, what am I going to do?" Overwhelmed, she grew light-headed and pain radiated through her chest. With knees buckling, she slid to the ground. The coolness of the concrete felt good to her sweating skin. Looking up at the fluorescent lights, she saw someone hovering over her and thought she heard her name being called.

"Val!"

Someone smacked her cheek not once but several times, the last swipe was hard. She stared at the person who was hitting her, and then blinked her eyes.

"Val! Are you okay?" Gwen yelled. "You scared the crap out of me. I was looking everywhere for you and I finally saw you standing here. And then I watched you fall to the floor!"

"I'm okay," Val whispered.

"Are you sure? I think I should get some help."

"No, please don't." Val put her hands to her eyes and started to cry.

"What's wrong?"

Through the sobs, Val told her about her meeting and the realization she was going to be fired and possibly killed. "If he finds out I've been helping Jack and Thomas get evidence against him he's going to kill me too. Just like he killed Julia. He's guilty. I know he is. It explains all of this."

"If he's coming after you, he's coming after me too. We have to stick together."

The thought of death made Val want to unburden herself, clear her conscience from the lie she told. Though she wanted to tell Gwen how she was hired and come clean, she hesitated confessing that she'd never met Oliver Solaris. The words just wouldn't come out. Gwen had been a good friend to her and the one thing she didn't want to lose right now was that friendship.

"Gwen, what are we going to do?"

The two women sat on the floor, backs against the wall, knees bent. "We have no choice. We have to find out how he fits into all of this."

"Yes, we do." After a few minutes Val finally stood. "Well, we'd better get back to work."

Gwen also stood and began brushing dirt off the back of her pants. She stopped mid swipe and said, "Oh, I almost forgot. It's the reason I went looking for you in the first place. Zoe, the toxicologist, asked where you were. She needs to see you right away."

25

Val ran towards the toxicology lab, eager to hear the news waiting for her. There would be only one reason Zoe would need to see her. The drug testing was complete on Samantha Ritcher. As she walked through the doorway to the lab, she fought to catch her breath, and hoped that her eyes had dried out enough so that it wouldn't look like she had been crying.

Zoe pulled out a chair so that Val could sit and then smiled as she explained her findings, "Samantha Ritcher had the curariform drug pancuronium bromide in her system," she announced triumphantly. "That's what she was allergic to. It took some digging but I found it. There were traces of it in her urine sample. Not much though, the drug was essentially wearing off. It doesn't last long after injection, typically only about a half hour. I compared pancuronium to her post-mortem serum and got a hit on the drug sensitivity."

Val was confused. She was aware of curare-type drugs and had a rough idea of their effects and uses. One fact stood out: people don't use them to get high. "Why on earth would she be taking something like this?"

"Beats the hell out of me. It's a pretty powerful muscle relaxer. Actually, muscle paralyzer would be a better description. These drugs are used during surgical procedures. It's risky to take it outside of a hospital setting. You need some means of artificial respiration available. It freezes all skeletal muscles including the diaphragm, in the right dosages. Once the diaphragm is inactivated, the person can't breathe on their own anymore."

"Wouldn't her breathing have stopped right away, then? Wouldn't she have died by asphyxiation and not anaphylaxis if that were the case?" Val said, the words tumbling out. She wondered if Blythe got the cause of death wrong. But then she remembered that Zoe confirmed that it was anaphylaxis. Samantha's enzymes and antibodies were telltale for it.

Zoe pulled off her glasses and rubbed the bridge of her nose. "The diaphragm is the last muscle to become paralyzed, so dosage is tricky. An amount that inactivates the muscles of the hands leaves the patient's breathing reduced by about twenty-five percent. So, if she didn't have a high enough dose, she still would have been able to breathe. And we know that she was breathing up until she had the allergic reaction."

So, she had just enough to incapacitate her.

Though Val wanted to believe that Samantha was murdered, and looked for anything to point in this direction, she maintained an open mind for the moment and searched for a plausible, simple explanation for all of this. She needed to cover all the bases and not jump to conclusions because if Samantha took the drug willingly, then her death was an accident. Val needed to rule this out.

Working with Thomas and Jack was certainly helping her learn her job. She was becoming good at asking the right questions. "Samantha had a history of a bad back. Any possibility this might have helped with it?"

"God no. This wouldn't be the drug for that. It has no effect on pain."

Val felt her pulse pick up a few paces. The theory of *taking the drug willingly* just went out the window. And she was happy about that. "Then what does it do?"

"It doesn't affect consciousness and causes complete paralysis of muscles—motor function only, not sensory. So, she would have been fully awake, unable to move and still feel everything. This should have freaked her out."

Val's thoughts spun rapidly. "How long would it have taken from the time she was injected until she became paralyzed?"

"A couple of minutes."

A needle wasn't found in the house. Samantha couldn't have disposed of it herself. Someone got rid of it. Samantha definitely wasn't alone. After all of this information though, there was no proof that she was murdered and no way to link her to the other women. This was still death by allergy. The manner couldn't be changed from accident to homicide without more to go on.

Val thought for a minute. "Too bad it's impossible to see if all of the victims had this drug in their system. Then it would prove Samantha's death was connected to them."

"It may not be impossible," Zoe said bluntly as if this was common knowledge.

Val sat upright. Zoe had her full attention. "What do you mean it's not? We only have skeletal remains from the other victims."

"You have the skulls from the victims, right? The flat bones are a good source of red bone marrow. Red marrow is highly vascular. It has lots of blood vessels and drugs get into the blood supply. Anywhere there's a source of blood we might be able to find drugs. That's the premise of this technique."

Val liked the idea and pressed Zoe further on it.

"It's kind of a new procedure but it's been getting good

publicity lately. There's been success with opioids and some sedatives. No one has tried it, to my knowledge, with muscle relaxants." Zoe sat forward, excited. "Hey, it might not show anything, but I'll give it a try. If it works, we could have a pretty nice presentation for the American Academy of Forensic Science meeting next year. Not to mention a good journal article. We could work on this together. It would really jump start your career in this field to do things like this. Getting published gets your name out there."

"What do we need?" Val said, willing to do anything.

"I'll need a piece of each of the skulls."

Val's optimism flatlined. For her to sneak a piece of the skulls from under Dr. Blythe's nose, would probably be as difficult as snatching the Mona Lisa from the Louvre. She had no idea how she was going to go about getting this.

She did know one thing, though. She needed another look in Samantha Ritcher's apartment. Her death couldn't have been an accident. And Val knew exactly what she needed to see.

26

Val waited outside Samantha's residence. Samantha's boyfriend, Eddie, looked at her skeptically. He sized her up and down, deciding whether to let her in or not. Val had no authorized documentation to gain entrance to this house. She'd only be let in by his invitation and her ability to convince him to extend this to her.

Jack and Thomas had told her that she needed to do this on her own. Since she was still working this case officially as a death investigator, she had a better chance of appearing legitimate if she didn't have an entourage with her.

"We think she died of an allergic reaction and we just need to find out what that was. It would be a great help if I could take another look around to see what it could have been. That way we could prove it was an accident and not homicide," Val lied, not letting on she already knew how Samantha died. Dr. Blythe still hadn't signed her death certificate. There was no way Eddie could know this. He had been considered a suspect in Samantha's death early on and he seemed to relax once Val mentioned "allergic reaction" and "accident."

"I guess it'll be okay. Will it take long? I have some work to do on my truck." He motioned towards an old red pickup sitting in the driveway and then moved out of the doorway to let Val enter.

"Oh, I can go through her medications myself. You can take care of your truck and I'll just call you if I need to," she said, hoping to get him out of the house. She wanted a few minutes alone. It would be much easier to do what she came here to do if Eddie was outside, out of her way.

He shrugged his shoulders and seemed undecided on where he was going at this point. "Where were you thinking of starting?"

"The bathroom would be best, that's probably where any pills would have been kept."

He silently led Val to the bathroom. She stayed a couple of steps behind, trying not to get too close, but when they reached the entrance he turned, blocking the doorway.

"It's not all that clean in there," he warned.

"Don't worry about it, you should see my place." Before he had a chance to say anything more, Val boldly slid past him and walked inside. She immediately wondered if she'd done the right thing or not. She was confined now.

Eddie leaned against the door watching her every move. It was obvious he wasn't going to leave and she needed to do something to get rid of him. Fast.

She nervously put on latex gloves and began poking through the medicine cabinet. Every container or tube was an over-the-counter drugstore item, but Val picked each one up, inspecting the label, writing down the name of the product, opening it, looking at it and smelling the contents. She progressed through this task in a purposely agonizingly slow rate. She could see Eddie shifting his weight from one foot to the next, crossing and uncrossing his arms, then glancing at his watch. He lost his patience when Val opened the box of Band-Aids and began removing them one at a time.

"Look, I really need to get to my truck. I have to work at four and if I don't make it in on time my boss is going to fire me."

Val let out a deep sympathetic sigh, shook her head and stated, "I know what it's like. My boss is a real prick too. Why do you think I have to do all of this crap?" She pointed to the healthcare products spread out on the counter and gave him a knowing scowl of asshole bosses and oppressive working conditions, hoping to win his trust.

It worked. Eddie gave her a grin and the tension eased.

Val said encouragingly, and with a smile, "Go take care of your truck. I'll get what I need and be out of your way in no time. Hell, if I don't clock back in by four, my ass is toast too."

He didn't move and Val wasn't sure what he was going to do. "I'll be right outside, just let me know if you need anything," he said.

She continued to smile and said assuredly, trying to hide any apprehension in her voice, "I'll do that."

He finally left the house.

From the window, Val had a partial view of the driveway. She waited until she saw Eddie walk towards his truck then hurried out of the bathroom and headed toward the bedroom; the room she really wanted to check.

In the bedroom, she had a much better view of the driveway and watched him pop the hood, beginning work on the pickup. She waited again, making sure he was involved with his job. Though it seemed safe, Val kept an eye on the window, glancing frequently to make sure he was still outside.

Quickly, she slid the bottom dresser drawer open. The last time she searched in here was the day Samantha was found dead. She was looking for drugs then. Today she wanted something else, and it was what she saw in this drawer that she needed to see again. Luckily, all of Samantha's belongings appeared to still be here.

As she moved items around, her fingers finally hit something large and rectangular. Val smiled as she pulled out what she was hoping to find—Samantha's photo album.

The person who killed Samantha had to have also known Francine too. Their deaths must be connected somehow. But the last time Samantha communicated with her sister was when she was a teenager. The link to this crime had to have roots extending at least that far back. Val needed to find something, anything in Samantha's past that could put the two murders together.

Some of the pages were old and yellowed with age. The pictures probably dated from the mid to late eighties judging by the clothing and hairstyles depicted. There were several of youngish-looking teenagers. Val lingered on these.

There was one photo of three young girls that caught her eye and after it did, she just stared. It was grainy and hard to discern clear facial features, obviously a result of photography at least thirty years old. Val needed to remove it to see it better and felt around the corners of the page, carefully lifting the cellophane. Her fingers stopped midway, a noise from outside had grabbed her attention as a car door slammed.

Her hand was frozen as she watched Eddie wave to the man next door, who had just gotten out of his car. They talked for a few minutes. She let out a sigh of relief when Eddie finally resumed his work. All attention went back to the book. Her hands trembled as she pulled the picture free.

The girls were around the age of twelve or thirteen. One was much smaller than the other two and had dark hair. Val brought the photo close to her face, her heart pounding. It was no use, no matter how hard she looked, there was no way to be sure. There just wasn't enough detail. She was so young. But it was just so bizarre that she would have such a strong resemblance in demeanor, such an uncanny way about her. In the photo, the girl's arms were crossed over her chest and she was leaning against a tree.

All Val could see as she stared at this girl—this girl with her dark hair, small stature and crossed arms—was Julia DeHaviland, her arms crossed, leaning on a gurney telling the story of how she met her husband Colin. Julia looked vulnerable then. The girl in the photo depicted that same vulnerability.

Val flipped the picture over. The writing on the back read; *Me and my best friends—Frannie and Sam, August 1987.* Why would Samantha even have this? It obviously didn't belong to her. It belonged to the small dark-haired girl who made the inscription. Val began scouring through the rest of the album, her thoughts racing. She needed to know who this girl was.

The three girls were in several other shots. They appeared younger in these, and this time they were standing around a boy. Val guessed the girls were about ten and the boy about seven or eight. She put the picture with the inscription to the side and was just about to pull this other one out of the album when she heard a noise coming from outside. She looked out of the window to check the whereabouts of Eddie.

Val saw the truck only.

A second later she heard the front door to the apartment slam and her pulse exploded.

As quickly as she could, she placed the picture back in the album, pulling the cellophane cover over it. Then she hesitated, taking the picture back out, holding it firmly in her hand. She needed this.

"Are you finding what you need?" Eddie called to her.

"Yes. I'm just finishing up," she yelled as she put the album back in the drawer, her fingers fumbling nervously as she heard him coming towards her, not sure what to do with the picture.

Not to mention how to explain why she was in his bedroom. Val no sooner had the dresser drawer closed and the picture hidden in her pocket when Eddie appeared in the doorway.

"What are you doing in here?" he asked.

Val couldn't read the tone. It wasn't accusatory or angry. It simply asked the question.

"I didn't find anything in the bathroom. A lot of women keep medicine in the bedroom. It's pretty common. I do it myself," she said, hoping that he believed her. "I thought maybe she had something in the dresser." Val's heart was beating hard enough to leap out of her chest.

"Did you find anything to help with what happened to Samantha?"

"No, not really. But I'll keep looking into it." She got up off the bed and walked out of the room and headed to the front door. All she wanted was to get out of the apartment now. Eddie followed close behind.

"You know, Samantha was cremated and I spread her ashes in a place that was special to her. She told me it was special to Francine too and I know Samantha would want her sister to be with her. Do you know what happened to Francine's remains? Could I get them? I know I'm not family, but I could spread her ashes with Samantha's," he said.

"That's really nice of you to do that for her." Val wondered if she'd misjudged Eddie. He seemed to really care about Samantha. "I'll check to see what's going on and let you know."

"Thanks. I'd appreciate it."

Val paused, her hand on the doorknob. "By the way, where was this special place?"

"It's where they used to play when they were kids. They grew up in Orchard Park, not far from Chestnut Ridge Park. They kind of built this fort out of tree branches just off from one of the hiking trails. Samantha told me they used to hang out there all of the time. Francine and her had it bad growing up and it was kind of like a safe place for them to be."

"Could you tell me just where in the park this fort was?"

Eddie explained and then said something far more interesting.

27

"Well," Gwen blurted before she even had her jacket off, "what happened?"

She'd arrived at Val's house only seconds behind Jack, who was already looking at the picture that Val had taken from Samantha's apartment.

"She just looks so much like Julia," Val said of the person in the photo.

"How can you tell? You can't really see her face. Plus, this person is pretty young. A lot happens in thirty years," Jack stated plainly.

"I can't explain it. It's the way she's standing. To me, it's just Julia." Val felt a need to defend her opinion, but really couldn't. Neither Jack nor Gwen had ever met her. They didn't know her. Though Val's own interaction with Julia was short-lived, what they confided in each other was not trivial.

"Unfortunately, this doesn't prove anything," Jack said. And it didn't. No matter how hard Val tried, there was nothing more she could really say to be convincing.

Gwen took the picture from Jack. She turned it over and said, "These girls were best friends. Val, wouldn't Julia have said something if she once had known Francine Donohue and Samantha Ritcher?"

"I know. It's a long shot and if that's Julia, if she was keeping this secret, it changes a lot with this case," Val said.

"*Secret* is an understatement. To hide a piece of information this big? Why not tell Detective Gavin?" Gwen said.

"Maybe she was afraid to do so," Val replied.

"I agree with you, this is a long shot," Jack said. "But, let's take it into consideration for now. We have to because Julia and Francine have been the focal points of this crime. DNA evidence ties Colin as the suspect in their deaths. He's set up to take the fall for both of them. Also, circumstantial evidence links him to Samantha through phone records. The killer knows Colin. This killer also knows, at least, Francine, Samantha and Julia. They have to be connected some way. Why not like this? It's odd that there's nothing to tie him to Jeanne's death yet, so we don't know how she fits in with all of this."

"Maybe Jeanne Coleman is why Francine was in Eastville to begin with. She knew Jeanne. Jeanne's personal documents were in her ceiling. They were hiding them from someone. Jesus, they themselves appeared to be hiding in the Eastville Projects," Gwen said. "They all had to have been afraid of someone."

"Whoever wanted them dead knew a lot of personal information about them too. Old information. Well, Francine and Samantha, at least," Val blurted, finally getting the chance to tell them what she learned from Eddie. "Samantha's boyfriend told me that they used to play in Chestnut Ridge Park, the same place where the first victim's skull was found, Jeanne Coleman's skull."

Both Gwen and Jack stared.

"And that's not all," Val said, and then told the rest of the story. "Francine and Samantha's parents eventually moved to

Niagara Falls and when they got older they hiked in Devil's Hole Park."

"So, remains of victims are found in places sentimental to Francine and Samantha," Jack said. "We still don't know who was in Devil's Hole but at this point, we have to assume it was someone they knew."

"No one can find any trace of Lorelei Sebastian. She's still missing. Her skull could be the one sitting in the medical examiner's office," Gwen said.

"The skull found in Devil's Hole would belong to the earliest victim. The first victim always puts a crime in motion. It sets the stage." Jack grew excited. "I asked you before if we could get another look at this skull. Can we do that? Do you have access to where it's kept?"

"Yes. We all do. Our swipe cards open all of the rooms," Gwen said.

"Good. I need to see it."

"Sounds like a plan. Let's go!" Gwen stood up and grabbed her jacket.

"Wait a minute," Val protested. "We can't just break in."

"If you have a key how is it breaking in?" Jack asked plainly.

"If we get caught, Dr. Blythe will fire me immediately," Val said.

Jack scoffed at the man's name. "Val, Blythe's going to fire you anyway, maybe not today, but soon. Ask yourself why is he trying so hard to get rid of you. You need to get him before he gets you."

Jack had a point, but still this was too risky.

"I just don't know about this," Val said.

"Five minutes. That's all I need."

"But what if we get caught?"

"You worry too much. Now how do we get in?" Jack was out of the door before she had a chance to answer.

The drop-off bay around the back of the hospital was the best way to get Jack into the morgue undetected. At this time of night there would be only one security guard on duty and he would be at the employee entrance.

The only problem was that given the late hour, the drop-off bay doors would be locked. They had to be opened from the inside. In order to do this, Val and Gwen needed to enter the morgue legitimately, which wasn't a big deal. They didn't need to sneak in. In fact, it was best if they didn't. But this meant that they would have to walk through the entrance in full view of the guard. He'd wonder why they were there.

"Just wait outside here and stand away from the door. We'll open it from the inside and let you in," Val said.

"Don't leave me out here too long." Jack looked around at the surroundings. The houses in the area were barely standing. Many had trash on the lawns. A group of teenagers sat on the porch of one building. Two of them pointed in Jack's direction. "I'm beginning to wonder how long it'll take before I'm mugged."

"We'll get you as soon as we can," Val said without compassion. She had her own worries at the moment and getting caught in this little escapade ranked at the top. Leaving Jack to fend for himself, she ran around to the side of the building. Gwen was waiting for her.

"I don't know if I can do this," Val said. "I can't feel my legs anymore and I think I'm going to throw up."

"It's going to be fine." Gwen's voice faltered. She sounded less than convincing. "Come on, let's go."

They walked in and waved to Ken, the night security guard. He peered over the top of his newspaper and waved back.

"See, this is going to be easy," Gwen whispered.

Val said hello to Ken each night she came to work and he knew her well. But for some reason she felt as if she was wearing a neon sign stating she was up to no good. They were nearly through the door and out of Ken's sight when he yelled, "What brings you ladies in? It's Howie's shift tonight."

Val's chest lurched at the sound of his voice and she stared at him, her mind blank. They were going to get caught if she didn't come up with an answer immediately. She forced herself to say something, anything plausible. "Gwen and I were getting some dinner and I remembered there's a couple of files I really need to have. I forgot to complete a report that Dr. Blythe's been on my ass about. If I get it now and finish before morning, maybe he won't put me through hell tomorrow." Val fought hard to keep her voice steady. Her heart banged fiercely as she added with a smile, "You won't blow me in, will you?"

Ken smirked knowingly. "Your secret's safe with me."

Val winked. "Thanks, you're the best."

Val and Gwen walked through the doors and into the morgue. As the doors closed behind them, Val took a deep breath. There was one more person they needed to be worried about. Howie. He was around somewhere. She looked up and down the halls for him.

"If we see Howie we'll use the same excuse that you gave Ken," Gwen said. "How did you come up with it? God, it was so plausible you even had me convinced that's why we're here."

"Lying is a skill I've been developing. It tends to come in handy."

"I should take some lessons. Convincing someone of something I'm not would be a pretty good talent to have."

Val almost laughed at the irony of the statement. "I'll let Jack in. Go to autopsy room one and meet us in there," she said, quickly walking down the corridor, heading to the drop-off bay. There was an odd stillness in the morgue. The night shift was always quite a contrast to the hustle that occurred during the day. Now, it was just eerily quiet and Val felt her skin prickle. No one was around.

As she was about to turn the last corner that would lead her to the doors, her motions grew slow. She thought she heard a series of pattering noises. Standing still, listening carefully, she heard it again. It sounded like someone walking, sneakers squeaking on the tiles. And it was coming towards her. Before she could do anything, Howie came around the corner and nearly collided with her.

"Val?" he asked, staring.

"Hi, Howie. I need a report for Dr. Blythe. I have to get it to him by tomorrow," she rambled. As soon as she said the words, she wished she hadn't.

"What brings you down here then?" He looked confused.

Her excuse, at this point, could only backfire—her office was down a different hallway. If she needed to get a report, there was no reason for her to be where she was. Val's eyes shifted past Howie. As she scrambled to think, she saw her answer. Pointing to a bathroom door that was about ten feet away, she said, "Ladies room. The one by my office didn't have any toilet paper." Her gaze went back to him and she waited to see if he bought her story.

"Are you okay?" he asked, staring again at her. "You look really pale."

"Just scared that's all. The morgue is scary at night."

"It's not the dead you have to be worried about, it's the living. You couldn't be safer here," he laughed. "You should know that by now."

Val crossed her legs and bounced up and down. She needed to get rid of Howie as fast as she could. "I don't mean to be rude, but I have to go."

"I won't keep you." He patted his pocket, the rectangular outline of a cigarette pack obvious. "I have to go too."

"I'll see you tomorrow then," Val said as she entered the bathroom. She waited a few seconds and then slowly looked back out. Howie was gone and she ran to the drop-off bay to grab Jack. The two slipped back into the main morgue area and made it to autopsy room one undetected.

"Hurry, let's get inside," Val said. She picked up her ID card with shaky fingers and quickly ran it through the swipe pad. The red light on the pad refused to turn green. It was still locked. She repeated the motion a second and then a third time. She could barely say the words. "It's not working. Gwen should already be inside. If she made it in, why isn't she opening the door?"

"Try it slower," Jack said.

Val ran the card again, slowly. This time the red light turned to green. She pushed on the handle, and as she did so, the door opened. Gwen was on the other side.

"Thank God," Gwen said. "I thought that was you, but I wasn't sure, otherwise I would have opened the door. What took so long?"

"Howie. But don't worry. I think he believed the excuse I gave him."

As soon as they were inside, Val turned on the lights. It was safe to do so. The door was sealed to keep any odors from escaping. It would also keep any light from shining round the perimeter. Unless someone walked in, no one would know they were in here. Her jaw dropped when she noticed what was sitting just a few feet in front of her.

Three skulls were on a small table. One was labeled Francine Donohue, the other Jeanne Coleman, and the third was marked as undetermined. Several containers, each holding human teeth, also sat on the table. Val couldn't believe what she was looking at. She had wanted to inspect the evidence with this case since her second day on the job and here it was. All of it within grabbing distance.

"Why are these still here?" Gwen asked, pointing to the ones belonging to Francine and Jeanne. "Shouldn't these have been released for burial?"

"Good question," Jack said.

All three of them put on a set of latex gloves. Gwen picked up the unknown skull found in Devil's Hole. "What do you think, Val? Were these teeth taken out or was this caused by the head being smashed on the rocks?"

Val reached for the skull, inspecting the part where the teeth would have been. "It's hard to tell. They could have been forcefully extracted. It looks like someone grabbed both the tooth and bone and pulled forward. But, it's so broken around this area I can't be sure. The damage is pretty bad." She turned it around, trying to get a good look from every angle. There was quite a bit of destruction to the bone. Multiple large cracks were evident and large pieces were missing, mostly around the region where the upper teeth once were. "There are no broken roots in the sockets, though. Rocks couldn't have caused this. I saw the same thing with Francine's skull. No broken roots."

Val tilted the skull and grew excited. "Look at this, the shape of the break here. The rectangular outline is obvious on these two sockets. It looks like the outline of the nose of a set of pliers." She remembered that Francine also had this kind of damage to her upper jaw and she quickly picked up Francine's skull, pointing out several patterns that were consistent in size and shape. "It's identical," she said.

"This one has to be connected to this case. It would be far too coincidental if it wasn't," Gwen remarked.

"I agree. A head bouncing around on some rocks could have easily caused the rest of this damage, but not in these two places.

There is no rock in the world that would make such a perfect rectangular pattern or dislodge roots from the sockets," Val said.

Jack reached for Jeanne's skull. "There are rectangular patterns on this too."

Val grew quiet. A unique opportunity was right in front of her and she couldn't afford to lose it. *Oh my God.* Zoe told her that if she had a piece of the skull, she could test it for the drug pancuronium. Well, here they all were. Proof that they may be connected.

"If I wanted to take a piece of this bone, how could I do it in a way that Dr. Blythe wouldn't notice?" Val asked. Jack and Gwen looked at her oddly, eyebrows raised and faces blank as if they hadn't heard correctly. Val explained why she wanted this and they both eagerly chimed in.

"The best way to do it is to take it from an area that has a break already. That way, it'll blend in," Jack said.

"What do I cut it with?" she asked.

"With those." Gwen walked over to a table that held an array of instruments. She picked up the garden loppers. "Would you like to do the honors?"

Val took the lopper. She was getting fairly acquainted with this tool, surprised by its many uses. One day she'd have to actually use one in a garden.

Gwen held the skull in place and Jack pointed out where to cut. Val placed the handles close together, wrapped the blades around the bone and in a quick push of the handle, a small section of the skull was free.

"Here." Jack handed her a paper towel. "Wrap it in this."

"I need to get a piece of Jeanne and Francine's too," Val said. The sequence was repeated and a small section of bone was removed. She grabbed a specimen bag and labeled each. After they were done, Jack was eager to get back to inspecting and comparing the skulls. So was Val, but the skulls weren't the only things in the room that caught her attention. The teeth did too.

Eyeing them, she opened the containers and took them out with a set of tweezers. She examined each tooth and root surface. Quite a few had portions of the jaw bone still attached, making it hard to view the entire tooth. But for the most part they were in good condition, especially given they had been ripped out of the victim's mouth. Surprisingly, none of the roots were broken.

Val picked Francine's skull back up and placed one of her teeth back in the appropriate socket. She continued with the rest, one by one. They all fitted neatly back into place. She smiled. This was something she had wanted to do from the beginning and now she had her chance.

"Can I have that for a second?" Jack asked Val. "I want to see something."

"Sure." She pulled out the teeth and handed him the skull.

Val picked up Jeanne's skull, repeating the same process by placing Jeanne's teeth into the sockets. No matter how she tried to get them in, none of them fitted. *That's odd.* For the hell of it, she picked up the unknown skull and tried to slip Jeanne's teeth in, only because some of the shapes appeared to be the right size.

After she placed the first one in, she tried another and then another. She thought for a long moment, trying to absorb what she was seeing and then stated, staring at the skull in her hands, "I have something to tell the two of you."

"What?" The statement obtained little interest.

"Jeanne Coleman's teeth fit into the sockets of the unknown skull. I don't care what the DNA or post-mortem interval results say. This skull, the skull from Devil's Hole, belongs to Jeanne Coleman." Val pointed at her find, her hands shaking with excitement.

Both Jack and Gwen snapped their heads in Val's direction.

"If that skull belonged to Jeanne, then it was detached from her body more than one year ago. How on earth could she have left an insurance policy to Lorelei Sebastian? That policy was written only six months ago," Jack said.

"Let alone apply for a passport recently," Gwen added.

"That's not all," Val said. "If the skull that was found in Chestnut Ridge Park doesn't belong to Jeanne, who the hell does it belong too? And who forged the DNA results?"

28

Val's first instinct was to go to Gavin and tell him about the discrepancy with Jeanne Coleman's skull.

"No," said Jack. "Don't. I advise you not to tell anyone—especially Detective Gavin—that we believe the unknown skull belongs to Jeanne Coleman."

"But this finding is huge!" protested Val.

"The finding is huge," said Jack, "but the evidence is shaky."

Val realized he was right. If exposed prematurely, it could easily be dismissed and ultimately lost. The fact that the teeth fitted into the sockets wasn't enough to make a claim that the skull was Jeanne's, especially with DNA stating the contrary. If they jumped too fast both Val and Gwen would certainly get fired. Dr. Blythe would know they broke into the autopsy suite. There was still so much to do and a connection to the medical examiner's office was key. Val saw Jack's point and agreed to keep her mouth shut. Particularly since the DNA could have been tampered with.

"If you were committing this crime, why let Jeanne's skull be found at all? Why risk it?" Val asked Jack. "What do you gain from that, even if DNA says otherwise?"

"Someone is way too confident about the crime they're committing." Jack said. "With no other leads at this point, and though it's a long shot, I want to visit Devil's Hole Park and see why this resting place was chosen for this skull, maybe find something of significance with the site since it had relevance to Francine Donohue and Samantha Ritcher."

Jack's phone buzzed and he pulled it out, glancing at his text messages. "Val, I have a favor to ask of you. When you were a dentist you prescribed medication, correct?"

"Yes." She wasn't sure where he was going with this.

Still staring at the screen, he said, "I want you to find out why Francine Donohue was taking the antibiotic doxycycline. I want you to call her doctor."

"Sure Jack, I can do that. Professional courtesy allows us to discuss mutual patients candidly. I'll just say Francine was my dental patient. Though I'm wondering why you want to know about this."

"It might be nothing but Thomas just let me know that he found out that Julia DeHaviland was taking high doses of the same drug six months before her death." He put away the phone. "But first, we need to take a trip to Niagara Falls."

Although they were still a distance away from the river, Val could hear the rush of water from where she stood, at the top of the trail in Devil's Hole Park.

Gwen tightened the laces on her shoes and then bent over, touching her toes, stretching her legs in preparation for the hike. Jack had a map and pointed out where Jeanne's skull was found, explaining where they would go once they reached the bottom of the Niagara Gorge.

They were about to enter the walkway leading down the

gorge to the water's edge. Val read the state park sign posted at the entrance to the trail. The Devil's Hole was a large cave that was once used by Seneca Indians as a hiding place in times of war. To keep the hiding place secret, all those who entered the area were killed and that section of the gorge quickly got a reputation as the home of a spirit of evil.

The notoriety was intensified when the Senecas and British soldiers fought a fierce battle there in 1763. The Senecas were about to lose control of their land. They ambushed a wagon train, scalping the troops that accompanied it and the oxen and carts were driven over the cliffs. This skirmish was named the Devil's Hole Massacre.

This place certainly has a violent past. Val looked around. The terrain was rough, aggressive almost. Dense foliage covered the walls of the gorge. Thick woods lined the slopes down to the water's edge. Leaves were budding, masking any view they might have had of the Niagara River from this vantage point. But you didn't need a view to know the Lower Whirlpool Rapids were below; the thunderous pounding was an obvious sign.

Val knew immediately this journey wasn't going to be an easy one. She skeptically evaluated the condition of the near-vertical winding stone staircase that would bring them to the river's edge. She examined the sign that stated the distance of the trail: "Two miles down."

Val reluctantly grabbed a rubber band from her pocket and pulled her hair into a ponytail. It was a warm day and she was already sweating. After some personal debate on the level of intense strenuous activity she was about to endure, she ventured down, slowly at first. The steep stones were in need of serious repair. They were jagged and worn away in many places, making the footing difficult. She slipped several times on just the first flight, becoming worried about breaking a leg somewhere on the rest of the journey. She stopped on the nearest landing, evaluating the crumbling condition of the next section. This wasn't going to get any easier.

As they made it farther, one landing at a time, the sound of the water grew louder, and at the one-mile marker Val looked back up to where they'd started, and immediately wished she hadn't. Though the trail was intimidating in the direction they were going it was much more so in the opposite direction.

"I'm more worried about the trip back to the top," she said to Gwen. "A two-mile grueling StairMaster trip like that might kill me." Val grew irritated as she watched Jack. He wasn't even out of breath as he quickly moved down the stairs.

"I'm already feeling like I could spit up a lung," Gwen said. "I don't know how I'm going to get back to our car."

They pressed onward, silently. The further she went, the worse it was getting. All Val wanted to do was reach the end. She was determined to just get this over with. She kept her head down, eyeing each stair, checking her footing to make sure she wouldn't fall.

When she finally reached the bottom, Val hobbled to the nearest rock to sit down. She rested her head and her hands, pushing the sweaty strands of hair that managed to escape from her rubber band, from her face. Her legs felt wobbly and she needed a moment to catch her breath. Gwen made Val scoot over and share the space on the rock.

Jack laughed at them and after a few minutes said, "Well, come on. We still have a way to go." He held the map out, pointing with his finger at their destination.

Val reluctantly rose from her seat. Gwen did too and they both followed Jack wearily down the trail along the water's edge.

The more Val walked, the better she felt. It was much cooler down by the water and the trail was fairly flat here. She looked around and thought the view really was breathtaking this close-up. White caps covered the rushing water as it sped past them at about twenty-five miles an hour. Ten- to fifteen-foot waves churned, rolling forward. It appeared as if they would swallow and destroy anything in their path. Val stared, mesmerized, when the sound of Jack's voice made her jump.

"There. That's where it was discovered!" he exclaimed.

"How do we get over there?" Gwen asked.

"I don't know. It looks kind of dangerous," Val said. She'd thought the walk down the stairs was treacherous but seeing where someone had to go to find this skull gave a new meaning to the term "unsafe terrain." Along this part of the trail a section of rocks jutted out into the river. To get to the water, you'd have to walk a short distance out onto the rocks, some of which were mostly covered by the rushing water. Though it was close to the shore, the likelihood of slipping and being swept away by the current was pretty big.

"How would a hiker have retrieved this? Who in their right mind would even go out there?" Gwen said. "The other remains have been purposely placed so they would be seen readily. But this is impossible to get to."

"A hiker didn't retrieve it," Jack said. "He saw what appeared to be a human skull and reported it to the police. The police recovered it."

"Why put it there then? Why risk your life to put it in a place where it was unlikely to be found?" Val asked.

"This is why you should always visit the scene. It was probably tossed into the water upstream, then hit the rocks and got caught. That could be how it got to be broken," Jack said. "So, the answer to your question, Val, is simple. I don't think this particular skull was meant to be found."

29

Val wasn't having an easy time checking on Francine's prescription for doxycycline. The doctor listed on the pharmacy records insisted that he had never prescribed it.

"Are you certain, doctor?" Val asked. "It was called into the pharmacy. Maybe you forgot to record it?"

"I don't forget to record medications I prescribe by phone." His answer was strong and to the point. The implication that the doctor could have made an error was not taken lightly.

"I'm sorry. I didn't mean to suggest any omission on your part. It could have been simply overlooked."

"Again... I do *not* overlook such issues."

"Of course," Val said diplomatically, almost humble at this point. Do you have any idea why she would need to take this drug? Did she ever complain of an infection?"

"No." There was silence after the one-word answer. Val sensed this discussion was over and thanked the doctor for his time.

Francine must have had an infection. Julia also had one.

They both needed the same antibiotic. They're both now dead, killed the same way.

There's another person connected to this case who currently has an infection, Val thought. *Colin Turner's girlfriend has one. The one that Julia was accused of purposely giving her.* This couldn't be a coincidence. Three women tied to this case that had infections? Two murdered? Why is this woman the only one still alive?

"Today," Jack told Val, "You are going to learn to question suspects." She happily agreed because that suspect would be Lauren Fitzgibbons, Colin Turner's girlfriend. Val was Thomas's and Jack's best choice to be at the interrogation. She had a good knowledge of drugs and infections, plus she had some insight from Julia DeHaviland herself that this woman somehow helped Colin set Julia up.

The big problem with all of this though: Dr. Blythe must not find out what Val is doing.

"Val, to protect your identity, you'll be working undercover," Jack further explained. He said it like this was no big deal.

To Val, it was huge. "Holy crap, what do I do?"

"Interrogation is all about asking questions that seem innocent. With some of them, you have better knowledge of than your subject. Some will make your suspect wonder how much you really know. When you jockey for control, that's when they mess up. But be careful. Never be too confident unless you know you can be."

Val took a deep breath: the instructions only made her more nervous.

"How am I going to get my money now *that the bitch* is dead?" Lauren wasn't a person who held back on what she was thinking. Her disfigurement could have easily caused this nasty demeanor, but equally possible was that maybe, she had always been this way. At this point, Val couldn't really tell.

A temporary prosthesis hid the lost section of her face, but the material gaped and the chin portion didn't fit properly. Lauren resembled a worn rag doll with a fraying face.

One of her wounds still wasn't healing and serious measures were being taken to keep it under control. She had what Val recognized as a catheter for intravenous antibiotics on her arm, an aggressive attempt to prevent the infection from spreading. Lauren explained that the infection had been waxing and waning for months, since the surgery. Luckily, it hadn't caused any further loss of tissue. However, it was obvious she wasn't out of the woods yet. Lauren confirmed, though, that out of all the antibiotics she was given none were doxycycline.

"Your lawsuit is something you're going to have to discuss with your lawyers. Colin hired us for other matters," Thomas said.

Val learned Thomas and Jack had questioned Colin at great length that morning about how Lauren acquired this infection. Other than his own opinion that Julia did it on purpose, Colin gave them nothing solid to follow up on. But, in the end he did say something interesting, though it took some pulling to get it out.

Colin finally admitted that when he returned home that night from Julia's, Lauren wasn't there. She didn't return home until the next day.

While she was crude, Val sensed that Lauren Fitzgibbons probably had a lifetime of men surrounding her. Several photographs were on display around the room, depicting the woman she'd been, and she had been gorgeous. Those days were certainly over and clearly her personality wasn't going to make up for her looks.

"Can you tell us what happened the night of Julia's murder?" Jack asked. Val knew her own questions would focus on three subjects: drugs, infections and Colin's affair. Everything else would be left to Jack and Thomas.

"She called and asked him to come over." Lauren seemed angry as she spoke, her arms crossed tightly, making it obvious she didn't approve of Colin's trip to Julia's house.

"Did he tell you at the time where he was going? Or did you find out later?"

"We have no secrets," she snapped. "I knew."

"You didn't care that he was going to his wife's house?" Jack raised his eyebrows.

"He only went there to find out what the hell was going on. We both knew she was up to something. He could have spent as much time as he wanted with her. I couldn't have cared less. I had no reason to be jealous of that nasty bitch." She glared at Jack. Her fingers began to drum hard on her crossed arms.

Jack just nodded in an exaggerated manner, emphasizing he didn't believe Lauren's response. "Did he call you before he came home?"

She hesitated.

"We can check phone records."

"Yes, he called." Her words were slow, cautious.

"What did he say to you?"

"He said Julia didn't have any money and she fixed everything to ruin us."

"What did you say to that? Were you angry?" Jack inquired further.

"Anybody would have been angry. You have no idea what she was like. She had everything planned. She wanted to destroy us. First me, then Colin."

"Weren't you trying to do that to her? Destroy her, that is. You were already having an affair with her husband when you befriended her," Val said. Julia had suspected Lauren knew that Colin was married. Val decided to see how Lauren reacted to the accusation.

"When *I* befriended *her*?" Lauren sat forward and pointed a finger at Val. "Where the hell did you hear that crap from?"

"Julia. That was her version of the story."

"I'll tell you what shit her version of the story was. She came up to me one day in the gym and commented on my haircut. She asked where I had it done. I told her the name of the salon. That's all I had to do with her." Lauren almost spat out the words.

"But then the two of you started to do things together," Val said.

"More like she wouldn't leave me alone. She started talking to me more and more at the gym and then she asked me to have lunch with her. I didn't know who she was. I didn't know she was Colin's wife. She and Colin have different last names and he never said her first name. He always said 'my soon-to-be-ex.'" Laurens's demeanor grew increasingly heated as she spoke. "Hell, I didn't even like her."

Val sat forward. "Then why go off and do things with someone you don't like? You *did* have lunch with her on more than one occasion, am I correct? In fact, you did many things with her; things friends do. That doesn't sound like someone you didn't like." Val remembered what Julia had told her and pressed Lauren on it.

Lauren appeared to be caught off guard. She sat back in her chair, seeming to search for an appropriate answer. "I found out she was a plastic surgeon. I don't know many plastic surgeons. So, I was interested."

"Interested in what? What she could do for you?" Jack said.

"Interested in having a fellow professional friend." Lauren glared at Jack.

"Oh yes, I'm sorry. You found it necessary to have a professional equal as your friend. And might I ask what your profession is?"

Lauren didn't answer. What remained of her jaw clenched hard.

"Were you even employed when you met Julia?" he asked.

Lauren lurched forward, looking as if she wanted to tear Jack in two.

"When did you go to Julia's office for the first time?" Thomas spoke up quickly.

Lauren's chest heaved with anger. Thomas repeated the question, once and then a second time.

"She asked me to work for her. She asked me to stop by and check out the office. Later, she offered to remove my mole free of charge, practically insisted on it." The words were rattled off in quick orchestrated succession. Val couldn't help but think that this wasn't the first time Lauren had said this explanation.

"And you agreed to it?" Thomas asked.

"Yeah, she was going to do it for free and it's something I'd been wanting to do for a while. If I had known who she was, I never would have let her touch me. I started with the infection the next day. She did it on purpose. She knew who I was." Lauren sat back in her chair.

"Did she ever say that to you? That she knew?" he asked.

Lauren paused.

Thomas said it again. "Did she ever tell you that she knew you were having an affair with her husband?"

"Christ, she had to have known. No one is that stupid."

"What would make you think that?"

"Colin was out almost every night with me. You don't think

she was suspicious? If my husband was out every night, I'd wonder where he was going."

"When did Colin leave her?"

"Right after I got the infection," Lauren said. "He was going to leave her anyway. This just sped things up. He saw her as a monster for doing this to me. He couldn't stand her after that."

"That's awfully convenient then, isn't it? You just said it 'sped things up.' Made him not stand her. Maybe he wouldn't have left Julia otherwise," Jack said.

"Colin loves me! Not her. He was just worried about hurting her feelings!"

Jack opened his mouth to respond, but Thomas intercepted. "How long were you with Colin before he left Julia?"

"About eight months."

Thomas's eyes opened wide. "You were with Colin *before he married Julia*?"

"Yes," Lauren said with confidence. Her eyes were piercing, challenging him. Daring him to ask more.

"How did you feel when he married her? Had you expected him to call off the wedding and marry you instead?" Val asked.

Lauren scoffed. "No. Colin and I weren't serious at the beginning. It was just a fling for both of us. I couldn't have cared less that he was getting married. Do *you* want to marry someone after you've only known them for about a month? I'm not some psycho-bitch."

"But, you continued the affair," Val said.

"Yeah, the sex was good. I didn't fall in love with him until later."

Val thought for a moment and then asked, "How did you two meet?"

"It was at a convention. My boyfriend was off somewhere doing God knows what and I was bored. I met Colin that night at the bar. His fiancé had gone to bed."

"That fiancé was Julia?" Val asked.

"I told you I didn't know who she was at the time." The words were venomous.

"I see. Let me get back to the night Julia died. What did Colin say to you on the phone that night when he called?" Jack said.

"He said he needed time to cool off, to think before he came home."

"Did he tell you he was going back to talk to her?"

"No. Why the hell would he do that?" Lauren looked disgusted.

"He wanted to try to get his wife to take him back," Jack answered, carefully leaving out the part that Colin was only pretending to string Julia along.

"That's a lie."

"We have a neighbor who saw him go back to the house," Thomas said.

"That's hardly the same as trying to get her to take him back. Did he tell the neighbor that's what he planned to do?" she said sarcastically.

"What would you say if I told you the neighbor didn't tell us that part?" Jack asked.

"See, you're making shit up. That's what you're doing."

"No, the neighbor didn't tell us that. Colin did. He admitted that he wanted to try to get her to take him back," Jack said.

"That's a lie!" Lauren shouted. Her face grew red.

"He did go back and then Julia died shortly afterwards," Jack stated.

"After he called and said he needed time to cool off, what did you do?" Thomas asked quickly.

Lauren looked lost, unsure of which way to turn.

"Where did you go? Colin told us you weren't home and that you didn't come back until the next day," Jack pressed.

"My sister wasn't feeling well. I went to check on her and ended up staying the night."

"Could it be possible that you left because you were angry with Colin for going back to Julia? He informed us that he told you what he was doing. Weren't you suspicious of why he was going back?"

"NO! You're making it seem like we're guilty. Why would we want Julia dead? How do I get my money now that she's dead?"

"You weren't going to get anything if she was alive either," Jack said. A moment of cold silence could be felt in the room.

"Why was Colin at this convention? The convention where you met him?" Val asked.

"He was there with Julia. She was the one attending the convention. It was all about pathology." Lauren's words were clipped.

"It was a pathology convention?" Val inquired. "So, you were there with a pathologist. A pathologist from Buffalo?"

"Yes. Why on earth would I be there otherwise?" she said quickly, maybe a little too quickly. She appeared to want to pull the words back in. The next question was unavoidable.

"What's this pathologist's name?"

Lauren hesitated again, staring at Val. Val repeated the question.

"Phillip Blythe," she said.

30

"So, the elusive Dr. Blythe has finally agreed to talk to us." Thomas turned towards Gavin. "Thank you for making this arrangement."

The three men stopped just outside the doctor's office. "Dr. Blythe has agreed to meet on an informal basis. I hope you won't resort to any line of questioning he might find offensive," Gavin said, stressing the unofficial nature of the interview. "If there is a possibility that he's going to be blindsided, especially without a lawyer present, there will be hell to pay."

"Of course, Mitch, I would never do anything offensive," Thomas said breezily.

As they entered the room Dr. Blythe stood up and welcomed them in a friendly manner, seemingly relaxed and not worried. They each took a chair around his desk. After a few thanks to the doctor for his time, the meeting began with Blythe speaking first. "I hear this meeting is about a woman named Lauren Fitzgibbons."

"That's correct."

"I knew her a long time ago," Blythe admitted.

"In what sort of context did you know her?"

"We dated," Blythe said, calmly. He appeared to have no guilt about it.

"How long did you date her?"

"On and off, probably about a year. Our relationship was more off than on. Lauren liked to play the field. She went where the money was. When she finally realized I didn't have any, we were officially off."

"When was the last time you were *on*?" Jack asked.

Blythe took a moment to think about the answer. "That had to be about eight or nine months ago."

"Do you still keep in contact?"

"No," he said flatly.

"Did you know about Julia's *problem* with her?"

"She told me about the lawsuit one day. I think she just wanted someone to talk to. I listened."

"Did you tell Julia about your past relationship with Lauren?"

"No, I saw no reason to. I hadn't spoken to or seen Lauren in a while. There was no reason to upset Julia."

"I can understand that you wouldn't want to upset Julia." Thomas purposely waited a moment before he asked, "Wasn't she in charge of reviewing your cases?" Thomas knew he was stepping over the line with this question. Gavin shot him a look of warning.

"Yes," Blythe said slowly.

"Yes?" Thomas raised his eyebrows. "Didn't that make you *a little annoyed*?"

"I wasn't happy with the situation but I had nothing personal against Julia." He looked over at Gavin. The severe glare indicated that he'd better not let Thomas go any further.

"It wouldn't be strange if you were annoyed. It would be normal to be irritated with the person who is... How should I say this? *Looking over your shoulder*." Thomas pressed on, ignoring the eye contact between Blythe and Gavin. Gavin, though, remained silent and Thomas didn't know why.

Phillip Blythe became visibly agitated but he took a second and composed himself. He tented his fingers together, inhaled deeply and answered, "Julia and I shared an amiable professional relationship. I respected her opinion. If I had done something wrong, I would have valued her judgment on the matter."

"She agreed with many of your reports, especially about this dog attack on a two-year old boy." Jack opened a folder and flipped through the files.

Blythe just shrugged his shoulders. "So?"

"Let's discuss what she said in some of these other reports. The ones she handed in to your superiors." Jack read from the documents in front of him. "It appears as if Dr. Phillip Blythe may be overworked. He has made several serious errors in judgment that are hard to overlook. I wouldn't expect these types of mistakes from a medical resident let alone the chief medical examiner." Jack glanced up from the folder and stared at Blythe, waiting for a response.

Phillip Blythe's face went white, his eyes opened wide and it took a second before he said, "I never saw that report."

"Now, sir, this is dated almost two months ago. Someone must have reviewed this with you since that time. I'm sure you have been privy to this. You must have known what she said about you."

Blythe stared blankly. "I had no idea." He sounded genuinely stunned.

"Okay, I think this line of questioning has gone far enough," Gavin finally announced.

"Of course. I'm sorry, doctor, I didn't mean to imply anything improper," Jack said.

Gavin got up to leave, indicating they all should follow. Both

Thomas and Jack rose, but after taking a few steps Thomas stopped. "You took Lauren to a pathology convention. Am I right?"

"Yes," Blythe answered, his tone questioning.

"Did you continue your relationship with Lauren after it?"

"Not for very long."

"Why was that?"

"We broke up. She found someone else." Blythe's response came out sharp. It was obvious that Lauren's brush-off hadn't sat well with him. Thomas decided to continue the interrogation, ignoring the looks from Gavin. He had Blythe right where he wanted him.

"She found Colin Turner, didn't she?" Thomas's words were to the point.

"I have no idea who she found after me." Blythe again appeared completely surprised.

"Lauren tells us she met Colin at your convention. You left Lauren alone and Julia had gone to bed early. Lauren went to the bar and met Colin."

"I didn't know any of this!" Blythe just stared at the two of them, his mouth open.

Gavin tried to grab Thomas by his arm to escort him out, but couldn't quite manage it before Thomas spoke again.

"Lauren left you for Colin and Julia was checking over your shoulder. Now, let's see, what happens next? Julia is killed. Colin's in jail, and Lauren loses half her face to an infection. What brilliant payback you must feel."

"How dare you!" Phillip Blythe jumped up. "I'm not listening to any more of this crap." He stormed to the door, yelling at Gavin, "The next time you want to talk to me it will be through my lawyer. I'm not through with you yet, Mitch, coming in here with this shit! How dare you! Just wait until I'm through talking to your supervisor: you'll be writing parking tickets for a living by the time I'm done." And with that Blythe walked out of the office, slamming the door hard enough to rattle the hinges.

31

"I thought that meeting with Dr. Blythe went well," Jack said to Thomas. The tone was tongue-in-cheek. He sat back on the couch in their hotel room and kicked off his shoes.

"I'll have to agree. It wasn't *all* that bad," Thomas added in dry sarcasm. He opened a bottle of scotch and poured a drink for Jack and himself. He knew what happened with Dr. Blythe wasn't good and hoped the alcohol might help dull the pain. That was his best suspect and any hope of questioning Blythe again, or really even investigating him further, especially without any concrete evidence, was gone. He shook his head as he handed Jack the glass. "I thought we had him back there."

"We had our one chance, we jumped, and we fell flat on our faces. It happens. We were overconfident." Jack motioned towards a large envelope Thomas was holding, an envelope that was waiting for them when they arrived back at the hotel. "What's in there?"

"Probably more bad news," Thomas said, and then rather than opening it, he tossed it onto the coffee table. "This case is so close and yet so far. It's swimming all around us and yet I can't grab hold of any part and reel it in. Why is this one so slippery?

What are we missing?" He took a large sip from his glass. "Damn it! How in the hell did we not win that battle with Blythe?"

"Are we overlooking another possible suspect? Are we being too narrow-minded?" Jack asked. "Who besides Blythe had motive?"

Thomas just gave him an uninterested look. "It's not just motive. This crime also has *ability* with it. Someone has to have had the ability to pull it off. Blythe is top of the list for ability. He's a doctor for Christ's sake. And he definitely has motive. Losing Lauren to Colin, Julia reviewing his cases. These are big reasons. Who else has motive and ability? No one."

Jack was silent and Thomas knew he was right. There was no one else. Jack finally said, "So, you never told me what was in the envelope?"

"Julia DeHaviland's financial records."

"That finally came?" Jack sat up and eagerly reached for it. "God, we asked for that when we first arrived, almost three weeks ago. Detective Gavin's been holding onto it for so long that I thought he would never give it to us."

"Yes, it was about time Gavin handed them over. Funny that he didn't say anything about this when we were with him earlier," Thomas said without any emotion. If Gavin had finally given these records to him, with no discussion about them, it was because they had no real impact on this case. Colin was still very guilty.

Jack opened the seal and slid out the documents. He looked through them for a while and then exhaled slowly before setting them aside. "Julia DeHaviland gets the last laugh."

"How so?" Thomas's eyes were fixed on Jack, waiting for the answer.

"First, there's no trail in her bank records indicating movements of large amounts of cash in or out. Nothing to show that she was hiding anything. According to this, she made very little money. She was basically broke all along."

"That can't be right," Thomas said, stunned. "How could a plastic surgeon not have any money?"

"Oh, the account was opened with a fairly large sum. It covered the down payment on the house and also the expenses for a few months. But there are no deposits until Julia was hired at the medical examiner's office. The only deposits were her paychecks from there. And what she earned wasn't enough to cover the bills each month by this time. Some bills were paid, others weren't. Then she just stopped paying everything altogether. The collection notices started quite a while ago and have just been multiplying."

"There must be another account."

"Not according to all of this." Jack pointed to the papers that were strewn across the coffee table.

"Is it possible that Julia placed all of her wealth in her assets? That she didn't have a large amount of liquid cash?"

"No. There's really no equity in these assets. She owed a lot of money on them, especially for the building she was constructing for her plastic surgery practice." He held up the loan papers so that Thomas could see.

"My God, look at how much money she borrowed. How do you get that without some type of collateral?"

"Maybe plastic surgeons are considered a good risk?"

"Unless they die." Thomas exhaled. "Well, that explains why she wasn't making anything. She was in the process of building this practice."

"So, the woman Colin is trying to screw over for her money was poorer than a church mouse. What an unlucky bastard." Jack laughed and pulled out another document. "And on top of that, here's the cancellation notice for her malpractice policy—

and he thought that she was bluffing with this. She wasn't giving him a penny. Not that she had one to give."

"As I told you, Jack, this is all just more bad news. In fact, it's very bad news. These documents only add to the proof that he's guilty. He said he was a player. The reason he gave us for being innocent was that he needed Julia alive. He wanted to string her along so she wouldn't ruin him financially. If he found out she had nothing all along, that there was no way he could possibly get a cent from her and that he was already financially ruined, that's motive to kill her. His excuse goes out the window. This is why Detective Gavin finally gave these to us." Thomas sat down on the couch. "Colin's screwed. Hell, maybe he should be."

Jack's phone rang and he looked down at the text. "It's Val. She's in the lobby. I almost forgot that I told her to meet me at this time. I thought I'd have some interesting news to tell her about Dr. Blythe. Well, I guess it could still be called *interesting*." He took one last swallow from his glass, finishing the contents. Then slid his shoes back on. As he was leaving he took one more look at Julia's documents and picked them up. "Maybe Julia spoke to Val about some of this," he said. "It wouldn't hurt to ask. We have nothing to lose at this point."

32

Val sat uncomfortably in the hotel lobby chair. The Naugahyde felt sticky and smelled of stale coffee. She had hoped that Jack was going to tell her what happened with Dr. Blythe. But instead he asked her to look at Julia's documents.

Julia's finances were laid out in front of her. She almost felt guilty for looking at such personal information, peering into a very private matter that her friend probably fought hard to keep hidden. No matter how hard she looked though, there was really nothing that she could add.

"Jack, I told you the first day I met you that Julia never said to me what she did with her money. How she planned to win the financial battle with Colin was something I don't know. I'm not sure how going through her paperwork will help."

"According to this," said Jack, "Julia never really had any money at all. Is this a possibility?"

"It's a possibility, but I really don't know." Val sat back from the table and crossed her arms.

"I knew it was a long shot." Jack looked into her eyes and then laughed.

"What's so funny?" she asked, wondering where he was finding humor in this situation.

"You didn't like me very much on that first day, did you? The day when we first met in your very small office."

Val felt her face get hot. He was right. She hated him that day, and for a few more after that.

"You don't have to answer," Jack said. "You *do* like me now?"

Her face grew hotter. He was good-looking, famous and smart. He treated her as an equal and had been interested to get her involved and hear her opinion. Despite that, he had never asked her about her scar, and why she wasn't practicing dentistry anymore. For Jack, who was always inquisitive, always challenging, this was the one detail he didn't seem to need to know and Val had no idea why. Maybe he was allowing her personal space and he wasn't going to intrude. Maybe, the person she once thought was an egotistical bastard was a nice guy, when he wanted to be.

She didn't hesitate when she said, "Yes, I like you now."

"That's all that matters." He smiled.

She smiled back. Trying to control her emotions, she picked up Julia's malpractice notice, hoping to distract herself long enough to get over the attraction she was feeling towards Jack. She glanced over the explanation for the cancellation. It was all pretty standard insurance company verbiage. After a few minutes, she finally collected herself enough and was ready to move the conversation on to something else. Val was dying to know what happened with Dr. Blythe. She went to set the document down, but her hand stopped midway to the table.

"Hey, wait a minute." Val's gaze fixed on a few key phrases and numbers. "This can't be correct."

"What is it?"

"She cancelled the insurance policy."

Jack had a blank expression. "I don't see the significance.

Julia told Colin that she did so that he couldn't get the money. We know that already."

"Look at this date." She pointed the numbers out to Jack. "The date of the cancellation."

Jack narrowed his eyes, peering at the line Val had her finger on. She could tell that he still didn't see the point.

"It's before the lawsuit started," she said. "Why would she have done this?"

"She must have known it was coming. That it was inevitable. Val, she cancelled this policy because she wanted to have nothing to give Colin. It all fits with her plan."

"There's a problem with that plan," she said, and received a quizzical look from Jack.

He leaned forward. "And what would that be?"

"The day she died, she told me that she was meeting with her lawyer." Val shook her head in astonishment. How did she pay this person? The malpractice policy would have covered all of her legal fees. If she cancelled the policy the lawyer wouldn't have been paid through the insurance carrier. This would have been out of her own pocket."

"And this would have been expensive?" Jack said enthusiastically.

"Hell, yes."

Jack's face lit up, and as he put his hand to his forehead, Val prodded his arm and said, "Care to tell me what's going on?"

"Of course, but let me ask this question first. Are you interested in working undercover again? Because what you did with Lauren Fitzgibbons the other day was utterly brilliant."

33

J ack's compliment about her undercover work hit home, and Val rode with it. She wanted to do this. She hungered for it. She had once felt passion for her profession as a dentist, but this surpassed it. The night before she was to meet Julia's lawyer, she barely slept. Adrenaline was fueling a high that was hard to come down from.

"Mr. Underwood, how did your professional relationship with Julia DeHaviland begin? You were the defense attorney for her lawsuit, correct?" Jack asked.

Tracking down the name of Julia's lawyer hadn't been easy. She didn't have it listed in any of her records. Jack had finally managed to get it from Lauren Fitzgibbon's attorney, who had met with Bradley Underwood just before Julia's death.

Val sat next to Jack, trying to relax as she waited her turn. She was introduced as his partner. She was supposed to ask her own questions, and was keen to do so. Val was very familiar with malpractice insurance. She had to have a policy when she was in practice, so she knew the dos and don'ts. Cancelling a policy with the threat of a patient bringing a lawsuit would be a stupid thing to do. Sure, it would ruin the plaintiff's chances of getting a large sum of money from the deep pocket of an insurance company, but the person being sued would ultimately be responsible for any payout, not to mention all the legal fees. Those legal fees alone could easily run into six figures.

In essence, Julia cancelled the policy so that Lauren and Colin wouldn't benefit from a multi-million-dollar award, but she hired a lawyer that would have cost her a considerable sum. This meant that she had the money to pay him.

"She called my office one day and made an appointment. It was that simple." Bradley sat behind a cheaply made desk, which Val guessed was veneered and not solid wood. The carpeting in both the office and hallway was standard industrial-grade steel gray, worn in many places by years of traffic. Mass-produced art hung on the walls. As she looked around at the unimpressive surroundings, Val couldn't help but wonder how and why Julia picked Bradley Underwood as her lawyer.

"And you were paid privately?" Jack asked.

"Yes."

"What is your retainer?" Val joined in.

"Twenty thousand."

She was stunned at the amount and fought hard not to show it on her face. "Is that all you asked for in this case?"

"No. I also have an hourly fee once the retainer is exhausted. I usually ask for this to be paid as a lump sum at the end."

"How much did that total up to the date she died?" Val asked a little too quickly, not thinking the question all the way through.

Bradley looked at her oddly. "I'm really not at liberty to divulge that kind of information."

Val took a deep breath. "Okay. Hypothetically, if someone were to hire your services, and you were to put in the same amount of time as you did in Julia's case up until her death, what would a ballpark figure be?"

Bradley shrugged his shoulders.

"Over twenty thousand?" Val pressed.

"Possibly. Give or take." Bradley smiled and Val couldn't help but think that amount was definitely on the *give* end.

Val decided to go out on a limb here. "Didn't you think it was strange that she gave you cash and not a check for the retainer?" It had to have been in cash. There was no record of Julia paying by check.

"No. She was going through a divorce, as you must know. Her husband was after her money and it was easier for her this way."

Julia paid twenty thousand in cash? Val thought.

"As far as the lump sum payment at the end then, weren't you worried how Julia would be able to pay? I mean, how could she compensate you in the end if she also had to give Lauren a large award? Julia would be broke. Neither of you would get anything."

"What do you mean?" Bradley shook his head in confusion. "Julia's malpractice policy would have covered any award."

Val grew puzzled. "But Julia had no malpractice insurance."

"That's incorrect. She had a pretty large policy. Ten million from what I recall," Bradley said confidently.

"Oh, it's very correct. She cancelled it. Cancelled it before she hired you." Val's thoughts quickly fired. *How could he not have known this?*

Bradley got up from his chair, walked over to a filing cabinet and began thumbing through the folders. He pulled one out. "I have a copy of her policy right here."

"I can also show you a copy of the cancellation notice for that," Val said. "If you thought Julia had a policy, didn't you find it was strange that she would hire you privately? The insurance carrier would have assigned a lawyer to her. It would have been covered under that policy."

"She told me she didn't like the lawyer they picked for her. In fact, Julia said she couldn't stand her." Bradley sat back down. "Look, she never said anything to me about not having malpractice insurance. Not once. In fact, at every meeting we had she led me to believe that she had it. Jesus, the day she died, I advised her to settle the case. She had no chance of winning. Julia did this procedure as a favor to Lauren and probably should have waited until the office opened. It really was her downfall."

"Excuse me? This was done in an office that wasn't even opened yet?" Val asked.

"Yes, it was still being built. All of the equipment was in. I think all that was left to do was place some fixtures in the bathrooms, hang wallpaper and lay a rug in the waiting room. So basically, it was close, but there was no staff to witness the event. Julia hadn't hired anyone because she wasn't treating patients yet. She was alone with Lauren when she removed the mole and alone with her when she did the follow-up visit. There was no one to support her story."

"Why would Julia do this?" Val said more to herself than to those in the room.

Bradley Underwood said, "In Julia's defense, she thought Lauren was her friend. I've seen many doctors screw themselves because they take care of so-called friends after hours in less-than-ideal settings."

"Where was Julia practicing before this incident?" asked Val.

"Julia used to belong to an organization that performed medical services in developing countries. It was tough work. She got burned-out and decided to go back to the US and set up her own office. So, she had no prior practice."

"And she never opened *this* office?"

"No. The problem with Lauren stopped that," said Bradley. "Instead, she got the job at the medical examiner's office. She also had a degree in pathology and thought it would be better to work on the dead. The lawsuit really destroyed her confidence.

It's not uncommon for someone who is accused of malpractice to shy away from his or her profession for a while. Julia was done with shying away. She wanted to fight Lauren and Colin and be a plastic surgeon again."

Once they were outside, Jack patted Val on the shoulder. "I'm impressed, Val. That was awesome questioning."

She loved the compliment, but something bothered her. "I can't get over the fact that she cancelled the policy, for whatever act of revenge she hoped to get by doing this. All she does is screw herself. If Julia wanted to be a plastic surgeon again, if this was her reason for hiring Bradley Underwood—so that he would fight this case—why cancel the policy? Why cancel it before the lawsuit even started? A lawsuit she knew she was going to lose. After this was over, there would be no way in hell Julia would ever be a plastic surgeon again. She would be broke, a bad credit risk and basically uninsurable again. But my bigger problem is that she lied to Bradley about the policy to begin with and that makes me feel that she also lied to him about her reasons for wanting to fight this case. Why would she have done this?"

"We still haven't answered our original question either. Where did she get the money to pay Bradley, especially if she had no previous plastic surgery practice?" Jack added.

34

I t was only 9am and Val had already consumed four cups of coffee. As she ran down the hall to the ladies' room she looked at her phone. There were two messages from Jack and three from Gwen, all within the last couple of minutes. She was about to read them when she bumped into Zoe.

"I've been looking for you," said the toxicologist. "The results on the testing of the samples from the skulls for the muscle-paralyzing drug pancuronium are finished."

Val completely forget about the need to pee. "*And*?"

"The unknown skull found in the Devil's Hole Park was inconclusive for it, and so was the first one found—the one discovered in Chestnut Ridge Park. I'm not surprised by that, though. It was pretty dried out and that could have had a big effect on the testing. But Francine Donohue was positive for it. This new test actually seems to work. According to this, both Samantha Ritcher and her sister Francine Donohue had this drug in their system."

Val wanted to hug Zoe for giving her such good news but then Zoe said something that made her legs feel weak.

"But Dr. Blythe isn't buying it."

Dr. Blythe knows about the drug testing, thought Val, horror mounting.

Zoe must have seen Val's face, because she added quickly, "I only said anything to him because I thought he would be interested to hear that this type of analysis was possible and that it suggested Francine had this drug in her system too." She sighed. "But he was concerned that this technique was experimental and he couldn't possibly accept this as scientific proof. He needed more to go on to consider Samantha's death related to Francine's, let alone prove Francine had something like pancuronium in her system." Zoe ended by stressing to Val that Dr. Blythe was really upset that she would even do this kind of testing. "He wants to know why I did it."

The pit of Val's stomach dropped. Dr. Blythe would certainly find out she also was involved with this experiment too, if he didn't know already. He must have asked Zoe how she got the bone specimens. *Oh God, does he know I gave them to Zoe?*

"He's going to rule Samantha's death an accident," she said. "Sorry, I thought we had something there."

Zoe started to go into more detail about how mad Blythe had been. Val couldn't listen anymore. With each word she knew how dangerous the situation was becoming and made an excuse to be on her way. She needed to think this through. Quickly.

Val was almost to her office when she heard someone yelling her name. It was Candace, calling for her to stop. Val halted and turned. When she did, her pulse exploded. Candace had a slip of paper in her hand.

"You received this message today." She handed Val a note. "The woman seemed a little irritated that you haven't returned her other messages."

Val exhaled so strongly that she almost became light-headed. Candace made no mention of any skull specimens. And she didn't say that Dr. Blythe wanted to see her about said skull specimens. Val read the message and she tried to comprehend what she was seeing. "Did this person say what this was in regards to?" she managed to ask.

"No, but she did say she needed to talk you immediately."

What on earth could this be about? Val didn't want to deal with out-of-the-blue problems right now. Unfortunately, she had to. The message was from the Florida State licensing department. They had questions about her dental license. Val had no idea what they could possibly want. She walked away from Candace without any further conversation and went to her office. At this point it was hard to even think straight.

She punched in the phone number and after a few rings someone answered.

"Division of professional regulation, board of examiners for the State of Florida, Stephanie Carter speaking, how may I help you."

"My name is Dr. Valentina Knight. I received a message to call you back."

Stephanie was quiet for a couple of seconds. Val could hear computer keys clacking in the background. "Ah, yes, Dr. Knight. I have been trying to track you down. You're a hard one to get a hold of."

"I'm sorry, what is this in regards to?" Val was curt, wanting to know why this woman was calling her. There was a lot on her mind and she wanted to get this nuisance out of the way.

"We're going to need you to fill out a new application. It's because of the lapse, you see. You can't just renew anymore if it's after one year of the expiration date."

"Renew what?" Val responded, thoroughly confused.

"Your license to practice dentistry."

"My dental license? I'm not renewing my Florida license," Val said.

Stephanie ignored her response and continued. "If it was less than a year on the lapse we would just need a continuing education record and a CPR card to prove your cardiopulmonary resuscitation course was taken. You've sent both, but unfortunately, that won't be enough."

"There must be some mistake, I never filed paperwork for the renewal. I never sent you anything." Val's voice wavered. She started to grow worried.

"I have an application right in front of me. You *are* Dr. Valentina Knight?" She spelled the last name and then read Val's Florida license number.

"That *is* correct." Val's heart started to pound. This wasn't some simple mistake. "Can you tell me the date on the application?"

Stephanie stated the date and Val nearly dropped the phone. It was filed a few days after she was hired at the medical examiner's office.

"Thank you very much," Val said, her voice trembling. "But I've changed my mind on the renewal." She didn't give Stephanie Carter time to say much more before hanging up.

Val just stared at the wall in shock. Someone was trying to renew her Florida license. Someone sent in her personal information to do so. Someone also sent in a CPR card and continuing education record. She hadn't taken any continuing education in over a year and her CPR certification was out of date. Val cupped her hand over her mouth and sat in the chair. Her skin felt prickly as every nerve came alive with fear. *What in the hell is going on?*

"There you are. I've been trying to call you," Gwen said as she entered the office. "I heard from Jack. He's been trying to reach you too. Why haven't you answered your phone? He and Thomas are on the way to interview Colin again as we speak, and that's not all!"

Val felt her head spinning. So much was happening all at

once. Her thoughts quickly leapt from one nightmare to the next and she tried hard not to break down.

"Lauren Fitzgibbons is back in the hospital. Her infection just worsened!" Gwen said.

"Is she all right?" Val managed to get out.

"No. She's critical."

35

C olin slumped over the table in the interrogation room. A month in prison had taken its toll. He looked tired and defeated. Arrogant smiles no longer stretched across his face, the cocky attitude had been replaced with the solemn image of hopeless desperation. When told of Lauren's condition he didn't seem to care and appeared far more concerned with his own fate.

"I told you before, I don't know how that other woman's DNA got on my clothing," Colin said. Thomas and Jack had been questioning him for nearly two hours and were no further along than when they first started. Gavin sat quietly in the corner. He hadn't said two words since they began.

"I think my client's had enough," Colin's lawyer said firmly.

"He's *my* client too." Thomas's tone was sharp. He pulled a handkerchief from his pocket and wiped his forehead. He hadn't felt well all morning and this interview was draining what little energy he had left. Turning to Colin, he stated as strongly as he could, "Tell me again how Julia's blood got on your clothes then. Let's start there."

Colin put his hands to his head, running his fingers through his hair, holding the strands back from his face. He sat up and continued. "I got her blood on me after I grabbed her wrist. She had a towel wrapped around it and it was dripping with blood. Now that I remember, it wasn't just wet with blood. It was soaked with water too. She was washing her wrist under the faucet and had the towel wrapped around it. The bloody water from the towel splashed my shirt and I know at some point I wiped my hands on my pant leg."

"What happened next?"

"She ran to the bathroom, I followed her and—"

Thomas interrupted him. "Did you do anything before going after her?"

"I opened the cupboard door to grab another towel for her."

"Okay, then you followed her to the bathroom."

"Yes, I stood outside the door trying to get her to let me in."

"How long before she opened the door?"

"Not long. She yelled out that she was okay and she was bandaging her wrist. She came out a few minutes later."

"She didn't want you to take her to the hospital?" Gavin finally spoke up.

"I suggested it. She was embarrassed about what she did and didn't want anyone to know. She said she took care of it and wasn't worried."

"Your wife cuts herself badly enough to get blood all over you and she's not worried about it?" Gavin said. He stared at Colin, challenging him.

"Look, like I told you before. She was a surgeon. Who the hell am I to argue with her about things like that?" Colin snapped.

Gavin got up from his chair and walked over to Colin. He stood within inches of him. "What a convenient excuse."

Colin lurched forward but the shackles kept him confined to

his seat. His lawyer grabbed him by the arm to keep him from saying anything more.

"What happened after she came out of the bathroom? You stayed for quite a while," Thomas said.

"We talked about old times, like when we first met. We drank some wine. I thought she'd forgiven me."

The room went silent for a moment. Thomas reached for a pitcher of water that sat in the middle of the table and poured a glass, drinking nearly all of it in a few gulps. He felt a little light-headed now and hoped the cool water would help.

"Did you know Julia had a life insurance policy?" Gavin asked.

Colin wasn't put off by the question. In fact, it appeared to be the easiest one of the day and he answered without hesitation.

"Yeah. She had the policy before we were married. She left the money to a friend of hers."

"Who was this friend?"

"Molly Dolan."

"What can you tell us about her?"

"I never met her."

Thomas couldn't help but feel that Gavin was fishing with this question, looking for another reason to prove Colin guilty. Colin wasn't getting his wife's life insurance either. And he knew it.

"Can you think of anything else? About Julia? About that night?" Thomas asked, picking up the water pitcher again.

Colin shook his head. "But I have a question for you." He pointed to Thomas. "How the hell did her DNA stay on my clothes when she washed them?"

"She washed your clothes?" Gavin nearly laughed out loud. "This is ridiculous. Your wife goes from trying to ruin you, to doing your laundry all in a matter of what, an hour or two?"

Jack's head immediately turned towards Thomas, and their

eyes locked, the disclosure was a revelation. Thomas shook his head, signaling for Jack to not say a word.

"Yeah, she did my laundry," Colin sneered. "I couldn't go back to Lauren covered in blood and Julia offered to do it. That's why I was there for so long. How do I have her DNA on my clothing if they were washed?"

"I'll look into it," Thomas said.

They wrapped up the questioning and everyone exited the interrogation room. Gavin caught Thomas and Jack in the hallway. "That was the biggest bunch of laughable crap I ever heard from a suspect. If you ask me, he did his own laundry to get rid of the DNA and is upset because he didn't do a good job."

"Unless an oxygen-producing detergent was used, the DNA wouldn't have been removed," Jack said.

"Obviously. Only he didn't know that." Gavin walked away and left Thomas and Jack standing in the hallway.

"Thomas, are you all right? You've looked pale all during the interview. But now you look worse. In fact, you're sweating quite a lot."

"I'm fine. They just need to turn some air conditioning on in this goddamn hot building." Thomas put his hand to his head and wiped his brow. He moved his hand to his chest and looked for a place to sit down. There was a chair a few feet in front of him. He collapsed before he made it.

36

Val couldn't sit still. Someone had tried to renew her dental license, sending in false documentation to do so. Someone was after her, confirmed, and had been for some time.

She slowly walked into Detective Gavin's office. He had asked her to meet with him and she wasn't sure what to make of the invitation.

She'd been avoiding him because lately it was impossible to talk with him about anything without him warning her to stay away from Jack and Thomas. Whatever suspicion or thought she tried to share, his response was the same: "They're putting *fantasies* into your head." To Gavin's mind, Colin was guilty. End of story. The two criminal investigators were in this only for money and fame. Not justice. "They'll do anything to spin the story in Colin's favor," he said. "If Colin goes free, they endorse their celebrity status. It attracts more high-profile, hence higher-paying, customers. This is their game, Val."

So this time Gavin caught her off guard when he asked how Thomas was doing.

Val sighed. "There's no change. Thomas had a heart attack

yesterday afternoon, but then slipped into a coma last night. The situation is critical. Jack's with him now and has pretty much been at his bedside the whole time."

Val had offered to come to the hospital to keep him company but Jack declined. He'd prefer to be alone, he said, adding, "I'd rather you and Gwen were following up on that lead about the washing machine."

A washer readily transfers DNA. In this case, all that would have been required was to throw something into the load containing Francine's DNA—for example, her missing bloody sheet—and it would deposit on everything in the machine. Regular detergent does not destroy DNA—only an oxygen-producing one does. Her DNA ended up on Colin's pants—the same pants that supposedly came out of Julia's washer.

"I'm very sorry to hear about Thomas," Gavin said with genuine sympathy. "Did Julia ever mention a Molly Dolan to you?"

The name meant nothing to Val. She shook her head, no. "Why do you ask?"

"Julia had a pretty big life insurance policy. Ms. Dolan was her friend and former co-worker. She's the beneficiary. She knows that you were also a good friend of Julia's and wanted me to let you know that she'll do good things with the money, in Julia's name of course."

"Why did she leave it to a friend? Had she recently changed it from her husband?" Val sat up straight, interested, and moved to the edge of her chair. An insurance policy linked Jeanne Coleman and Lorelei Sebastian and here it was again. Her heart began to beat faster.

"She took this out before she married Colin. He was never an intended beneficiary. Ms. Dolan told us what she believed Julia's motivations to be. It seems Julia discussed this matter in some detail with her."

"Which was?" Val's thoughts fired in rapid succession.

"Molly Dolan works for an organization that provides medical and dental care to people in developing countries. Julia worked with her on these missions quite a bit. She left the money to help Molly with this cause. Julia was quite the humanitarian."

Val remembered that Bradley Underwood had said the same thing about Julia's previous employment. "How much was the policy for?" Val asked.

"Three million dollars."

Val just stared, boggled by the amount. "Isn't that a reason to have some concern about Ms. Dolan? Three million dollars is quite a lot."

"That kind of money certainly could make her a suspect, and we did investigate that likelihood. But there's nothing in her background to tie her to this case. She's a well-respected missionary who devotes her time and expertise to helping the poor." Gavin stressed, "She is *not* a person of interest."

Val could see it in his eyes as he spoke. Molly Dolan definitely had some influence somewhere with someone. Gavin had no intention of pursuing her. He had probably been warned by his superiors to do no such thing. Gavin kept talking, telling Val about Molly's accomplishments, but Val really wasn't listening. Her mind was elsewhere.

"She couldn't argue when I mentioned that Buffalo was experiencing spring weather as warm as Florida's," he said.

The words caught Val's attention and she snapped, "Excuse me?"

"Oh, I'm sorry, I forgot to mention this. She used to live in the Clearwater area of Florida too. She thought it was odd that the both of you would have that in common. She joked about Floridians having to endure weather like Buffalo's. She told me to share the joke with you. That you'd understand."

"That I'd understand?" Val could barely say the words. Her thoughts spun to the day in Julia's office, the day of her interview. She had told Julia that she lived in Clearwater and now this Molly Dolan knew too.

"Yes. She lived in Florida for almost ten years. She's only in town because of the will. She's leaving for South Africa early next week."

Ten years? The same amount of time I lived in Florida? Val swallowed hard. "She's here? In Buffalo?"

"I think she's staying in Ellicottville actually." Gavin took a look at a pad on his desk. "Yep, Ellicottville."

Val couldn't help but notice an address and phone number written on Gavin's pad. She took note of them, and then made an excuse about needing to return to work. As she turned to leave, he had one more announcement.

"Oh. They finally found out what species of bacteria is causing Lauren's infection. It's *Vibrio vulnificus* . The doctors are pretty shocked because it's so unusual. Given her circumstances, they have no idea how she would get something like this," he said. "Anyway, they're giving her a new antibiotic and it seems to be working. They think she's going to pull through."

"What antibiotic are they giving her?" Val asked, waiting anxiously for the answer, sensing what it would be.

"High doses of doxycycline."

37

"Val, we should wait for Jack to return. This isn't a good idea," Gwen said. She couldn't hide the uncertainty in her voice.

"We can't bother him, not with the condition Thomas is in," Val replied, fighting hard to hold everything together both mentally and physically. She hadn't slept in two days and felt like someone had rubbed sand in her eyes, grating them to the point of rawness. Fear and paranoia grabbed control of her judgment.

"Gavin told me that Molly Dolan's going to be leaving the country soon. Once she's gone, she could go anywhere. We may never have the upper hand like this again. We don't know when Jack's coming back. We know where to find her right now. I'm going there, with or without you."

"I have no intention of letting you do this alone," Gwen said, and then let out a deep sigh. "Val, I'm on your side, I really am. I just don't see why you're so suspicious of her. Honestly, you could be wrong, very wrong about this. And if you are, things are going to get bad."

Val was borderline hysterical, her voice shrill. "I'm not

wrong. She knew that I lived in Florida. How did she know that?"

"Julia obviously told her," Gwen said in a calm and even tone. "She was her friend, a friend who was also from Clearwater. It must have come up in conversation."

"But she wanted Gavin to tell me. She wanted me to know this. She said that 'I'd understand.'"

Gwen just stared and Val couldn't help but think that Gwen regarded her as crazy. Val tried to explain. "Let me ask you this. Why is someone trying to renew my Florida license by pretending to be me? Don't you think it's odd that right after I was hired someone tried to do this?"

"Val, anyone could have done that. The fact that you have a Florida license is listed in your employee file. You yourself told me that. Blythe could have seen it."

Val shook her head. "That fact is listed in my file, and Blythe could easily have seen it, but there was only one person who heard a simple lie that I told about it. And that person wasn't Blythe. It was Julia."

Gwen's eyes narrowed in confusion. "What do you mean?"

"The truth is that I don't have a license anymore. It's expired." Val nearly laughed. She'd been so worried that someone would find out about the whopper she'd told about Oliver Solaris she didn't even think about this small one that she'd told about her license. It came out of her mouth in a moment of desperation and was so insignificant that it was easily forgotten, until this point. The license number was listed on her résumé and after she was hired no one asked her to produce any documentation to show if it was current or not. A Florida dental license had no bearing on her position at the Erie County Medical Examiner's Office.

"During my interview, I told Julia that it was due for renewal in a month. It was actually expired, and had been for a while,"

Val said. "Only Julia, or someone she talked to, would think that it needed to be renewed this soon because no one else could have known about it. That's not written anywhere in my employee file or even on my résumé." Val could see that Gwen was starting to understand the significance and she kept the momentum going. "Hell, I didn't even tell *you* that fact until now."

"What do you suggest then?"

"I'm going to meet with Molly Dolan, unannounced. What better opportunity than to just show up on her doorstep? I'm going to call her out."

Gwen grabbed Val's shoulders. "Val, that's what makes me worried about all of this. If she's involved with this, why would she purposely want you to know about living in Clearwater? If she is the one trying to renew your license, impersonating you to do so, wouldn't she want to keep this a secret? It just doesn't make sense."

"If she's involved with this case, she's crazy. She kills people. I would have to say that she doesn't engage in rational behavior."

"But Val, you usually do engage in rational behavior. Though today, I will admit, what you're doing is testing that claim to the limit." Gwen sighed. "Think about it. If she is part of this, and she's crazy, then you're not calling her out. She's calling *you* out."

38

M olly Dolan was staying in an expensive Airbnb in the trendy town of Ellicottville, NY. The drive took about an hour. Gwen sat behind the wheel, discussing the best way to handle the situation. Val eventually began to listen to some reason, confirming they would approach this in a cautious manner. This seemed to calm Gwen down.

Though, thought Val, *I really didn't promise anything.* "The next house should be hers," Val said. "Slow down."

Gwen slowed the car and parked. "Now what?"

Val's pulse raced. She started to have second thoughts about knocking on the door, possibly going inside the house. And possibly being trapped. It would be two against one, but they might not be a match for a woman expert at ripping people apart. "We wait for her to come outside."

Three hours passed before the door opened and a woman walked out.

Molly Dolan worked in developing countries but she looked as if she'd stepped off the pages of a fashion magazine. She had dark red hair cut short, pixie style, and her clothing was straight off the Burberry line. But there was something else about her, and the chic appearance didn't hide it, really it couldn't.

Val's heart began to bang hard. "Holy crap, it can't be. It simply can't be!"

"Can't be what?"

Val jumped out of the car. She was shaking so strongly that she almost fell once her feet touched the ground. Stumbling, she ran forward as best she could.

"Val!" Gwen jumped too, running after her. "Val, stop! What are you doing!"

Molly snapped her head in their direction. Then quickly retreated, backing away in obvious fear of the two women coming at her. She looked towards the door of the house. There was no way she'd make it in time. She put her hands up defensively as Val approached her.

Val stopped within a couple of feet of Molly. "I know what you've done! Why don't you just admit it?" Val yelled.

Gwen's eyes went wide. She grabbed Val's wrist and tried to pull her away. "What in the hell are you doing?" she said through clenched teeth.

Molly put her hand to her chest, her mouth hung open in shock. She looked in Gwen's direction for some explanation for Val's outburst. "What are you talking about?" she asked, frightened. "Who are you?"

"It's Val. Like you don't know."

"Val? Valentina Knight?" Molly narrowed her eyes. She looked thoroughly stunned. "Julia's *friend*?"

Val glared at Molly. "I know everything about you! I've got you!"

Molly jumped back. "Oh my God, you're insane! Stay away from me!" she yelled, quickly reaching for her phone. "Get away from me! I'm calling the police!"

Val broke out of Gwen's grasp and lunged at Molly, trying to pull the phone from her hand. She continued to spew accusations as she yanked at her. Val didn't stop struggling until she felt an intense pain on her arm, forcing her to release the grip on the phone, and Molly. Molly had bitten her.

Val screamed loudly and continued to scream as Gwen grabbed her, dragging her away as Molly ran towards the house, and inside the front door.

"Get a hold of yourself, Val!" Gwen yelled. Her hands were firmly on Val's shoulders, shaking her, trying to drive common sense home. "What happened back there? You're losing it. Jesus Christ, Val, you know I thought this was a bad idea all along. It's just gone from bad to worse. In fact, it doesn't get any worse than this."

"You're right it doesn't get any worse than this. That person isn't Molly Dolan. I knew it from the moment I saw her."

Val couldn't help but notice that Gwen was looking at her as if she was out of her mind.

"Who is it then?" Gwen asked, exhausted.

"Julia DeHaviland!"

39

Over the next hour, several angry messages were left on Val's voicemail. All from Gavin. Molly Dolan had called him. He knew what had happened, and in detail. And he was pissed. Without some proof to support her suspicions though, Val was screwed. She had nothing.

Maybe I am going crazy, Val thought. Molly really appeared stunned by the accusations.

Gwen sat on Val's couch. "Val, procrastinating like this isn't going to change the situation. I wish I could say more, but I never met Julia DeHaviland. I don't know what she looked like."

Val knew Gwen didn't believe her. Hell, at this point, who would? Val finally picked up the phone, calling Gavin to get this part, the reaming-out part, over with.

She winced as he spoke. "Val, did you visit Molly Dolan?" His voice was on edge.

She didn't respond.

"Were you incendiary and accusatory? Did you come off looking like a raving lunatic?" Gavin's anger came clearly down the line.

"Maybe." She faltered. She knew the problems she had just caused for herself and the medical examiner's office.

"She called and complained and is threatening a lawsuit. I can't even repeat what she said about you. She wants a restraining order. She's afraid of you."

"She's afraid of *me*! That's the best crap I've heard in a while. Take a look at her and tell me that you don't believe this isn't Julia!" Val continued to defend herself before he finally managed to interrupt her.

"Val, I can't protect you. You're damn lucky she hasn't pressed charges against you. It's only a matter of time before Dr. Blythe hears about this, if he doesn't know already."

She continued to listen but didn't say anymore. What could she say? With a threat of a lawsuit, Gavin wasn't about to go near Molly Dolan. It was only after he had assured her she wouldn't be bothered again, and Val would be dealt with, that Molly backed off on her threats. Gavin made it clear that this woman was to be left alone.

"What do you think?" Val turned to Gwen for comfort after ending the call. "I guess I'm swimming with the sharks now."

"If you're going to swim with the sharks, you really ought to make sure you don't chum the water," Gwen said, and then put her arm around Val's shoulder. "Dr. Blythe's going to fire you."

"I know."

"Well, I probably won't be far behind."

After Gwen left, Val walked into her bathroom. Her arm throbbed in pain. The bitten spot was red and swollen and a bruise was already forming. Luckily the skin wasn't broken. Inspecting the bite, Val had an idea and knew what she needed to do. Time was ticking. She was due to report for work in the next hour. Dr. Blythe would be waiting for her. She reached into her cupboard and pulled out a box of Q-tips. Softening the tips under the tap water, she swabbed the bitten area for salivary DNA.

When Val arrived at the medical examiner's office Howie grabbed her as soon as she walked in. "I wanted to get you before Candace did. She's looking for you. She's eager to let you know Blythe wants to see you in his office as soon as you get here." He started to say more but Val didn't need him to soften the blow: she knew what was coming.

She thanked Howie, hugging him for his sincerity, deciding not to prolong the inevitable. She looked at her small office space and thought it wouldn't take long to pack her belongings. After her meeting with Dr. Blythe, Val knew she'd be out on the street. Holding her head up as high as she could, she went to his office.

"Dr. Blythe, you wanted to see me."

"Valentina, come in. Please shut the door behind you." As she approached his desk, he pointed to a chair. "Sit."

The event seemed surreal. She was moving in slow motion. Val only hoped that she wouldn't be escorted out by security. She wanted to leave with what little was left of her dignity.

"Why have you been harassing a Molly Dolan? She's phoned me directly and lodged a fairly serious complaint against you and this office. She's even moved out of the Airbnb she was renting so that you couldn't find her again."

Val just shrugged her shoulders. She had no idea what to say, how to respond without sounding crazy.

"Valentina, there's a reason for it. And if you tell me, I'm willing to listen." His voice was searching and his eyes locked on hers. If ever Val had a positive moment with Dr. Blythe this was it. The way he looked at her, the tone in his voice, the fact that he hadn't fired her and showed her the door already, made Val pause. Should she trust him?

"Are you going to fire me?" she asked.

"Not yet. For now, I'm going to place you on a leave of absence, pending review of this matter. This will buy some time." He leaned towards her. "Val, if you can think of anything you need to say, tell me. I'm very interested in anything pertaining to Julia. I might be able to help."

His words were comforting, lulling. And oddly, he hadn't fired her immediately. She thought about the DNA swabs, but just couldn't confide in Dr. Blythe. Not now. She was walking around so many traps that she didn't know which one was ready to grab her. The DNA was something she knew she had to take care of herself.

Val silently left the medical examiner's office. Before heading home, she had one stop—the Erie County Crime Lab. It took less than an hour to drop off her DNA samples, though she did hold one back. The request on the testing was stat. She listed her cell phone number as the point of contact. As a death scene investigator, dropping off samples for testing was common. No one questioned her. No one knew what her current employment status was. A leave of absence was a far cry from termination.

I've got her now! Val almost said it out loud.

Several days later, The DNA results came in. They were negative, proving that Molly Dolan and Julia DeHaviland were not one and the same. Val didn't know which way to turn. This was just impossible.

She had one last hope, something else to test for, but there was no way she could do this without Dr. Blythe's help. Should she take it? He was the only one who could do what she needed. She wished she could talk with Jack but that would be impossible. Today, Thomas was undergoing bypass surgery and she couldn't bother Jack now for guidance. Val needed to stand on her own two feet. She knew she had to, and she knew she could do it. She'd learned to interrogate people, sense deception. Val finally confronted Dr. Blythe.

"Why do you want to help me, Dr. Blythe?" she asked.

"Because she's after me too, Val. She was reviewing my cases and, for some reason, she's after me."

For some reason, she's after me. Val had the same problem. This, they shared.

40

Val put her phone down on her couch. She'd been speaking to Dr. Blythe for nearly a half hour. The last test result was finally in and he explained everything to her. Now to tell Gwen, who was in the chair opposite her, eating some dinner.

A pizza and a box of chicken wings sat on Val's living room coffee table. She and Gwen had already polished off one bottle of wine. Val began to open the second one.

"Only in Buffalo could you find a vintage that's advertised as going well with pizza and wings," Gwen said. Gwen had been staying with Val for the last few days. Val lived in constant fear and until Julia was caught, she didn't want to be alone.

"I think this is cheap crap," Val remarked about the wine as she filled both of their glasses.

"It's called Hot Stuff and has a picture of a chicken wing on the label. What did you think you were going to get when you bought it?"

"Hey, I'm more than likely on a murderer's hit list. I can have what I want to drink to ease that stress."

Gwen didn't laugh. "Val, do you think it's a good idea to trust Dr. Blythe?"

"Absolutely. He just gave me information that shows Julia DeHaviland and Molly Dolan must be one and the same. In fact, he's already told Gavin about it."

Gwen gave a skeptical look. "How did Blythe do that? DNA said they're different people."

"She passed the DNA test but failed the antibody test," Val said.

"Antibody test?"

"Yes. The infection Lauren has. The species is *Vibrio vulnificus*. This one is a rare and virulent strain found in warm water mostly in the coastal area around the Gulf of Mexico. This bug can enter the body one of two ways, either ingestion of contaminated seafood, which makes you physically ill, or through an open wound. We know Lauren got her infection through an opening in her skin during her surgical procedure. Infection of a wound with this kind of bacteria leads to a rapidly spreading skin infection."

Gwen listened carefully as Val continued to explain. "The person, who's claiming to be Molly Dolan had the same infection. She has antibodies to it, antibodies to the same rare strain of *Vibrio*. Her saliva sample proved it. There's a special type of oral fluid that flows out of the gum tissue around the teeth. It's called crevicular fluid. It's clear, and looks just like saliva, but it's similar in content to blood since it's derived from blood plasma. Antibody concentrations are high in this fluid and can be used to detect diseases that an individual has been exposed to."

Gwen looked shocked as she started to see the significance of what Val was telling her.

"Lauren hasn't been outside of Buffalo in over two years, Colin even longer than this. Only one person could have given Lauren this type of infection. Only the person who removed

Lauren's mole could have done it. Julia must have had the infection herself first, then took care of it right away with the correct antibiotic," Val said. "Oh, by the way, they use doxycycline to fight it."

Val took a sip of her wine. "And if you need more to convince you Julia and Molly are one and the same, let me try this. There was only one person again who could have infected Lauren and also have known about my Florida license. There is also only one person who could have done all of this and incriminated Colin by washing his clothes. What are the chances now this is someone other than Julia?"

"Julia passed the DNA test. How did she do that?"

"I think it all has to do with the blood and teeth found in Julia's house. They did match each other, as well as the bloody fingerprint that Colin left, but that crime scene was staged. Thomas and Jack knew it was. If this is true, it's pretty clever because it throws all suspicion away from her. In fact, for all practical purposes, it proves that Molly Dolan and Julia DeHaviland *can't* be one and the same because the evidence left in that house doesn't match Molly."

Gwen's eyes opened wide. "The teeth and blood belong to someone else."

"They have to. Gavin only had the crime lab compare the DNA of the blood and the teeth to other personal items in the house to confirm the identity of Julia. That's pretty standard." Val shook her head. "Even if they were to look for *Molly's* DNA there, *Molly* was Julia's friend. And if *Molly's* DNA *is* found in the house, so what, she visited her friend. She's covered her ass any way you look at it."

"Jesus Christ, Val, this woman is dangerous."

"Dangerous is an understatement. She kills people to get what she wants. She's smart and her moves are calculated. I think she purposely bit me because she knew DNA would clear her. There's no way that was an accident."

"What do you think she wants? I mean, what or who is she after?"

"I think this case is mostly about the insurance money. It's a deadly scam. But the bizarre part is that there are two trails to the same scam that don't seem to come together. Think about it. Jeanne Coleman, leaves her insurance money to Lorelei Sebastian, a woman no one can find. Francine's hiding the documents: she was in on this. She had to have been. And here is where the tree starts to branch. Francine and Julia must have been childhood friends: the picture found in Samantha's apartment suggests it. They were taking the same antibiotic, doxycycline. They must have had the same infection. They're connected. Connected on this scam, somehow. Now Julia leaves her money, a lot of it, to Molly Dolan." Val drained what was left in her glass. "As far as who she's after, I'm on her list."

"Is there enough evidence to at least arrest her?"

"Jesus, I hope so."

41

The car was parked about thirty yards away from the house. The woman who said she was Molly Dolan sat behind the steering wheel, waiting, watching for the right time. One by one the windows had gone dark as the lights were finally turned off. They had been that way for nearly an hour. The people inside should be asleep by now.

After the confrontation at her rental in Ellicottville, Molly made sure to find out who Gwen was. She'd only seen Gwen going into the house tonight. This meant that there were only two of them inside. This should be easier than expected.

Slowly, Molly opened the car door and stepped out. She shut the door softly, then quickly crossed the lawn, rounding to the back of the house, stopping just outside the back door.

Now, how to get in?

That would be simple.

She had been prepared for this moment for a while now. *One should always make things as simple as possible.* She thought back to the day at the medical examiner's office when she had taken Val's keys from her jacket pocket and had a copy made. She had been taken aback when she went to return them and saw the jacket was missing. But she'd always been quick-thinking, so she'd decided at that moment to place the keys on the floor as if they had slipped out of the pocket.

Silently, she entered the kitchen and walked through to the living room. Quickly, she made her way up the stairs, to the bedrooms. There were two. In the first one Gwen rested soundly. Molly pushed open the door to the second; here Val tossed and turned but she didn't seem to be awake.

Molly went back to the first room and watched Gwen for a few minutes, making sure she was soundly asleep. She reached into her bag and pulled out a syringe. Then she hovered over Gwen, waiting for the right moment. She aimed carefully. Then in one quick motion, plunged in the needle.

Gwen eyes flew open at the sting. She stared at the woman who stood over her, as if trying to comprehend what she was seeing, but before any sound could come from her mouth, Gwen's eyes rolled back.

"You're going to be out for a while," Molly whispered. She'd given Gwen a sedative that took effect almost immediately, and more importantly was metabolized completely. In a few hours, it wouldn't be detectable in her system anymore. For now, an earthquake couldn't wake her up. Molly needed Gwen alive. Gwen, in this crime, was going to be the assumed assailant, suspected of killing Val.

In Val's room, the plan was a little different. She wanted Val to truly experience terror before she was ripped apart. So, timing was far more important with the drugs she planned to use now. What strategy beats a victim who can't fight back? It would take almost two minutes for the pancuronium to incapacitate her. That was long enough for Val to fight back and Molly just couldn't risk it.

To solve this problem, she first placed a rag soaked in chloroform gently over Val's face.

Molly couldn't do this with Gwen. There would be a possibility of the chloroform being detected in Gwen's system. For Val, it didn't matter. If drugs were found, it would only incriminate Gwen further.

Val's body jerked as the rag was held over her mouth and nose. She finally went limp as she passed out. Next, Molly gave her the pancuronium and waited.

"Time to wake up, sleepyhead."

Someone was patting Val's cheek. It took a couple of taps before her eyes slowly opened. She tried to lift her arms, to turn her head, but she couldn't move at all and immediately began to panic. Her lungs attempted to inhale as she gasped for air. She felt like a fish out of water, gills moving, but completely ineffectively.

Again, the cheek patting. "Val. Pay attention now. It's Julia. Are you afraid of me?" The tone became taunting. *"You should be."*

Val stared blankly. Her heart banged against her chest. She heard Julia's voice. The sound of it was terrifying. Struggling to move, to do something, to just get out of this, Val realized it was no use. She was trapped.

"Actually, I'm the person you knew as Julia. I stole her identity a long time ago. As you know, I'm calling myself Molly now."

Desperately, Val tried to breathe but it felt as if she had a thousand pounds sitting on her ribcage. Swallowing was also difficult and the back of her throat began to fill with saliva, making her panic more.

"What happened to the real Julia DeHaviland? We both worked for the same organization. Julia made the mistake of telling me about this big new house she had bought in Buffalo.

She was really looking forward to moving into it. She was also getting ready to set up a surgery practice. Julia had quite a large sum in savings, which made it easy for her to do all of this, and easy for me to do what I wanted to do. Two weeks after our mission, we went back to the States. I asked Julia if I could stay with her for a while. She agreed." Molly went quiet for a few seconds and Val couldn't tell what was going on, where Molly was. "After I killed Julia, a friend of mine got me the job at the medical examiner's office and then helped me do the job."

The word *friend* caught Val's attention. She thought, *Oh my God, did I place my confidence in the wrong person?*

Molly laughed, "You know Julia's biggest worry about coming back to the U.S. was that she didn't know anyone in Buffalo. She said that making friends was hard for her. She was happy to have me with her. Honestly, Val, she wasn't a good judge of character."

Val's chest ached terribly and saliva had pooled to the point that she felt like she was drowning. The pain was becoming unbearable. *I have to fight this, or I am going to die.* Val forced herself to pay less attention to the agony and more to the person speaking. There was only one way to escape from this lunatic. And Val had to be ready.

"Why did I kill Julia? It was nothing personal, I just wanted her identity. She was part of my brilliant plan to become wealthy. Do you know how easy it is to assume someone's identity and then make a lot of money? I mean, actually become that person and then become rich? Let me tell you. It's so easy, it's almost shocking, especially if you know what you are doing... *and have the stomach for it.*"

Val begged for her body to move but the drug had to run its course. Molly seemed to think there was plenty of time, because she wasn't in any rush. Val knew she had to let Molly keep believing this. It was the only way out. Val knew how pancuronium worked: she read up on it after she learned that this drug was used on Samantha Ritcher, and this knowledge was going to get her out of this hellish nightmare.

"So many people with this identity theft thing are such small potatoes it's laughable. I don't want your credit card to go shopping for trinkets, or even use your name to get a mortgage. If I want to become you, and if you're still alive, what use is that to me? If you're dead, you can be worth your weight in gold to the right miner."

Val's chest continued to quiver. After a few minutes, the vibration slowed and she was finally able to swallow. Her lungs started to suck in a little more air, and when they did, she inhaled as deeply as she could.

"If you're under the age of fifty, getting a life insurance policy is a pretty uncomplicated thing. Fill out a form, have a visiting nurse come to your house, pee in a cup and bingo, and they'll give you as much as you're willing to pay for. After I became Julia DeHaviland, I bought a three-million-dollar policy. Hell, the insurance company wanted me to buy more. They expect someone with a medical degree to get a large amount of coverage. So, what do I do next? I name Molly Dolan as beneficiary on the policy, and after an appropriate amount of time, Julia's death is staged to look like it just happened. Once she's found dead, I get a big fat check. It was such a brilliant plan, so simple. The only problem is that my partner decided to double-cross me and screw everything up. That partner was Francine Donohue."

Val lay still. The drug was already starting to wear off and the effects would only continue to weaken. Molly couldn't see this happening. She had to think Val was more incapacitated than she actually was.

Lie still.

Don't move.

Don't blink.

"You see, about a year ago, we had this plan set with another person, Jeanne Coleman. She was killed, her teeth removed, her body dismembered, and whatever parts we thought weren't necessary we destroyed. Those we wanted to use at a later date to stage her murder, we stored. We chose her teeth and skull for that part. Of course, we had to clean the crime scene. We couldn't have bloody walls and floors in the apartment. Francine was going to assume Jeanne's identity and had to live as her for a while, long enough to get an insurance policy. In the end, the money would be left to me and we would split the payout."

Molly walked around the bed. Val listened to the sound of her voice, tracking where she was in the room. How close she was to her. She seemed further away now and Val frantically tried to tell what Molly was doing.

"I decided at the last minute not to go through with it, even though we had the insurance policy for Jeanne Coleman. I wanted to save this plan for Julia. The money was a hell, and I mean *a hell*, of a lot more. Francine disagreed, and we argued quite viciously about it. Her rationale was that we were all set, why change it now? My rationale was the payout with Julia would be so much higher. There couldn't be two sets of deaths like this. It was one or the other. Francine was a bitch and so completely unreasonable. Didn't she know whose idea this was to begin with? I couldn't have cared less that she was a dentist and came up with the part of the plan to leave the teeth on the pillow. God, she was acting like she was the mastermind because of this. So, I broke off my partnership with her."

The room went strangely quiet and Val couldn't tell what was going on anymore. Her heart raced. *Was this it? Was Molly going to kill her now?* There was a moment before Molly continued. Val purposely made her breathing shallow.

"Francine went behind my back and changed the beneficiary

on the policy to someone named Lorelei Sebastian. She staged Jeanne's death with the teeth and then began a claim on that insurance policy as Lorelei!" Molly's voice rose dramatically as she spoke. "She jeopardized everything I worked for! For her betrayal, well you know what happened. I thought it was ironic to rip out her teeth and leave them behind. The fact she was a dentist and had her teeth on her pillow threw a wobbler for the investigation now, didn't it?"

Molly kept yelling. "After I killed Francine, I tore that house apart and couldn't find the personal documents she had for her identities of Lorelei and Jeanne. I knew she'd hid them somewhere. I was desperate to find them. They had to be destroyed."

There was almost no hesitation as Molly continued. "I was already living as Julia DeHaviland. I had to change the plan quickly and this took a little creativity. Francine and Julia's murders were now going to be the same as Jeanne Coleman's. It was going to look like a series of murders occurred, a serial killing, and they all were going to be pinned on some unsuspecting fool. That fool was Colin Turner. When I met him at that singles event, I knew he was the one who was going to take the fall for Julia's death. Why not a couple more? He thought he married me for my money. Well, I married him because I needed someone to frame for murder."

Val's eyes blinked reflexively. Her heart pummeled as she prayed Molly hadn't noticed.

"It's even easier to frame someone than to steal their identity. Isn't that a scary thought? You could spend the rest of your life behind bars, or worse yet be sentenced to death, because someone is smart enough to frame you. When I killed Julia, in addition to her sheets, I saved a towel soaked in her blood and a few items that had spatter on it. The blood dried out but that didn't matter, in fact it was a good thing. Dry blood is a good source of DNA evidence, and items like this worked very well in staging a crime. I kept bloody items from all of the victims for this reason. Jesus, you never know what strange courses an investigation will take. The sheet thing eventually was thought of as a signature of the killer. It was never planned as that. Taking the sheets was just a necessity."

Val's thoughts flashed to that day she was in Julia's bedroom, nearly collapsing when she saw blood on the spattered lamp, feeling devastated that Julia was dead. She choked on that memory now.

"The night I staged Julia's death, I had the bloody towel wrapped around my arm, running it under the faucet, soaking it. I told Colin I'd slit my wrist. The water mixed with Julia's blood and hence her DNA. He grabbed the towel to check what I did, to make sure I was okay.

"He's a real prince, isn't he?" Molly said sarcastically. "Anyway, the bloody water was running all over the place. I made sure plenty got on him. Later that night I washed his clothes with the bloody sheet I kept from Francine's apartment. Now, Francine's DNA is on him too. Oh, after I killed Francine, I threw a chewing gum wrapper with Colin's DNA under her bed. It all worked like a charm."

Val's arms felt lighter and she thought if she tried, she could move her hands. Molly's voice was to the left of her. Now was her chance. She quickly tried to wiggle the fingers on her right hand. They moved.

"I kept Francine's skull and arm, stripping the skin on the skull but baking the arm. I thought hell, why not. Honestly it was just meant to be a red herring. I actually got the idea from Phillip Blythe. He thought the first skull found, the one he claimed belonged to Jeanne Coleman, was baked because the post-mortem interval was too long. The post-mortem interval *was* too long!" Molly walked closer to Val and stopped talking for a second. Val wondered if Molly was assessing her for any movement and she remained as still as she could.

"I held my breath during the analysis. It could have killed my entire plan. And when he explained it away for this cause, I nearly peed my pants. What an idiot. This skull belonged to the real Julia DeHaviland and she was dead way before I placed it in Chestnut Ridge Park. I had no choice but to use Julia's. I had no idea what Francine did with Jeanne's actual skull. Well, not until after it was found in Devil's Hole Park. For the DNA comparison, I substituted a piece of the bone surrounding one of Jeanne Coleman's teeth. They were all in autopsy room one."

Suddenly Val felt her entire body tingling, feeling like it was becoming her own again but she continued to be as still as she could.

Molly was right next to the bed. "It was all going well. I thought my new plan was back on track until Francine's sister Samantha bumped into me. She came into the medical examiner's office to find out about getting Francine's teeth released for burial—this was before her other remains were found. She recognized me and asked what the hell I was doing. Why was I calling myself Julia DeHaviland? I gave her a hundred bucks and told her she'd get more if she kept her mouth shut. God, what a drug addict. She was pretty out of it the day she came in. I managed to steal her cell phone when she wasn't looking. I don't even think she knew I took it. I called Colin from it, making it seem like she was corresponding with him, incriminating him further. I also did the same thing with Francine's phone."

Val fought the urge to blink, the urge to move, to test how much mobility she had regained. Right now, she knew she had control of her fingers. Nothing else was confirmed. Unless she could jump out of this bed, she wasn't risking anything.

"Samantha had to die after that meeting. She promised me she wouldn't tell anyone who I really was, but do you think I was going to believe that junkie bitch? I could just see her trying to blackmail me. When I injected her with pancuronium, I never expected she would have an allergic reaction to the stuff. It wasn't my plan to have her die that way."

Lying still, Val listened. Molly's psychopathic and narcissistic personality was evident. She only cared about herself and was only paying attention to herself. This is why she wasn't noticing that the drug was wearing off. Val needed her to keep doing this for a little longer.

Molly leaned on the bed and slowly crawled in, curling up next to Val. She was inches from her face as she spoke, practically whispering in her ear. She reached a hand to Val and softly stroked her hair. Val forced her eyes to stay open. Under no circumstances could she blink now.

Her hand hesitated on Val's head. "I knew as soon as I saw you on the day of your interview I was going to kill you. That's why I hired you. I needed your identity. You'd be a pretty easy one to assume." She let go of Val's hair. "I do have a question. How on earth did you make it this long without getting fired? You getting fired was pivotal to the next phase of my plan. I thought for sure Blythe would have gotten rid of you after *Julia died*. He resented you so much. I made sure of that. What the hell was taking him so long to do so? Phil can be such a putz."

She resumed petting Val's hair, twirling strands between her fingers. Val's eyes ached to blink and she didn't know how much longer she could hold them open.

"After you got fired, the story would be you were so distraught you moved back to Florida. Only in reality, you were dead and I was you living in Florida. But you are a nasty girl. You lied to me about your Florida license. I've had a devil of a time trying to renew it because it's expired. But that's not the worst thing you did. What did you think you were doing showing up at my house with that bitch Gwen? She saw me and I'm sure you told her about me. Were you screwing with me?"

There was a moment of silence. Like she was expecting Val to actually answer.

"I don't tolerate people who screw with me." Molly laughed, tugging hard on the hair in her grasp, jerking Val's head towards her. "Just ask Lauren Fitzgibbons how I take care of those who want to screw with me."

She pulled Val's hair harder.

"I know what you're thinking! Oh, don't you feel sorry for her. She's not innocent at all. I believe one hundred percent she tried to befriend me on purpose, to check me out after she stole my sorry excuse for a husband. So, I got my revenge my way. If she had just stayed away from me, she'd be fine."

Molly stretched out on the bed and let go of Val's hair. She stayed close though. "I had to come out in the open because of that. I was going to be sued and I wasn't ready to stage Julia's death yet. I had to buy a lawyer so that I could drag this out a little more." Molly sounded angry again and she took a few deep breaths.

Val resisted every urge to blink. It was unbearable now. She didn't think she could hold out much longer.

"Why did I do it? Why infect her? Why would I jeopardize my plan, bring the Julia DeHaviland alias out in the open, and have some link to the real me?" she yelled. "Do you think I was going to let that silly bitch get away with trying to screw with me? Lauren's punishment was that she lost her face. There's a lesson to be learned for trying to screw with me. Unfortunately, it's a lesson you're going to learn too, *the hard way*."

Val couldn't control it anymore. As Molly lunged at her, Val finally blinked. Molly saw the movement.

"You're beginning to come around."

Val felt her arms being poked, her ability to move being assessed.

"We still have some time. But really I should get started."

Val knew Molly miscalculated how much time she had.

In the kitchen, Molly rummaged through drawers looking for a knife that would do the best job. After killing Val, she would put Gwen's fingerprints all over it. Some of Val's blood would be placed on Gwen too so that Gwen would be the obvious suspect. The majority of the evidence will incriminate her. She'll never be able to prove that she didn't do it. She can plead until she's blue in the face that she's innocent. Molly laughed when she thought, *Gwen can write to Colin in jail and the two of them can bitch over being set up.*

Molly was ready to return upstairs, but a knock at the back door made her jump. She turned her head towards the sound but remained still, hoping the person would just go away.

The person knocked again and then yelled, "Molly. I know you're in there. Let me in."

She recognized the voice but was really surprised to hear it. How could he have known to find her here? She wasn't prepared for this. The man knocked for a third time, louder.

Before the neighbors could hear the commotion, Molly placed the knife on the counter next to her chloroformed rag and opened the door. She didn't say anything when she saw Howie standing in the open doorway. He walked in and shut the door behind him.

"It's good to see you, Julia," Howie said. "I'd have thought you would have been long gone by now."

"I'm doing what I always have to do, Howie. Fix problems."

"You told me we were going to let Val live."

"Don't be a fool. We can't let her live. She knows too much."

"Not about me."

"Since when was this ever about *you*? I think it's almost sad how you care about her."

"So what if I care about her."

"What did you think? The two of you were going to ride off into the sunset together? God, that's pathetic."

Molly eyed the knife sitting on the counter. She wasn't sure what Howie had in mind with this visit. The more he talked the angrier she became. He was wasting time. Val was only going to be incapacitated for so long.

"I can't let you do it. You're not going to kill her."

Molly hissed, "What a complete idiot you are. This is my game and I make the rules. Your stupidity isn't only dangerous to you, it's dangerous to me too."

"Don't call me stupid! You would've never been able to carry this off without me. I'm the one who got you the job at the medical examiner's office and I'm the one who helped you do the job. You never could have done it without *me*!"

He was right and she needed to calm down, think clearly. She knew what she needed to do to control this situation. There was only one option. "Howie, we shouldn't be arguing over such things. We're in this together. If you want Val to live, we can do that. We just have to figure out a way to make it work for both of us." She patted the kitchen chair and motioned for him to sit. "Let's talk about this."

He did as he was told and sat down at the table. When his back was turned, Molly grabbed the rag from the counter and reached around Howie's head and put it across his face. It only took seconds before the chloroform took effect and he slumped at the table. Then he slid to the floor.

"This is going to hurt me more than it hurts you."

Molly picked up the knife and stabbed him in the stomach. She pulled the knife out and stabbed him again.

"You see, Howie, you became one of my loose ends when you decided to screw with me. This has to be done."

She held the knife up, ready to plunge again, when a loud thud came from upstairs causing her to divert her attention away from Howie. She took the bloody knife and walked towards the stairs. "My, my, sleeping beauty's awake."

Val, still wobbly and dizzy from being drugged, knew she was trapped. There was nowhere to run. The only way out was down the stairs and at that moment, Molly was coming up them.

As fast as she could, Val staggered to the bedroom window. Her hands grabbed the sash, pulling upwards, opening it as far as it would go, hoping to make it look like she escaped out the window.

She heard Molly approaching the top of the stairs. With no time to lose, Val ran to the closet and hid, keeping the door ajar so she could see what was going on. Shaking, breathing hard, she sat curled on the floor of the closet feeling around for any type of weapon she could find. Her hand searched frantically. It froze as soon as she saw Molly enter the room.

Molly walked straight to the window and looked out. It took a second before she slammed the sash down and turned her attention to the room.

"Please, do you think I'm stupid? Jesus Christ. Are you under the bed or in the closet?"

It was a matter time before she would be found. In the closet, she was a sitting duck. As Molly bent down to look under the bed, Val stumbled out, hoping to get to the door and down the stairs. She made it about five feet into the bedroom before she lost her balance and fell to the floor. The effect of the pancuronium still overpowered her. After a few more stumbles, she managed to get up.

The two women stared at each other. Julia held a large butcher's knife. Val stood defenseless.

"Honestly, Val, I must admit that what I'll cherish about the time we've spent together is how much you amused me. You really are precious, in a pedestrian kind of way."

"You were my friend," Val cried out.

"You weren't *mine,*" Molly responded, matter-of-factly. Unfeeling.

"I shared things about myself with you! I trusted you!" Val screamed.

"I know, and in return I gave you back your life by hiring you. You showed up on my doorstep, pathetic as you were and I helped you out, and this is how you repay me! And you want to say we were friends. Is this how you treat your friends? Because maybe this is why you didn't have any."

"You only hired me because you wanted to kill me."

Molly tilted her head, and pursed her lips, thinking about Val's comment. "True."

"You're one sick bitch!" Val yelled.

Molly lunged forward with the knife. Val placed her arms up defensively, and the knife tore through her left hand. With her other hand, she swiped Molly across the face with a clenched fist.

The shock of the blow caused Molly to drop the knife and reach for the hand that hit her. She had Val's wrist in her grasp and held firmly; she pulled back, twisting it as hard as she could.

Val screamed in pain, and tried to lash out, struggling as best she could, but the twisting continued; Julia wouldn't ease up on her grasp. Val finally managed to break free, but not before she felt the snapping of bones.

"I'm sorry. Was that your bad hand or your good one? I can't remember which one is which."

Val cried out in pain, curling on the floor. Molly picked the knife up and came at her again. Val felt a burning sensation as the knife penetrated her arm and the warm oozing of blood as the weapon slid across her skin.

"I could have killed you already, but now I just want to make you suffer." She sliced the knife again into Val's arm and then her leg. "I'm going to filet you like a fish." Each time the knife came at her, Val tried to defend herself.

In her fury of attack, Molly suddenly stopped and composed herself. Her lips curled into a sinister smile. She brought the tip of the bloody knife to Val's face, turned it over and ran the blunt end down, not cutting her but leaving a trail of blood from the dripping weapon down her cheek.

"Where on that pretty face should I start first?"

She was close to Val this time and Val cupped the fingers of her undamaged hand into a fist and hit Molly across the jaw as hard as she could, stunning her for a second, but this was enough time.

The knife fell again.

Val picked it up, cowering defensively with it. Pointing it outward, shaking, afraid Molly would come at her. She didn't have to wait long. Molly ran forward.

With what little strength she had left, Val lifted herself up and plunged the knife into Molly's chest. Her eyes were wide and locked on Val's as the knife went in. Her hands went to the knife as she collapsed to the floor.

Val hobbled out of the room. *Gwen! Where's Gwen?* Val found her on the bed in the room next door. She felt for a pulse; there was one, a strong one.

Val rushed down the stairs as quickly as she could, almost falling several times. She could barely feel her gashed leg anymore. Her phone was in the living room and she needed to get to it. When she reached the bottom of the staircase, she noticed someone lying on the kitchen floor. She limped forward, her heart racing. As she got closer, she nearly collapsed. It was Howie, lying in a pool of blood.

"Oh my God no!"

She felt for a pulse and found one. It was weak. He was still alive but barely. He tried to talk. His lips moved but what little sound came out was incoherent.

Val shushed him. "Howie, save your strength. Don't talk."

"I... have... tell... Val..."

"Howie, not now! I'm going to get help for you," she said frantically. She needed to call an ambulance.

Blood dripped from Val's leg. She was dizzy and stumbled to the living room where she left her phone on the couch. She grabbed it then staggered back to the kitchen, to Howie. Her fingers acted like they were moving in slow motion as her brain tried to instruct them to push the numbers.

"911, what's your emergency?" the operator responded.

"Help. I've been stabbed," Val's voice whispered. It was all she could get out.

She collapsed to the floor, barely conscious now. The phone still in her hand, the dispatcher was yelling in the background.

"Ma'am! Ma'am! Are you there? Stay on the line! Help is on the way!"

Val dropped the phone. A pool of red was beneath her. She was bleeding out.

She pictured Dr. Blythe filling out his report. "Cause of death: exsanguination. Manner of death: homicide." She pictured herself lying on the cold steel table of the morgue.

She turned her head and looked at Howie. He was lying next to her on the floor. His eyes blinked and his chest rose up and down, and then without warning, both movements stopped. His body appeared lifeless. His head was turned to the side with eyes fixed in her direction, chest still. She had seen this look enough to know what it meant. She tried to reach out to touch him, but her hand wouldn't reach.

There was a slamming of car doors and a commotion of people in haste. Lights flashed in her windows and sirens were reeling.

Val's back door flew open. Emergency medical technicians rushed to her side and immediately started to inspect her wounds. Another technician went to Howie and felt his carotid for a pulse.

"He's dead," Val tried to tell the E.M.T. No sound came. The man pulled his finger from Howie's neck and came over to Val, but she couldn't speak: she was starting to lose consciousness.

People began to shout. She had no idea who they were.

"Jesus Christ! Get a tourniquet on that leg now or she's not going to make it." It was last thing Val heard before the room went dark.

42

Val stayed in the hospital for almost a week. She recovered quickly and the doctors were pleased. She'd have scars on her leg and would have to walk with the aid of a cane for a while, but it looked like she would have no permanent nerve damage. Her wrist was broken. The doctor said physical therapy would help with recovery, giving her back any lost mobility. Val wasn't optimistic. She'd heard that story before.

Right now, three weeks later, she stood outside of the one-way glass of the interrogation room. There was no way she was going to miss this. Molly Dolan was being questioned by Detective Gavin. Val wasn't allowed in. Which wasn't a bad thing. She didn't want to be in the same room with that woman, even if Molly was wearing restraints.

Molly had been released from the hospital that morning. She sat at the interrogation room table dressed in an orange jumpsuit, her hands shackled to the belt around her waist. Her lawyer and a psychiatrist sat on either side of her.

"What's your real name?" Gavin asked.

"Molly Dolan."

Gavin sat back in his chair and crossed his arms. "DNA says you're not."

"Your tests must be wrong."

"That's impossible."

Molly laughed wryly. "You've been wrong before, Detective Gavin."

"Not this time. You're not Julia DeHaviland. You're not Molly Dolan. And you're not Lorelei Sebastian. Who are you?"

"If you don't believe I'm Molly Dolan, that's your problem not mine," she said with an amused smile. "I can show you all types of physical documentation."

Gavin slammed his hand down on the table. He knew this was going to go nowhere. This woman was a narcissist and a psychopath. Probably the coldest and most calculating one he'd ever seen. She actually gave him the creeps as she sat innocently smiling in a challenging manner, daring him to try to place a name on her face. He stared at her, trying to picture the Julia DeHaviland he knew. The woman he liked and respected. All he could think about was how she'd fooled him. The sheer mastery at deception, the ruthless and emotionless killer hidden just under the surface, was frightening. *Jesus, you really don't know the people you associate with.*

Molly narrowed her eyes, as if trying to read his thoughts, perhaps to stay one step ahead? Beat him at his own game. It wasn't going to work. This ended now.

"Whatever you want to call yourself, it doesn't matter to me because you're going to prison regardless. I don't care what your name tag reads when you get there." With that, he got up and exited the room and entered the adjoining one where Val was standing, waiting for him.

Val didn't turn her head when Gavin came in. She couldn't keep her gaze off Molly, who was staring right at Val. Slowly Molly cocked her head, narrowed her eyes, and curled her lips up in a smile. It was as if she knew Val was on the other side of the glass. The reaction sent shivers down Val's spine.

Gavin grabbed the cord for the window curtain and pulled it shut. "Val, don't look at her anymore. That's what she wants. She wants to control the situation. Control you."

"What's going to happen now?" Val said, terrified. The thought of Molly loose was more than she could handle.

"She'll be arraigned, then without doubt, tried and convicted. Then hopefully sentenced to prison for the rest of her life."

"What about an insanity defense?"

"Of course, they'll try that. We just have to be ready for it."

"Will you ever be able to find out who she really is?"

"Her DNA is in no database and her fingerprints are not on file. So, it's unlikely, unless someone who knows her comes forward and says who she is. Then we can test her DNA against that person. But honestly, it doesn't matter if we know who she is because we know what she is."

"She's pure evil."

"Of the most dangerous kind. This kind of criminal enters people's lives unsuspectingly and steals them easily. She has no conscience, is manipulative, and can gain someone's trust easily. It's anyone's guess how many identities she's stolen. Hell, she herself probably doesn't even know who she really is. Chameleons, that's what this type of psychotic is called. It's so rare to catch them. Val, you're damn lucky to have escaped her."

"Thomas was well enough to travel home yesterday," Jack said on the way to the airport. "He should be resting for a few more weeks, but if I know him, he'll be at it by tomorrow. We have a case waiting for us when we return."

"Is there a time when you two never have a case?" Gwen asked jokingly.

"When the time comes, that's the time to retire," Jack said. "I will say, this one with Colin was one of the more challenging in a while. We couldn't have done it without you, Val."

"That's because I had some very good teachers," Val said. "What about Colin? How is he adjusting to what happened?"

"He might not be behind bars anymore, but he will be captive in other ways. He'll be in quite a financial hole for some time. He's still responsible for all of "Julia's" debt, though he's fighting it. Thomas and I have been partially paid, but I doubt if we'll see the rest of it. He's going to file for bankruptcy. Oh, by the way, Lauren left him."

"I'll bet that's the smartest thing she's done in a while," Val said.

"So, Dr. Knight, what lies in store for you after your recovery? Are you eager to get back to your job at the medical examiner's office?" Jack asked.

"With my job, I've been attacked, battered and then stabbed. Yes, I'll have lovely stories for my grandchildren." Val smiled when she added, "I can think of safer professions to have, but none quite as challenging. So, what's in store for you and Thomas? You mentioned that you had a case waiting for you."

"We received a phone call a couple of days ago to continue an investigation we were working on just before we came here."

"What happened in this one?"

"We were looking into the possible murder of a man killed by arsenic poisoning. But, the levels of arsenic found were consistent with levels in the soil and in the drinking water. They weren't high enough to kill him, or really make him sick for that matter. Only now the dead man's adult son went missing last week and small bits of him were found just this morning in plastic bags floating in the local river."

Jack glanced at his watch. "I'd better run if I'm going to make it through the security line in time for my flight."

"Well, Jack Styles, maybe one day we'll work together again," Val said.

"Yes, perhaps we will." He then hugged Val and Gwen goodbye.

Val watched Jack walk away. She turned to Gwen and found her colleague staring at her oddly.

"Val, there's something I've been meaning to bring up for a while but never found the right time. I know if I wait any longer I won't be able to do it."

"What is it?" Val asked, her voice hesitating.

"It's about Oliver Solaris," Gwen said in a serious tone.

Dear god, here it finally comes. Val grew increasingly worried. This was the last thing she wanted to hear.

It seemed like forever before Gwen spoke. "The truth is I really didn't know Oliver all that well. Actually, I barely knew him. I met him at a seminar and talked to him briefly. He was such a nice man, so willing to help and he really believed in giving someone a chance. He mentioned there was a position available at the Erie County Medical Examiner's Office. I wanted so much to change professions that I jumped at the possibility. I hope you don't hate me for lying." Gwen smiled sheepishly. "It all worked out in the end because they gave the job to you over me anyway."

Val looked at Gwen for a second and then burst out laughing. "Then, you knew him better than I did, because I didn't know him at all!" Val confessed everything. "If he believed in giving someone a chance, he gave that to both of us. Well, me unintentionally."

Gwen grabbed Val in a big embrace. "Cheers to Oliver Solaris!"

THE END

ACKNOWLEDGEMENTS

My deepest gratitude to Bloodhound books for being willing to give me, an unpublished author, an amazing chance. Thank you to Betsy Reavley and Fred Freeman, Tara Lyons, Clare Law, Heather Fitt, and the rest of the editorial, design and publicity team. You are fantastic. I can't thank you all enough at Bloodhound for bringing *A Simple Lie* out in the world and helping me make it the best it can be.

Thank you to all who gave me information and advice on drugs and medications that are outside of my area of expertise. I did tweak some of the details—don't want to give anyone any ideas now—so, don't try this at home! Being a Buffalo NY native I did keep the geography and locations as accurate as possible but some places were changed and or invented as necessary. Also, thank you to those who've helped me with my forensic questions. I tried to keep the facts as real as possible. Any errors, or stretches of the imagination, are my own. Fiction is as fiction needs.

For my late brother Michael, who read early drafts of this novel and made excellent comments and gave me spot on advice. Mike, the changes have been made. I still have your edited documents and will always cherish them. Cancer is an ugly disease and hopefully one day we'll find the cure. For today, we still fight the battle. And to my mother, who continually cheers me on, it's finally happened!

Thank you to my dear friend, colleague and "partner in crime", Dr. Ray Miller for your encouragement and advice, being willing to lend an ear when needed and just giving all around support. Don't worry, I'll give *your* character a dog soon. I think I promised that a while ago. English bulldog, right?

To my friends, colleagues, co-workers, former and current students at UB, the encouragement you've given is amazing. Thank you all!

Finally, to my husband Peter, who after reading early drafts of my book, brought home a computer, set up our spare bedroom as an office, and made me become serious about being a writer. You believed in me, my characters. My writing. Thank you for your dedication, love and support. I couldn't have done this without you!

CPSIA information can be obtained
at www.ICGtesting.com
Printed in the USA
FSHW021615210220
67397FS